THE BATTLING PROPHET

In this series:
The Sands of Windee
Winds of Evil
Mr Jelly's Business
The Bone is Pointed
Bushranger of the Skies
Death of a Swagman
The Devil's Steps
An Author Bites the Dust
The Widows of Broome
Man of Two Tribes
The Battling Prophet
The Mystery of Swordfish Reef
The Bachelors of Broken Hill
The Will of the Tribe
Murder Must Wait
The New Shoe
Bony and the White Savage
The Lake Frome Monster
Venom House
Wings Above the Diamantina

If you have difficulty obtaining these titles from your local bookshop, write direct to Angus & Robertson Publishers at:

Unit 4, Eden Park, 31 Waterloo Road, North Ryde, NSW, Australia 2113
or
16 Golden Square, London WIR 4BN, United Kingdom

Arthur Upfield

THE BATTLING PROPHET

All characters in this book are entirely fictitious, and no reference is intended to any living person.

EDEN PAPERBACKS
an imprint of Angus & Robertson Publishers

Unit 4, Eden Park, 31 Waterloo Road, North Ryde, NSW, Australia 2113; 94 Newton Road, Auckland 1, New Zealand; and 16 Golden Square, London W1R 4BN, United Kingdom

First published in 1956
Arkon paperback edition first published in 1972
Reprinted 1981, 1983
This Eden paperback edition 1989

ISBN 0 207 16218 2

Printed in Australia by The Book Printer

CONTENTS

Chapter One

A REGRETTABLE DEATH

THE coach captain was young, smart in the grey uniform of the company, and a facile talker. It was obvious that his female passengers found him disturbing; that he was being mentally seduced by those in whom hope was waning and those whose husbands had exhausted their repertoire.

The voice from the amplifier was pleasing, and grammatical errors easy to condone. There was little of the bored tones of the guide, and more often than not the man spoke as though to close friends, as, indeed, the majority of the passengers had become, for they had left Sydney ten days before on this tour to Adelaide and now were on the return journey. Only one man had joined them at Adelaide.

"We are now approaching Murray Bridge," announced the captain. "As you all know, we are returning to Melbourne via the Princes Highway, and here at Murray Bridge we halt for morning tea. I know you understand how we must keep strictly to schedule, so please don't go wandering down the street."

"Not unless you go with me, Captain," said a middle-aged woman who was good for a solid tip at the end of the tour.

Again on the road a man remarked:

"Country looks terribly dry even this far south." And the amplified voice said:

"Droughtiest year for the last seventeen. All across South Australia and Victoria, and high into New South Wales, the man on the land is being hard hit."

"Old Ben Wickham was right again," a woman said, and her travelling companion added:

"He's been right for years, but this time all the farmers believed him. Pity he died."

Both before and after leaving Border Town the effect of the drought was apparent. There was no new fallow; the grass paddocks were burned brown and patchily bare; there were no green crops. It was as though this were the end of summer and all the thirsty land awaited the autumn rains. But it was early spring, when all the world should have been bursting with vigorous life. Brown was the universal colouring, broken only by the dark of pine plantations and the barbered gardens of neat homesteads. The district was almost denuded of stock. Of human activity there was none to be seen.

Mount Gambier was ever a thriving town, and important as a police administrative centre. The passenger who had joined the coach at Adelaide changed here to an old bus that connected Mount Gambier with the small fishing village called Cowdry. The way ran over the low hills and climbed to the famed Blue Lake, into which, so said the cynical driver, the Mount Gambier people emptied tons of washing blue every six months. Beyond this serene pool the road crossed bare uplands where even the occasional tree seemed lifeless.

"Depressing, isn't it," observed the man from Adelaide, who was seated immediately behind the local driver.

"Yair, looks grim all right," agreed the driver. "Still, there's no argument. Old Wickham predicted the drought, and them who wouldn't believe him deserved what they're getting. There's lots of people who howled him down for crying drought, and lots who've been on his side. Would have cheered him up if he'd lived."

"His home was down this way, I understand," said the Adelaide passenger.

"Yair. Place about twenty thousand acres called Mount

Marlo. You can see it ahead just right of that line of pines. They took his body to Adelaide for cremation, and flew the ashes back and scattered 'em over Mount Marlo. Nice-lookin' place from the road. I'll pull up and let you take a peep at it. You're staying with John Luton, you said. You get off at the bridge."

"Thanks. Yes, Mr. Luton invited me down for a few days' fishing. The kingfish are in, he tells me."

"Coming around. Bit early this year. Where you from?"

To this frank question the passenger proffered a lie, as the driver's curiosity was due to habit. They came to the line of pines bordering the road and offering a magnificent windbreak to the pasture-lands beyond. Then into the line of trees grew the white sandstone pillars of a gateway, where the bus stopped.

From this point the plebs could get an eyeful of Mount Marlo. The wrought-iron gates were swung wide; the driveway ran straight between wide borders of flowing daffodils all the way to the large house crowning a low hillock. There were people on the wide patio, and the oblique rays of the sun gleamed on the chromium of several cars standing against a green wall of lambertianas. To the right of the house of Colonial architecture squatted an observatory as though denying all interest in the heavens, and still farther to the right was a long building flanked by rows of white boxes on stands and white-painted cylinders elevated like mortar barrels.

There had lived and worked Ben Wickham, who had had many enemies and many followers; a famous meteorologist whose death terminated a stormy career marked by professional jealousy, governmental stupidity, and by fierce opposition from commercial and certain financial interests. From this Mount Marlo had been flung challenges; from it had issued defiance of obstruction; to it had looked, with ever-growing confidence, farmers and graziers from all over Australia.

Ben Wickham had predicted that last year would be very dry over certain areas. He named days when slight and useless rain would fall. It was so. He had predicted that this year would be disastrous in named areas. His forecasts had proved to be one hundred per cent accurate. And then, having removed the gamble on the weather for the man on the land, he had died.

The circumstances of his death were not, it might well be said, quite respectable for one of his affluence and renown, and no newpaper reported them. The local doctor did not hesitate to sign the certificate, and the relatives readily carried out the dead man's wishes regarding the disposal of his ashes . . . according to the newspapers.

"Yair. Nice place," repeated the driver, and drove on beside the wind-break following the gentle decline to the bridge which crossed a royal river. "You get out here, sir. That side track'll take you to Luton's cottage. Less'n half a mile. See you again some time."

The passenger stood beside the highway and watched the vehicle cross the bridge before taking up his battered suitcase and turning to the unmade road skirting the river-bank. Here grew great gums, and between the trunks the sheen of water dappled with sunlight caught his eye, and that same eye noted the fallen tree litter and the ants working close to their nests, for when the sun set it would be cold.

The river drifted beyond screening gums and lower bush, and presently the track debouched on to an open place where three evenly spaced tree giants guarded the river to the right, and a white-painted picket fence guarded a small weatherboard cottage to the left.

At sight of the stranger, two dogs bounded from the broad veranda to race to the gate and bark with more welcome than hostility. When the wayfarer spoke, they turned themselves into the shape of an S, and escorted him along the cinder path dividing plots of growing vegetables. Reaching the veranda ahead, they barked again, and this time there was the faint note of house guardians.

Then the front door swung open and on to the veranda stepped a man.

He was twice the traveller's weight, seemed half as high again, and was certainly twice his age. The white hair, clipped short, was plentiful. The full white moustache failed to hide the stern mouth and the rugged chin. Most men begin to decline at forty; this one hadn't begun to decline at eighty.

"Good 'day-ee!" drawled the traveller in the manner of the inland. "Are you John Luton?"

"I was this mornin' when I woke up," replied Mr. Luton, examining his visitor with eyes extraordinarily clear and vital. "I think I know who you are, but tell me."

"I am, of course, Detective-Inspector Napoleon Bonaparte." The faint bow which accompanied this statement appeared to pass unnoticed by Mr. Luton, who said warmly:

"Glad to meet you. Come on in and we'll boil the billy."

The dogs stood aside to permit Bony to step directly into the front room. It was an ordinary room, obviously devoted to comfort during winter evenings, the only objects of note being several photographic enlargements of bullock teams attached to table-top wagons loaded with mountains of wool, and two great bullock whips arranged like crossed swords against one wall. Above the small radio on the mantel was suspended, of all things, a bullock yoke.

Bonaparte was conducted to the kitchen-living-room beyond, where Mr. Luton filled a jug from the bench tap and switched on the current. From the cold stove he took a teapot to the back door, tossing the leaves outside and narrowly missing a huge black-and-white cat. The cat came in, the fur on its back standing upright. It was more hostile to the visitor than the dogs had been.

"You got my letter," remarked Mr. Luton, spooning tea into the pot.

"How did you know I was in Adelaide?" Bony asked.

"Seen your name in the paper. It said you was mixed up with the investigation into a smuggling racket. Glad you came, Inspector. I been more'n a bit worried over Ben Wickham, as I wrote. He was a fine feller. They don't breed 'em like him these days."

Mr. Luton was standing with his back to the stove, seeming to tower over the seated Bonaparte, who was rolling a cigarette.

"Excuse the question," Bony said, "but how old are you?"

"Me? Eighty-four. Nothing namby-pamby about me Wasn't with Ben Wickham, either, and he was seventy-five. Heart failure, the quack said he died of, due to alcoholic poisoning. Alcoholic poisoning! You ever had the hoo-jahs?"

The hazel eyes regarded Bony with interest and anticipation. They were the eyes of the voyager by land or sea, eyes accustomed to searching beyond horizons, and the years had not come between. The impressions they were now receiving were not indicated by the weathered features, but the alert mind was summing up the visitor—his light-brown face, his blue eyes, the straight nose and slim nostrils, the level brows, the sleek-straight, black hair. Even by European standards, the female partner in this unusual creation must have been a fine-looking woman. When Mr. Luton was obliged to switch off the electric jug, D.-I. Bonaparte said:

"My varied experience does not include delirium tremens. Your letter indicates that you have studied the subject."

"How many times I've had the hoo-jahs, Inspector, I'm not admitting, being a humble man. I could fill a book about the hoo-jahs, all sorts of 'em, and their effects." Mr. Luton vigorously shook the teapot to induce the leaves to settle. "I might find it a bit hard to prove it, but I will."

"You do not look an alcoholic."

"Not at the moment, Inspector." Mr. Luton smiled and away sped fifty years. "You wouldn't deny me my claims if you happened along when I was on a bender."

The tea was poured and a plate of sweet scones placed within reach of the visitor.

"I've a troublesome corn on a big toe, Inspector. That's all that's wrong with me. I can read the papers without glasses, and I can hear the wireless without it loud. I can drink myself into the hoo-jahs when I like, and I can ride the water-cart when it suits me. I can take only one night-cap, and I can work up for three bottles of grog a day—after a bit of practice.

"My old friend, Ben Wickham, was as good as me on all them points. All that was wrong with him, when he died of something give to him, was a touch of lumbago. They said he died in the hoo-jahs of alcoholic poisoning. He was having the hoo-jahs all right. We both were at the same time. But he didn't die of 'em. I told the quack that. And the policeman. And all I got for me trouble was a threat to have me put away in an old men's home in Adelaide."

"You think you might convince me?"

"Yes. I'm betting on it."

"On what grounds?"

"You being a bushman, like me. That covers a lot, Inspector. Ben wasn't exactly a bushman, but near enough. I'm asking you to believe I'm not shouting down a rabbit hole. Do I look like a ruddy lunatic?"

"On the contrary. It was not your thesis on alcoholism which induced me to apply for ten days' leave. The doctor's reputation is high in those quarters able to assess it. The policeman's record is without blemish. But your reputation, Mr. Luton, is—shall we agree?—just faintly tarnished."

"I've never robbed a man," shouted Mr. Luton, eyes blazing. "I owe no man anything. I've always . . ."

The arched brows, the coldly analytical blue eyes, which only a moment before were warm and friendly, stopped Mr. Luton's outburst. He sat opposite his guest, applied a match to his pipe, and admitted calmly:

"You're about right, Inspector. I'm not much account locally. Still, I done no man wrong, not even Ben. I know what I know, and what I know no one will believe . . . exceptin' perhaps a bushman. A bushman can understand other bushmen and their ways. So I'm still hoping."

"You will, at least, find me sympathetic, Mr. Luton." And Mr. Luton remembered how astonished he had been at what he had seen in those deep blue eyes, and was relieved that those same eyes were again expressing warmth.

The cat had subsided on the hearth before the cold stove. The two dogs were squatting that they could watch both their master and the visitor. Bony struck a match, lit a cigarette, puffed out the flame and balanced the stick on the heeler's nose. The dog played along, moving only his tail.

"You got a way with dogs," observed the old man, faintly impatient. "I hope you will be stayin'."

"Perhaps, Mr. Luton. Even the coach driver assured me that the fishing was good. Ah! Someone coming."

Chapter Two

HOO-JAHS

BEYOND the door appeared a man, who called:

"Hey, there, John! You around?"

The frame of the door darkened and there stepped into the kitchen a man tall and lean and weather-bashed. He was wearing a suit of dungarees so often boiled that the colour was like blue-veined stone. Smiling, obviously embarrassed, he sat on a chair near the door and fondled the dogs.

"That," remarked Mr. Luton, pointing the stem of his pipe at the caller, "that is my neighbour up-river a bit. Name is Knocker Harris. He believes in no one and nothing. It was him who recommended I write the letter to you, Inspector."

"That's me, Inspector," agreed Knocker Harris. "Pleased to meet cher. Me nephew, Frank Lord, you put away for his natural, always said you're a top detective, and if he hadn't sort of accidentally shot that prospector in the bush, you wouldn't have been on to the job and he wouldn't have been nabbed like. So we reckoned you are the man to understand John's ideas about the jerks. Not that Ben wasn't murdered. Got too dangerous for the politicians, he did. I told him more'n once to go easy, but he would never listen."

"You talk too much," Mr. Luton asserted severely.

"That's me," ruefully agreed Mr. Harris.

"Knocker is given to making wild statements," Mr. Luton said, accusingly. "I like to keep to a bit of reason, because people might say we're old and mentally wonky. You heard

Knocker say the Government murdered Ben. Then again the Commos could have done it, hoping to get what he'd worked out. Ben wasn't just an ordinary bloke, like us."

The fishing was slipping from Bony's mind. He said:

'Mr. Wickham told you something of his work, it would seem."

"During the past half-century or thereabouts," replied Mr. Luton. "If you read the papers you'll know that three years ago he made it public that, given fifty years of weather records, he could forecast for sure what the weather would be like four, five, six years ahead. No matter what part of Australia, no matter what part of the world, providing he had them fifty years' records. Not what the weather was likely to be, but what the weather would be, any particular day or night. He predicted this drought, even the days when the rain threatened and didn't come. You know what happened?"

"What did happen?" replied Bony.

"The farmers didn't do any fallowing last summer and autumn. They didn't sow crops this winter. So they didn't buy any super-phosphate and other manures. They didn't buy any machinery last year, and they won't be buying any this year. They sold their stock and sacked their hands. And the graziers cut their stock down to barest, and put off their stockmen. And none of 'em, neither farmers nor graziers, lashed out a lot of money on work and wages and machinery just to watch it burned to dust by the sun. So none of 'em are in the hands of the banks and financial concerns. Instead of the drought bankrupting 'em, they're all living comfortably on their fat."

Mr. Luton regarded Bony with quiet confidence, and Knocker Harris said:

"And that's why Ben was murdered."

"Murdered because he assisted the farmers and graziers?" Bony expostulated.

"No, murdered because the finance companies, the big merchants and the banks couldn't sell their stuff and lend money to the farmers and graziers and make 'em their slaves for years to come, like they always did following droughts."

Knocker Harris again put in his oar.

"And the Gov'ment's in it, too, Federal and State. 'Cos why? 'Cos the men on the land threw thousands of men on the labour market. The machinery makers have their yards a mile high with rustin' iron, and the manure firms have mountains of super no one will take at any price, and the oil companies can't sell tractor oil. Y'see, Inspector, knowing what the weather is going to be this day next year, like, and this day the year after, is no damn good to lots and lots of people with lots and lots of money to lend out to drought-stricken farmers. So they bumped off poor old Ben."

Mr. Luton rose to knock his pipe against the stove. Bony slowly rolled yet another thing some persons might name a cigarette. The two men watched and waited as though for his verdict.

"The newspapers told me," he said, "that Wickham died in this house, and early one morning. The doctor stated, and so signed the certificate, that death was due to heart disease. You support a private report made to me that he died during a bout of delirium tremens. Well?"

"We were having the hoo-jahs. We were both getting over 'em," declared Mr. Luton. "We were at the tail-end of 'em when Ben died that morning. He should of come out of them hoo-jahs like he always did. Same as me. But he died instead. Of something else."

"The doctor said it was alcoholic poisoning," interjected Bony.

"The quack's a bone-pointer, like. He wouldn't know," argued Knocker Harris, savagely pulling at his dirty-grey ragged moustache.

"Mr. Wickham had been drinking hard for more than three weeks," Bony persisted.

"Not a reason," countered Mr. Luton. "We often drank hard for six weeks. Once for two months, solid. Nearly got carted off to hospital that time."

"Wickham was seventy-five."

"I'm eighty-four, Inspector."

"You told the policeman that that morning you woke from a good sleep. Feeling slightly better, you decided to light the stove and prepare something to eat. You were busy with the stove when you heard Mr. Wickham laughing. Mr. Wickham was occupying the front room. You went to him and found him sitting up in bed. He continued to laugh, and appeared to be unaware of your presence. You returned to the kitchen and brewed a pot of tea. When you returned to your friend with tea and dry biscuits, Wickham was lying back on the bed asleep. So you thought. You covered him with the bedclothes and left him for an hour. On again going to join him, you discovered that he was dead. Correct, Mr. Luton?"

"All correct," replied the old man, his eyes hard, his chin like a rock. "Still, Ben didn't die of the drink. He was pointing to things on his legs, and he was laughing like hell at what he was seeing. We had been boozing on gin for a bit more'n three weeks, and gin don't have that effect on any man. Want me to prove it?"

"If you can," Bony assented, "prove it."

"I will, when I've lit the stove. Switch on the light, Knocker."

The stove was already prepared for lighting, and the electric light pushed the dying day a million miles beyond the doorway. Knocker said, as though Bony might be doubtful:

"He can, too." He smiled brightly, and Mr. Luton, turning back to the table, saw the smile and stared disapprovingly. He was breathing a trifle fast, and the fingers loading the pipe shook a little, all telling Bony that this was the crucial moment for which Mr. Luton had hoped. He began slowly, a pause between each word:

"Back in the Year One, when I was wearing out me tenth pair of pants, I'd got sense enough to stick to whatever I started on, and found I could go further and stand up longer. You know how it is with us—a good, hearty booze-up every year, perhaps twice a year, very rare more'n three times a year.

"I haven't had time to tell you yet, but Ben and me was mates for something like ten years, flogging bullocks over the tracks back of New South. What I led with, he followed suit. When we boozed on whisky, the things we saw sort of grew before our eyes. When we blinked, they didn't vanish, but stayed on the table, on our knees, wherever they happened to appear and grow like roses on a bush. Following a spell on rum, the things appear suddenly and vanish suddenly after playing around like they wanted to bite you. The gin hoo-jahs is still different. You see them out of the corner of your eye. They always stalk you from behind, and when you turn to look at 'em, they aren't there. Understand?"

"Partly. Go on," Bony urged.

"Ben and me was drinkin' gin that time he perished. He was laughing at things he was seeing on his legs and feet, pointing at them, and laughing so he couldn't describe 'em to me. Them things wasn't caused by the gin, and they wasn't even the whisky hoo-jahs, 'cos you don't laugh at them. For two days we'd been seeing the gin hoo-jahs—things that creep up behind you and vanish when you try to look straight at 'em. So it wasn't the gin that tossed him."

"Throughout the day before he died, your friend was seeing things from the corners of his eyes . . . as you were doing?"

"That's what I'm saying, Inspector."

"What would he have been drinking to produce the effects on him which you saw that morning, when you found him sitting up and laughing and pointing to things on his legs?"

"General mixture of beer, spirits and sherry."

Bony pondered, and Knocker Harris brought his chair to sit at the table.

"Last night in Adelaide," Bony said, "I was introduced to several habitual drunks by a sergeant of the Vice Squad. One victim said that the hoo-jahs, to employ your name for them, always dropped on him from the ceiling. Another told us that the hoo-jahs came from nowhere and crawled all over him. Yet another victim said he had a pet hoo-jah with legs sticking up from its head and three eyes in its stomach. And so on. I have to admit that all these persons mixed their drinks, with the exception of a woman who invariably drank sherry. Have you ever had the hoo-jahs on wine?"

Mr. Luton shuddered.

"Once. A long time before I fell in with Ben. Never no more. They pulled my hair out in chunks, and then my whiskers. After that they nipped out all me body hairs, one at a time. And now and then they threw things at me—a bale of wool, a bullock, a planet. And never missed."

"You take a point," conceded Bony. And Knocker Harris cried triumphantly:

"There y'are, Inspector. Ben konked out on somethin' not gin. You got to study this killing to find the lay of it." His small eyes gleamed with sardonic humour. "Millions of people had no time for Ben and his weather-predictin'. And the politicians are in it, too. They were all agin Ben, like. He told us. The politicians would have their mothers murdered if they could hire someone to murder 'em for nineteen and elevenpence. As for the Jews . . ."

"You keep off the Jews, Knocker," roared Mr. Luton. "I'll have no sectarianism in my house. "You'll be . . ."

"Tell me about this last drinking bout," interposed Bony, and Knocker Harris was unabashed.

"Yes, tell him," he urged, and Mr. Luton said:

"It'll be easy. Ben hadn't been along for about two weeks, when he came down from the big house one afternoon. He didn't say, and I didn't ask him, but he was soured by something or other, and when I seen how he was, I suggested a bender as we hadn't had one going on for six months. First he says no, and then he says yes and to hell with everything, and so we got stuck into the gin."

"You happened to have a supply of gin on hand?" Bony asked.

"I did, Inspector. Well, after a bit we didn't want to eat no more. Now and then Knocker would call in and cook us a feed, but we didn't want it. Then he tried us out with soup, and after that he gave us up.

"Mind you, this was all on the programme. Nothing unusual. We talked about the old days. We sang all the old songs we knew. Now and then we took the whips down and went outside and flogged the trees, pretending we was once more on the tracks with the bullock teams. It ended like it always did. One of us got thinking about his mother, and then we cried and called each other drunken sots and swore off the booze for ever. That was two days before he died.

"You got to understand that once we swore off the drink, we had to take on the cure and stick to it. We'd never been that weak-minded that any justice could have put us on the Blackfellers' Act.* The cure was a small dose of the same every four hours. Between doses you suffer hell and you watch the clock like it was going to spit at you.

"I got the hoo-jahs that night, and Ben got 'em first thing in the morning, the same as me. He didn't tell me so. Had no

* In several Australian States, a magistrate is empowered to declare an offender an habitual drunkard, whereupon it is an offence for a hotel keeper to serve him with liquor. The aborigines are also debarred from hotels, and to serve them with liquor under any circumstances is an offence. Colloquially, the habitual drunkard comes under the Blackfellows' Act.

need to, or me to tell him. I knew by the way he kept looking sideways and back over his shoulders that he was having the gin hoo-jahs all normal and proper.

"Towards evening that first day, I made a fire in the stove and got us a hot drink of meat extract. We couldn't bear the stink of it. So we sat and called each other dirty names till med'cine time came round again. At midnight we had our doch-an'-doris. A real snorter for the night. I was a bit worse than Ben, so he seen me into bed, and, soon after, I heard him shout good-night from his stretcher in the front room.

"I had a cat-nap, but I was awake long before med'cine time at four in the morning. I waited till four to take the bottle in to Ben. He was sitting on the stretcher with his feet on the floor, and he was holding his head with both hands to stop himself looking backwards at them hoo-jahs. Y'see, after a day of doing that, your neck aches like hell. I gave him his snort, and had one myself. Then I covered him up after he got back on the stretcher, and went back to my own bunk.

"I had another cat-nap, and was woke by hearing Ben roaring with laughter. I asked him what he was laughing at, and all he could do was to keep on laughing and point at his legs, him sitting up and the bedclothes on the floor. I wasn't liking the way he was going on. I pushed him down and covered him up and left him, the time being just before half-past six, and one hour and a half off med'cine time.

"He stopped laughing as I was making a brew of tea, pouring as much water on the floor as in the pot. I was thinkin' then that if Ben didn't come out from them funny sort of hoo-jahs pretty quick, I'd break our rule and give him a stiffener to keep him going. It seemed that I needn't have worried, because when I went to him with the tea and the bottle, he was asleep and snoring. So I came back here and had a cup of tea and resisted the gin, deciding I'd wait for Ben to join me in the eight o'clock dose.

"Come eight o'clock, I went in to see how he was faring. He must have sat up again, for the clothes were half off him. He wasn't asleep then. He was dead. So I staggered up-river to tell Knocker to go for the quack."

"And the quack roared hell outer me, like," snarled Knocker. "Told me that Ben and his boozing mate oughta died a century back. And I oughta be ashamed of myself for associating with 'em. I told him to take a runnin' jump at hisself, and I went to the policeman, and he said he'd a good mind to lock us all up, includin' dead Ben."

Mr. Luton took over once again.

"They got here in the doctor's car about ten that morning. By then I'd done some tidying up, throwing the empties into the river, planting the full ones out of sight. I told the tale that Ben had brought the supply with him, and we'd run dry and was sobering up. We had a confab on the veranda after the quack had seen Ben and said he'd died of the booze. I told them about the right kind of hoo-jahs Ben had, and how he couldn't have died of 'em. They told me not to be a damned old fool, and that I ought to be put away for my own good."

"The quack said we both oughta be sent up to the Old Men's Home," supplemented Knocker Harris indignantly. "And the policeman backed him up. Ruddy bastards, both of 'em."

"You'd better get back to your camp," Mr. Luton suggested with some severity. "I got to fix us with a feed, and feed the fowls and the dogs. It's almost dark."

A smile of benign satisfaction spread slowly over the weather-bashed features of the neighbour. He said something about seeing them later, and departed. The dogs went with him, only as far as the garden gate.

"You'll be staying, Inspector, eh?" again pleaded Mr. Luton.

"Of course. You asked me down for the fishing," replied Bony. "I'm a good fisherman, Mr. Luton."

Chapter Three

THE PICTURE

THE night was peaceful and cold. The moon at zenith was almost completely triumphant, for the western sky was fast being drained of light. Beyond the garden fence the three mighty gums ruled a magic world of semi-tones, with the silvered pathway of the river in the distance.

This was not the picture Bony was seeing. He was looking at a picture sharp in places, blurred in others, an unfinished picture. A man had died, and he and those associated with him were the subjects of this picture. They were portrayed brilliantly, were at once recognisable. The circumstances surrounding the dead man's last hour of life were blurred as though befogged by Mr. Luton's claims of extraordinary knowledge, knowledge which, superficially, was as fantastic as the dreams of the modern artists. Superficially to everyone save those who, like Bony, were familiar with the extraordinary background of the extraordinary race of men represented by Mr. Luton.

This race has not entirely passed away. The last remnants are still to be found living in peaceful old age on the banks of inland rivers and near a township which they visit only on pension days. It was a race the like of which will never again be seen, for it possessed all the admirable attributes and but few of the human vices. They were born long before motor traction could weaken their bodies and the craze for luxury and mental distraction could weaken their minds. Life made upon them such physical demands that occasional intemperance had no lasting effects, whilst their dependence on one another in a world of vast, semi-arid distances gave to them a spiritual strength rarely found in city and town even in their own times.

John Luton's background applied only in part to Knocker Harris, a younger man, less intelligent, less stable. He had been brought up on a farm, whereas Mr. Luton had roamed the open spaces of the Interior. He had driven horses in a single-furrow plough, long after Mr. Luton had saved a little money from the pubs and purchased his first bullock team and wagon. Knocker Harris had prospected for gold in Victoria when Mr. Luton was punching bullocks on the far tracks of the Interior. But, like Mr. Luton, he had worked from dawn to dusk, and he had lived with those whose motto was: "If your neighbour needs a pound, give him five. If a down-and-out begs for a crust, give him half your loaf." There was no sentiment about it. It was just plain common-sensical insurance.

Ben Wickham had been a newchum, a towny, an outsider lost in a rough man's country. He was a full-grown man when Mr. Luton found him completely drunk on the wood-heap at the rear of a wayside hotel. The publican wanted Wickham away from his yard, and had no use for him in his bar, as he was broke to the wide, wide sky. Mr. Luton was conveying a mountain of stores and grog to far distant townships, and, the day before, he had left Broken Hill without his offsider, who had decided he couldn't leave the bright gas-lights of Argent Street.

Wickham was, of course, no use whatever to Mr. Luton. He was wearing a flash city suit, horribly soiled, and shoes, instead of he-man's boots. He had never seen a bullock yoke, and didn't know which end a bullock hauled with. Mr. Luton took the body off the wood-heap, nursed life back into it, and ultimately fashioned the best offsider he ever had. Twelve months later, Ben Wickham was driving his own bullock team in company with John Luton.

They worked together for ten years. For ten years, summer and winter, they flogged and cursed bullocks up and down all the tracks of outback New South Wales and Queensland, loading wool to the railheads, loading stores and building material and beer and spirits back to the growing townships and the ever demanding station homesteads.

Wickham had been a brilliant student and promised to become a brilliant scientist, and, like so many brilliant minds, he had a weakness for alcohol. Mr. Luton picked him off the hotel wood-heap just in time. Forced abstinence and gruelling work on the tracks, aided by his own intelligence and by Mr. Luton's remarkable influence, slowly brought Wickham into a world he could appreciate. He had accepted and profited by Mr. Luton's advice, which was: "Don't nibble at the grog. Have a gut-ful when you're at the trough, and then give it away for a spell." It was sound advice, too, when the visit to the trough lasted two weeks and the spell following it lasted nine or twelve months.

The partnership was broken when Wickham inherited his father's estate known as Mount Marlo, at the time when the motor truck was banishing bullocks to the abattoirs. Mr. Luton decided to buy a small grazing property, and Wickham took up his inheritance and his meteorological ambitions. What Bony knew of him were tiny pen strokes which brought him into clear perspective in this large picture he was now studying.

That Wickham had been a truly remarkable man was unarguable. He broke away from the orthodox science of meteorology, which was getting nowhere very fast and could only advise my lady what clothes to wear the next day, the airman what conditions he could expect to fly into during the next two hours, and the seaman whose barometer and radio contact with other ships could tell him more.

Like Sister Kenny, he battled with obstruction, a professional jealousy and spite. From a low percentage of accurate forecasts, he had ultimately claimed accuracy of one hundred per cent, and the two years before his death had proved his claim. Without doubt, Ben Wickham had been greatly admired and greatly hated. Twenty thousand people watched the plane rise from the airfield with his ashes to scatter them over the place where he had worked and fought and triumphed.

There was, of course, part of the picture so exceedingly blurred as to be almost undecipherable. Mr. Luton's idea, if it could be so named, that every spirituous liquor has its own distinct effect on the mind subject to its power—it could be accepted only as an idea, barely as a theory. Who on this earth, other than Mr. Luton, with the possible exception of Knocker Harris, would accept as fact that hallucinations created by whisky were distinctly different from those created by gin? Who else would be even faintly interested by this subject, this idea, this theory, this utter rot? A man aged seventy-five existed on gin and nothing else for three weeks. Of course he would have delirium tremens. What was more remarkable was that he didn't die before reaching that stage. He had had a sick heart. The doctor had warned him.

And still Mr. Luton stood forth in the picture, clearly sane, mentally virile, without question speaking of something in which he believed and of the truth as he understood it. He had sent for Napoleon Bonaparte, believing that only one reared in and habituated to the bush could be expected to believe that Wickham had not died of too much gin.

Well, it would be something to exercise the mind while he was fishing, and there were ten days of fishing ahead, a leave long due and, in his own opinion, well deserved. Ah . . . Then Mr. Luton's booming voice issued from the front door, calling him to dinner.

The kitchen was bright and warm, and Mr. Luton, wearing

a cook's apron, was serving fillets of fish, surrounded by crisp potatoes and garnished with lemons, from the Darling River. They discussed fish and fishing, when Bony learned that the Cowdry River was short and deep and wide, that it was not actually a river, although two streams entered it. In the long ago the sandstone cracked open to let in the sea and admit the kingfish, the flathead and the bream.

Cooking fish is an art distinct from cooking, and Mr. Luton was an artist. He certainly knew how to brew coffee, well laced with brandy.

"That was a truly satisfying meal," Bony told him when they lazed at table, and the black-and-white cat stretched on the hearth footing the hot stove.

"Plain and good," agreed his host. "You know, us old geezers in the old days lived on damper bread and meat, and nothing else except tomato sauce, black tea and pain-killer, and got along very well. Ben often trotted down here for a simple plain feed away from his own table, where only high-falutin muck was fed to him. One morning he came in and said: 'I've come down for a beer out of a tin pannikin. You got pint pannikins, haven't you?'"

"He liked everything plain?"

"Yes, took him back to the old days. In his own house he wasn't the boss, you understand. His sister was and still is. Sour old bitch about sixty. Only one man ever got into bed with her and he dropped dead the next morning.

"Not that she didn't run the big house all right. She always did that, the servants and all, including Ben when he was there. In the house he was a mouse. Outside he was a lion, and wouldn't allow her or anyone to say how he should manage his office and his staff. Give her her due, she always did believe he'd win out. She married a Parsloe, of Parsloe Jams, but, as I said, he couldn't stand it and shuffled off. There's others as well."

"Tell me," Bony prodded when Mr. Luton was about to remove the dinner crocks.

"Well, there's a sort of retired parson. Been there for a couple of years. Mrs. Parsloe invited him and he stayed on. Ben hated the Reverend, name of Weston. Supposed to be writing a book or something. Then there's Mrs. Parsloe's husband's niece, Jane. She married a doctor and kidded Ben to fork out the money to buy the practice at Cowdry."

"The same doctor who signed the certificate?"

"The same. Shire councillor. Runs the golf club. Knows everything—in his own mind. Name's Maltby."

"And they live at Mount Marlo?"

"Been there for four years. Surgery is at Cowdry, only four miles down-river."

"Oh! Anyone else?"

"One more. Lass by the name of Jessica Lawrence, Ben's secretary. He thought a lot of her. She's in love with Dr. Linke."

"One moment, please," interrupted Bony. "You said that Ben thought a lot of his secretary. Kindly be precise. In what way did he think a lot of her? For her work?"

"For her work and because he found her straight and easy to talk to. She even gets round me. About twenty-four or five. Started working for Ben four years ago last Easter."

"And this Dr. Linke?"

"Ben's chief assistant. Was with him five years. He and the second assistant lived in a house separate from the big house, and they was looked after by Mrs. Loxton." Mr. Luton chuckled. "If ever I'd have married I'd have chosen her sort."

"You imply that the assistants do not now live apart from the big house?"

"Correct. After Ben died, the second assistant was sacked by the Parsloe woman, so I understand. Dr. Linke's still there, and now lives at the house. He's fallen for Jessica, the secretary.

Foreigner. Comes from Germany, so Ben told me. Clever feller, again accordin' to Ben. Been here once or twice with Jessica. Very interested in the Outback."

While Mr. Luton was at the wash-bench, Bony pencilled notes in a slim pocket-book, and when Mr. Luton returned to the table he asked:

"Did your friend ever say his life was threatened?"

"He named no name, but you only had to read the papers and talk to people in Cowdry to know he was hated enough for some madman to be mean enough to kill him. Even the local Member of Parliament last year said Ben ought to be gaoled for what he was doing, arguing in the House that the country would lose heavily if Ben was wrong and had led the farmers and graziers to sort of go on strike."

"Who inherits the property?"

"Don't know yet. Haven't heard about a will so far."

"Did Wickham ever mention to what degree he had taken his assistants into his confidence?" pressed Bony. "I'll put it another way. Did his assistants know Wickham's ultimate calculations or formulæ, or whatever it is, making his forecasting a hundred per cent accurate?"

"I can answer that one, Inspector. No. That was his secret he kept to himself. Dr. Linke didn't tell me in words when he was down here a couple of nights back, but from what he did say I think they're looking for those calculations."

"You tell me you believe Wickham was murdered. Why was he murdered? To suggest that someone paid by the finance corporations, or by a big business concern, murdered him is really fantastic. If it was murder, there must be a motive. Was the motive to benefit from his estate? Was it to prevent him continuing his forecasting—which, as I have just said, is really fantastic? Was it to gain possession of his weather calculations? And that is more feasible. Are you a beneficiary under his will, do you know?"

"Could be, but I don't think so," replied Mr. Luton. "Ben wanted to put me down for twenty thousand quid, and I told him I had twenty thousand of my own and a bit more."

"You didn't quarrel with him during that last bender?"

"Quarrel with him! Me and Ben never once quarrelled."

"Did you and Wickham, or Wickham himself, ever quarrel with Knocker Harris?"

"Never. Knocker's always easy to get on with. Used to nurse us with food and soups and things."

"I have yet to learn this point, Mr. Luton. Did Harris drink with you and Wickham?"

"No. 'Cos why? Because he's got stomach ulcers and can't take it without sufferin' like hell. In fact, I don't think he ever took a drink in this house."

"You like him, I should think."

"Why not? Harmless sort of bloke. Always ready to oblige or do a good turn. Lives quiet and don't want for anything."

"Then it would seem that we have a murder without a motive, Mr. Luton. And we have a murder because you believe that when Wickham died he wasn't having an attack of the right kind of hoo-jahs. His body has been cremated and the ashes scattered over Mount Marlo, so that the remains cannot be pathologically examined. What have we left?"

Mr. Luton frowned. He said:

"Gumption."

"That might be the right answer, Mr. Luton."

Chapter Four

THE CONSPIRATORS

THERE was that about John Luton, ex-bullock-driver, D.T. expert, which forbade familiarity. It was the character of the man as presented in his eighty-fourth year, and was due only in part to his age. Seated in a high-back chair to one side of the sitting-room fire, he appeared to be relaxed though he sat upright, like a king on his throne. His eyes were steady. His great gnarled hands were passive. The expression on his large face was of calm confidence in his body and mind. It seemed that the natural form of address to this man, in acknowledgment not only of his age but of the inherent strength of character, was Mister Luton.

A man can be great though a bullock-driver. A man can be a king and yet a weakling. Mr. Luton had gained and was to retain Inspector Bonaparte's respect.

Bony sat on that side of the fireplace having his back to the outer wall, in which was the door and the window. The black-and-white cat lay curled on the rug, its broad back pressed against the carpet slipper of Mr. Luton's right foot, and not for twenty minutes had Mr. Luton moved that foot, that the cat be undisturbed.

He spoke of Ben Wickham as an equal, evincing no inferiority to the famous meteorologist, and Bony knew that this was the result of the man's distant background where all men were equal, and all men were respected, provided they were not damned by meanness of thought and of act. All else was merely incidental.

Speaking of Wickham disclosed Mr. Luton's deep affection for and loyalty to the dead man. And there was the wisdom of the old, which isn't tainted by intolerance, smugness, bigotry.

He talked about those old days, revealing to Bony a picture of a young man who was lost to himself—a self he could not understand, and another of that young man grown tanned and physically strong, striding the length of fourteen pairs of bullocks, and wielding an eighteen-foot whip swung from a twelve-foot heavy handle, and able to flick the thong against any chosen inch of hide, to contact the animal like a fly or a flail; a third picture, that of a heavier man, of flowing white hair and dark eyes alive with ambition and the joy of achievement, the square face and alert eyes of the man who learned to fight only late in life; and the last picture of a man wearied less of fighting than of the astounding mental narrowness and crass stupidity of those in political power. These pictures made vivid all those blurred sections of the greater picture Bony had studied earlier this evening, and now he was impressed by Mr. Luton's beliefs if not convinced by their relationship with fact.

"Ben Wickham was sleeping in this room, was he not?" he asked when Mr. Luton fell silent.

"Yes, on a stretcher by that wall where the whips are," replied Mr. Luton. "Camp stretcher." He nodded to the position and Bony noted it was opposite the front door and the one window and that a few feet from it was the door to the living-room.

"The table. In the same place then as now?"

"Yes."

"Was there a chair or a stand at the head of the stretcher?"

"Low packing case I'd covered with a cloth. It had a jug of water on it and a glass. And Ben's watch and a wallet. Of course, there was his pipe and tobacco pouch and matches."

"The front and back doors were locked when you retired?"

"Yes. But that window was up. Ben couldn't abide a room without a window open."

"When you sent Knocker Harris for the doctor that morning, it would be shortly after eight o'clock, I take it?"

"Would have been, because I came in here with the dose exactly on time. I'd be talking with Knocker within five minutes of eight."

"He walked to Cowdry for the doctor?"

Mr. Luton nodded, and Bony asked why Cowdry, when Dr. Maltby lived at Mount Marlo, and that eight o'clock in the morning would hardly find the doctor at his surgery in the town. The point brought a glint of approval into the hazel eyes, and Mr. Luton replied:

"When I got to Knocker's camp he'd just come back from looking at a set-line below the bridge, and when there he'd seen the doctor's car headed for town. Being that early in the morning, he half expected to meet Maltby coming back."

"At four in the morning, when you went to Wickham with the dose, was the light on?"

"Yes. Both of us slept with the lights on. Y'see we couldn't stand waking up in the dark, and find we couldn't sort of glimpse the things we knew were stalking from behind."

"And the light was on when you went to him at half-past six . . . when you heard him laughing?"

"Yes."

"Did he speak when you went to him with the dose at four?"

"Said it had been a hell of a time between drinks. Give me a 'thank-you' and then was willing to lie down, and closed his eyes."

"He appeared to be quite normal . . . in view of the, ah, circumstances?"

"Yes, nothing wrong at all."

"The dose. Did he take it with or without water?"

"Neat. We never ruined good grog."

"Why the jug of water on the packing case by the bed?"

"When you're sufferin' during a cure, a drink of water about an hour after a dose often gives the dose a renewed kick," grimly replied Mr. Luton. "I noticed the next morning when I was cleaning up ready for the quack that Ben had half-emptied the jug."

"You left the jug and the glass on the case, or had you removed them when the doctor came?"

"The jug, yes. The glass I took to the sink and cleaned it properly, knowing that Maltby would be bound to sniff at it, and took it back to the case and poured a little water in it. You see, when the quack came, all the empties were in the river, and the remainders put back in the cellar."

"Oh! Not a real cellar?"

"'Course. Under the floor. I dug her out and carted the mullock down to the bottom of the garden. The cellar's sort of secret."

"Answer this carefully, Mr. Luton. Had you gone to your friend, say at three o'clock in the morning, and suggested a drink, would he have accepted it?"

"Perhaps yes: perhaps no. I'd never tested the point. Having agreed on the cure, we never suggested to each other a drink between drinks."

"Yet you said that when he was laughing later, and you went in with tea, after he stopped laughing, you took the bottle as well, thinking he might be in such bad shape as to need a drink most specially."

"If I had told him then that he'd have to take a snort, Ben would have drunk it, knowing I'd not say so if I wasn't worried about him."

"Then, Mr. Luton," Bony pressed, "had you taken a drink to him at three o'clock, he would have accepted it."

Mr. Luton flushed slightly, whether from annoyance or embarrassment Bony could not decide.

"I think he would," he admitted. "You see, in the old days I was always the boss, and when I came down here to live because he wanted me to, he let me be the boss again. What I said regarding the grog always went with him."

"Did he drink when at home?"

"A glass of beer sometimes. Cocktail before dinner. Port after dinner. The Parsloe woman said it was the social thing. If it was social to drink coffee out of an old boot, they would have had to drink from old boots."

"Precisely, Mr. Luton. One more question I want answered with care. After you gave Wickham the dose at four o'clock, could he have obtained more gin without you knowing it? Assuming that you slept soundly. Or another kind of spirit, from what you had above floor, or even from the cellar?"

"Yes. I sleep in a room off the far side of the living-room. Ben could have gone into the living-room and had a swiftie from the stock in the cupboard by the stove. He didn't. I knew how many full bottles there were. They were all there when I looked. The tide in the opened bottle hadn't gone down since I'd lowered it at four. He could have gone down to the cellar and helped himself, but he didn't, because nothing had been opened. And I didn't sleep soundly. No one does when having the hoo-jahs."

"Thank you for your patience, Mr. Luton." Bony stood. "Let us make a call on Mr. Harris."

Mr. Luton was obviously astonished, but he stood without commenting and went for a muffler and hat. Bony followed him to the clearing and along the path he could but faintly see, which wound under the great gums and avoided dense clumps of brush.

Ultimately the path passed from thick timber to a small clearing bordered by the river to one side. From the middle of the clearing issued music, and, with startling impact, a dog barked ferociously. An oblong of light confronted them, and framed within stood Knocker Harris and the dog, the smallest Australian terrier Bony had ever seen.

Then Knocker Harris was inviting them into his mansion, and the dog was sniffing at Bony's heels and trying to grab a trouser cuff.

The kerosene pressure lamp blazed white light against the walls, walls built of odd lengths of milled timber, strips of thick bark, sheets of corrugated iron. The roof was of iron nailed to light logs with fencing wire. The table was of planks wired to cross logs, which in turn rested in the fork of the four legs planted in the hard earth. On the open fireplace a fire burned, and to one side stood a chair which had been fashioned from the stump and roots of a tree storm-blown clear off the ground. Two stools of similar fashioning completed the furniture, save for nine beer cases nailed together to serve as a pantry and dresser.

"How's things?" mildly enquired Knocker Harris. "Didn't expect you. Have a squat. Drink of tea?"

Without waiting for acceptance or otherwise, he filled a billy from a petrol-tin bucket. Mr. Luton gravely said it was a nice night, and expressed the hope that Knocker Harris wasn't being put to too much trouble. Bony gazed at a blank in one wall and guessed the darkness beyond to hide a gentleman's bedroom. The place, undoubtedly, was built with river jetsam and junk. Save for the sheets of iron, the wireless on the 'dresser' and the lamp were the only visible objects not fashioned with axe and saw.

"How's the fish biting?" politely asked Mr. Luton, who knew very well how they were biting.

"Bit lazy since the last tide," replied Knocker Harris. "How they doin' down your way?"

"About the same."

So they talked while Bony sat on a comfortable tree-root stool and rolled a cigarette, both merely waiting for the reason of this late visit.

"I suppose you are not often bothered with visitors," he said, having applied a match to an alleged cigarette.

"No, not much, Inspector," replied the host. "They come generally for bait-fish in the summer. I nets bait-fish for visitors, like. Never takes money. They make me a present of bread, or a cut of meat, or a bit of tobacco and what not, and I'm so grateful I make them a present of bait-fish."

"Barter trade, eh?"

"Trade! No! No trade, Inspector. Can't do no tradin', else it makes me in business and I gets taxed by the blood-sucking Council."

"How often do you go into town?" was Bony's next question.

"Once a fortnight, generally. To draw me Bachelor's Mite from the Post Office."

"What else do you do when you go to town?"

"Oh, not much," replied Knocker Harris. "Calls in at the chemist for pills and things, and at the sports store for fish hooks and lines. Then I have one small tiddly of rum to give me strength to get home, like, and I has a yarn with a few I know."

"A tiddly of rum!" snorted Mr. Luton. "When I offer you a proper snort you turn it down."

"Meaning not to be unneighbourly, John. Actually because I like a chip on me Pension Day, and me cobbers likes a drink at the pub." A wail crept into the voice. "I keep telling you I can't take the booze like I useter. It plays hell with me ulcers and things. Why ain't you got some ulcers, too? Why me, and not you? The way you and poor old Ben shoved it down, like, you oughta have no stomicks at all."

Mr. Harris served tea in jam tins fitted with fencing-wire

handles. He placed a tin of condensed milk on the table and with it an apostle spoon of bright silver. The sugar bowl was a fruit tin. The appearance of the spoon astounded Bony, but he said:

"When will you be going to draw your pension?"

"Next Thursday, Inspector. I walks in, but I often thumbs a ride out."

"I was wondering . . ." began Bony, when hell broke loose.

Outside a bullock bell began to clang and clang as though agony itself were tortured metal. The miniature dog yapped and twisted into an S and than a reverse S, in its excitement. The bell sounded as though tied to a bullock in convulsions.

Knocker Harris jumped to his feet.

"Got me a fish," he shouted. "Be seeing you."

Seizing the kerosene lamp, he rushed outside, leaving his visitors faintly illumined to each other by the fire. The bell continued its roar, and above it, Mr. Luton said:

"Could be a big fish. I'd say about fifteen pounds."

"Could be a 300-pound marlin," observed Bony. "I assume the fish is ringing the bell."

Mr. Luton chuckled and beamed at Bony. Abruptly the bell ceased its uproar, and he said:

"Knocker's as proud as a woman with a new baby when that bell goes off. Take a look at it in daylight. Bit of a character is Knocker. Harmless enough, though. Decent sort."

Presently the yapping dog came in, followed by Knocker carrying a bream. He assessed the weight at four pounds, and his friend argued it wasn't more than two. The discussion went on over the fish lying on the table, and twenty minutes were spent in gutting it, and then washing down the table.

"You was saying, Inspector, when that fish got hooked?" said Harris.

"Ah, yes. I was wondering if you would make a special

trip to town to-morrow morning. You could buy yourself a tin of salmon."

"Coo! Why the salmon?"

"Well, you might think of something you really want. You could call at the hotel for your usual tot of rum. You could call on the chemist for a bottle of cod liver oil. By the way, is a local paper published in Cowdry?"

"The *Cowdry Star*. Comes out every Toosday," proudly replied Knocker Harris. "I know the editor, like. Champion of the down-trodden toiler, he is."

"Excellent," decided Bony. "Perhaps you could pass to him an item of local news for his social column."

Two pairs of bright eyes watched the dark expressionless face of D.-I. Bonaparte. Two ancient men waited. He said:

"I would be greatly obliged, Mr. Harris, did you take a trip to town in the morning, and to everyone you know, including the newspaper editor, whisper that you understand a detective is staying with Mr. John Luton, and that you think he's come down from Adelaide about something concerning Ben Wickham. Just that, no more. And don't mention I asked you to do this, or my name."

They looked from Bony to each other. Knocker Harris nodded as though with dawning comprehension.

"Okay, Inspector," he said. "I'll be in town by nine o'clock."

Chapter Five

THE FISHERMAN

HAVING cast his baited hook into the river of humanity, Bony strolled beside the Cowdry River and communed with the birds. Having slept on several problems, he was, this scintillating morning, satisfied by his own approach to them.

His position relative to these problems was clear. The seconding to the South Australian Police Department having terminated, he had no official authority in this State. He had been granted absence of leave from his own State Department, and was thus almost a private citizen and could not approach these problems as he could in his own State of Queensland. To reduce the method of approach to the problems to its minimum in plain English: he could not go about stating he was so-and-so enquiring into the circumstances surrounding the death of Ben Wickham.

In fact, he felt no urge to do so, no urge to track a hypothetical murderer. He felt relaxed and the need for further relaxation, to take every ounce of benefit from the period of leave granted. Like the good actor, the good detective is emotionally taxed, and Bony yearned to do nothing but loll about and fish.

He had been thinking of nothing but fishing—for fish—when Mr. Luton's letter reached him. The writer's extraordinary thesis on delirium tremens was supported by the writer's obvious sincerity and the clarity of his mind, but perhaps what was even a greater inducement to accept the invitation to fish in the Cowdry River was his own instinctive loyalty to the race of men who had left their mark so indelibly on the Outback to which he was attached by ties never to be severed.

Mr. Luton, of that remarkable race, had appealed for help. Mr. Luton, living on the south coast of South Australia, was a stranger in a strange land, surrounded by foreigners incapable of understanding him. It was a plea for help which Bony, of the Inland, could not ignore, and the thesis, in which, it was alleged, hid a means to murder, could not be set aside by Detective-Inspector Bonaparte.

Having listened to argument in support of Mr. Luton's thesis, he was still wary of giving it support, but he was convinced that Mr. Luton was completely sane and truthful. Loyalty again to Mr. Luton was actually the mainspring of the decision to do something about it. But what? The body of the alleged murder-victim was but dust settled upon the pastures of Mount Marlo, and therefore nothing could be proved in opposition to certified medical opinion. There would appear to be nothing definite about the dead man's will, and no information about the dead man's recorded work in meteorology.

Thus the gentle prodding, per Knocker Harris. Thus to broadcast the fact that a detective was staying with Mr. Luton, and probably was working on Mr. Luton's silly idea that Wickham had not died of the booze but "of something given to him." And thus to withhold who the detective was, and the fact that the detective had no official authority, and was merely on leave of absence from a distant State.

So to wait and fish and loll about in the sun, to wait and see what kind of fish would jump.

The three ancient gums held his attention for several minutes. They were actually grey box. The bark was softly grey, and, at this spring-time, the old bark had been cast, since when the trunks had suffered assault. Not only were these trees evenly spaced fifty-odd feet apart, they also were in line, and up and down this line of gums two madmen armed with great bullock whips had skipped and screamed and thrashed the imaginary animals to haul the imaginary wagon from a sand-bog, or urge them round a bend of the track that the wagon wheels would miss a damaging obstacle.

Later, Bony wandered up-river to visit the camp of Knocker Harris. He was met by the man-eating midget dog, welcomed as a friend of the house, and inspected the 'grounds'. It was quickly evident that Knocker Harris had achieved almost complete independence of Man, for if the miserable pittance called the Old Age Pension were suddenly to cease, Harris could still exist.

Under a bark roof a bicycle without wheels was fixed to a heavy plank. Mr. Harris could sit on the saddle and pedal the normal way. The driving chain worked a roller and the roller motivated a chain of jam tins going down into a shallow well and coming up filled, to empty their contents into a trough at the highest point. Bony could not resist temptation, proving that the contraption worked, and sent water along a channel to reach a line of rhubarb crowns.

He wandered about the little garden which revealed tender care for growing things and a sense of order not apparent in the construction of the abode. There were rows of last season's carrots, and this season's turnips and radish. The parsley looked ragged, but the sage, thyme, and other herbs thrived. Knocker Harris actually stocked roots of horse-radish, and Bony stole a piece to wash and chew with relish.

Brushwood protected the garden from wallabies that were, however, given free access to the 'lawn', a patch of ground about a dozen square yards in area which, Bony had been told, Knocker Harris had carefully sown with the best grass seed.

Here and there, spaced like croquet hoops, were set expertly the snares so beloved by the old-time poachers.

Bony found the bell, a huge tempered-iron bullock bell weighing five or six pounds. Suspended from a cross-bar, it was worked by two sticks tied at an angle, and to the lower end of one stick was tied the fisherman's line.

He did not presume to enter the 'house', but he did look into a kind of cavern walled by a vast creeper bearing a red flower, and saw within the cold interior a hanging meat-safe made of boards and hessian bags. There was also a bench littered with junk: an iron pot on a battered primus, a bunch of dried lavender, a tangled fish-line, and bottles.

The little dog escorted him off the premises.

The path by which he had come did not go farther up-river, and having gazed with admiration at the landing-stage built of poles and planks and tree branches, and the trap built with odds of wire netting, he proceeded down-river till he came opposite Mr. Luton's cottage, where he found a fallen tree-trunk upon which Mr. Luton must often have sat and fished, for the past six years, so smooth was the log.

After lunch of cold mutton and a bottle of beer, he returned to the tree-trunk and expertly cast a line baited with garden worms. Like the morning, the afternoon was superb. The kookaburras were inclined to sleep, the lesser birds were busy, and to him came the large house-cat to sit by his side and purr its contentment.

Nothing happened for two hours. The sluggish river passed slowly on its way to the open sea. A tidal inlet, the water was of the sea, and yet within a yard of it it was possible to sink a shallow well for fresh water.

Nothing happened until into this sylvan silence there intruded the low throbbing song of a motor engine, and Bony witnessed the approach of an expensive convertible, all leaf-green and chrome and sparkling glass. The car stopped at the wicket gate, and from it stepped a man of medium build and energetic movement. He wore a light-grey suit, and was hatless.

That much Bony noted before turning to his fishing, winding in the line and examining the bait before making the next cast. He heard the wicket gate being shut, and the dogs barking to warn Mr. Luton, who was at ease on the veranda. He did not look round, even when the wicket gate was closed again ten minutes later. The cat, who had crouched with spine fur raised and yellow eyes blazing, now stood and arched its back, a moment later to race to a tree.

Then a man said, voice soft and cultured:

"Having any luck?"

Bony glanced upward to see the man in grey regarding him with clear dark eyes. About forty, he was well-knit, and the tiny dark moustache suited his handsome face.

"They say the kingfish came back into their river yesterday morning. Must give them a try. You get them big sometimes. Haven't seen you before. On holiday?"

"Yes, down for a few days."

The man waited as though for additional information from the stranger, but Bony did not volunteer it. So he said:

"Good healthy sport, fishing. Good because it relaxes the mind as well as the body. You staying with old Luton?"

"Yes. Where do you live?"

Bony caught the flash of hostility in the dark eyes.

"Oh, I live at Mount Marlo. I'm Dr. Maltby. Just trotted along to look up the old chap. Remarkably tough for his age. Interesting, and all that." There followed a pause. "Will break out on the drink now and then, and I'm a little afraid he'll walk into the river and be drowned. Oughtn't to live alone like he does—not a man of his years."

"Seems to be self-dependent, and a hundred per cent sane."

"Oh yes, he's all that . . . while he remains sober. Are you a . . . er . . . relative?"

"No. Mr. Luton asked me to stay with him for a few days. I met him years ago when he lived on his place above Wentworth."

"Ah yes, I fancy I heard some time that he owned a small sheep property up there. Are you in sheep?"

The question, like those preceding it, was easily put and entirely without offence. Dr. Maltby evinced no stiffness in his make-up, being accustomed to meeting everyone on his own ground. As easily, Bony said:

"Also met, when previously staying with Mr. Luton, his great friend Ben Wickham. I think Mr. Luton mentioned that you live at the late Mr. Wickham's house?"

"Yes. I'm by way of being married into his family. Fine old boy. Only one failing. The liquor. Must admit I couldn't approve of his orgies with old Luton. I suppose you know the booze killed him?"

"Not till last night. The papers said nothing of it; merely that he died in Luton's house. How old was he? Near eighty, I think the papers said."

"Seventy-five."

"Remarkable man. He certainly stirred up lots of people either to admire or detest him."

"The people on the land loudly praised his name," supported Dr. Maltby. "I don't know anyone personally who didn't take his advice and batten down the hatches against bad seasons, and so save themselves from near bankruptcy at least. A pity they can't understand the scientific formulæ on which he based his forecasts. Pity there's no one to carry on where he left off."

"I didn't know that," admitted Bony. "It would seem, then, that his admirers are despairing and his enemies triumphant."

"Looks like it, doesn't it. Back to the old gamble for the farmers. Back to the old grind of alternating prosperity and bankruptcy. Watching you fishing brings to mind the bit about Pericles. A disciple asked him how the fishes live in the sea, and he replied: 'Why, as men do a-land; the great ones eat up the little ones.' Well, I must go. See you again, perhaps."

Bony nodded quiescently, and Dr. Maltby strode back to his car.

He heard the car depart. His bait-fish was grabbed but he was too preoccupied to strike in time to hook the fish. Presently Mr. Luton came and sat with him.

"He wanted to find out if Ben left any papers with me," the old man said. "Seems they can't begin where Ben left off, up at the Mount. It's got 'em stonkered. Quack said Ben hadn't confided fully in Dr. Linke. Then he asked me who you were. Like you said if he did, I told him. What d'you think? He come to find out about the papers or to find out about you, having heard the furphy published by Knocker Harris?"

"Perhaps both with equal intent. What else did he say?"

"Only jawed me about the drink. Said he was glad to see I looked sober and healthy. Advised me to stay that way. Seemed a bit friendly this time. Funny how people can be friendly when they want. It's after three. What about a mug of tea? Shall I bring the billy out here?"

They had their tea on the veranda, and Bony went back to his fishing. He had been sitting on the log half an hour when there came up-river a smart motor-cruiser and, as it passed, Knocker Harris waved vigorously and yelled a "Good-dayee". After that the shadows spread over the water, and the kookaburras gained strength enough to chortle and chuckle. Near sundown, a second car came from the bridge and stopped at the wicket gate.

The gate slammed, and when Bony glanced back he saw a large man standing at the foot of the veranda steps talking to Mr. Luton. A minute passed, when the gate slammed again, and fifteen seconds after that noise Bony heard a heavy tread and a deep voice saying:

"Good-dayee!"

"Good-day!" replied Bony, glancing at the big man's thick legs and heavy boots. "It's been a nice day."

"Yair! One out of the mitt." The man sat on the end of the log and rolled a cigarette, and Bony slyly watched the thick and capable fingers. "I'm Senior Constable Ralph Gibley. That right you're down from the C.I.B.? Heard that you are. Could be wrong."

"Yes, I am staying for a few days with Mr. Luton. I am Inspector Bonaparte."

"Inspect . . . Did you say Inspector Bonaparte?"

"If my memory isn't faulty, I did. Why?"

"Ah!" The exclamation held a hint of satisfaction. "You wouldn't be imagining things, would you, er, Inspector?"

"Imagining what things?" mildly asked Bony.

"Imagining that you're an inspector in the Police Department. It happens that I know there's no Inspector Bonaparte in the South Australian Police Department. I know for sure the name of every officer, and would take a chance on knowing the name of every man. What d'you say to that?"

"Nothing of importance." The rod was placed on the ground, and then Constable Gibley was swiftly caught in the net of two startlingly blue eyes which seemed to grow large and larger and give him the feeling that his mind was being prised open to admit them.

"A caste, too," he managed to say. "What a yarn to put over!"

The eyes vanished, and he felt relief as though from physical pressure. Then he was looking at a police badge. Then he was gazing with mounting perturbation at a wallet open to show an identity card. He looked up and again encountered the eyes, and wished they were not there.

"Perhaps you would like to check by sending a telegram to your Divisional Headquarters? I understand that your D.H. is at Mount Gambier. I was talking to Senior Sergeant Maskell the day before yesterday."

"Yes, sir. My mistake, perhaps. But . . . how was I to know?"

"Merely by asking. D'you fish?"

"Fish! Yes, sometimes."

"I'm fishing for kingfish, and baiting for bream. Could I do better?"

"Don't think so, sir."

"I am, too, on a sort of vacation, so please omit the 'sir'. Your inaccurate summing-up of me, based on my birth, no doubt, is pardonable in view of the fact that only in the Queensland Department are brains recognised and encouraged. How many cases of homicide unsolved in South Australia these last ten years?"

"I don't rightly know," admitted the policeman, still jittery.

"There are eleven murder cases still to be terminated," went on Bony. "There are two in Queensland where I belong. I was prevented from concentrating on those."

The policeman obviously saw something beyond Bony, for he stood hastily, apology plain on his large and weather-beaten face. As the doctor had, so he now said:

"See you again sometime, Inspector. I must be on my way back to town. The parson's coming. Sort of character I can't stand at any price. If you'll excuse me . . ."

He left abruptly, and hurried to his car, which he turned and drove towards the bridge and the highway. Approaching from the direction of Knocker Harris's camp was a tall figure wrapped in an overcoat and wearing a shabby grey hat. He walked with ungainly gait, and he rested on one shoulder a long, stout fishing-rod, and carried slung from the other a fisherman's creel. He watched the river he was following, and appeared to start with surprise when encountering the still seated Bony.

"How d'you do!" he greeted, and came to stand before the fisherman who had caught nothing all day. "Any luck?"

"None, so far."

"Mind me casting here for a minute or two?"

"Not at all."

"Thank you, thank you." He baited his hook and prepared to cast. "I suppose that policeman told you I'm a blasted parson, eh?"

"He did so allude to you," smiled Bony, and the man chuckled to remind Bony of the kookaburras.

"He would. Mr. Gibley and I fail to get along together. I regret that his soul is helpless and hopeless. I'm the Reverend Weston, you know, of Mount Marlo. Could you reciprocate? I like meeting people."

He made the cast.

"I am Ins . . ." began Bony, when the parson hooked a whopper.

Chapter Six

THE BALL ROLLER

THEY stood with the fish dying at their feet, and when their gaze clashed, the small light-grey eyes of the Reverend Weston were impishly triumphant.

"A nice fish," he said. "A seven-pounder, eh?"

"Something like that," Bony agreed.

"Well, well! I was hoping for luck as we have had no fish for a week. Where are you staying?"

"With Mr. Luton."

"Luton, eh! Pliable . . . when he consents to remain sober. I trust you are not a slave to John Barleycorn."

The reverend gentleman knelt to fit the fish into his creel.

"Mr. Luton conforms to type," Bony said. "He's a relic from the old days when men worked hard and suffered Spartan conditioning, and broke wide open under grog after long self-imposed abstinence. At present Mr. Luton does not look like an addict."

"I'm glad to hear it. He is often a sot. Ah, why do men indulge like brute beasts? Why cannot they use God's gifts with respect? I like a glass of wine occasionally, and I think I am tolerant. Moderation in all things, yes. Immoderate drinking is as bad as immoderate preaching, and I know many such sinners. Now you will say I live in a glass house. I am, however, perturbed by Luton's outbreaks. My dear friend, the late Ben Wickham, was Luton's crony. He died over there in the house, in delirium tremens. I fear that Luton will go the same way."

"Not while I am with him," Bony assured the parson.

"Good man!" came approvingly. "Staying long?"

"A week or ten days, perhaps."

"From Adelaide?"

"Actually from Brisbane. I knew Mr. Luton several years ago, in New South Wales. In fact, it was there I met the late Ben Wickham."

"Indeed."

Mr. Weston was openly interested, but aware of the force of silence, Bony appeared to fall into the trap.

"I was on a case in New South Wales at the time, and since then Mr. Luton and I have occasionally corresponded. Having been seconded to the Adelaide Department, and having terminated my work, I accepted a long-standing invitation from Mr. Luton."

"Oh! Ah! To be sure!" The small grey eyes probed, betraying the hardness behind the high and narrow forehead. "What do you do?" was the well-timed question.

"I'm a police officer. I was about to tell you my name when you hooked the fish. Detective-Inspector Bonaparte."

"Oh! I'm happy to have met you, Inspector. Well, I hope you have a restful holiday and good fishing. Patience, you know. You must call on us one afternoon before you leave. I'm sure poor Ben's sister would be delighted to receive you. Now I must be going. Remember me to Luton, won't you. And do warn him against over-indulgence, and remind him of his years. I'm sure you could do much in that direction. Bye-bye! I hope we meet again."

The Reverend Weston took up his creel, shouldered his rod, smiled at Bony and departed, and, when slowly winding in his line, Bony watched the ungainly figure grow small as it passed under the trees towards the distant bridge.

"Quite a day," remarked Mr. Luton when Bony entered the kitchen to find him trimming lamb chops for grilling. "Any bites?"

"Yes, a bite by a fish under water. And several bites by fish out of water."

"Three of 'em," stated Mr. Luton. "A doctor. A policeman. A parson. Old Knocker Harris did his job all right, didn't he. A whisper down these parts is as good as a radio during a race meeting."

"I have been instructed to warn you against over-indulgence in the cursed drink. And, moreover, I have been requested to remind you of your years."

"Is that all?" exclaimed Mr. Luton. "Didn't he call me a sot?"

"I believe he did."

"Then why didn't you back me up by knocking him down?"

"Recalling how well you look, I accepted the charge as being amusing."

"And he caught a fish?"

"Yes. Made his cast within a yard of my bait."

"Parson's luck," snorted the old man. "You can't win."

"I shall, next time. Can I do anything?"

"If you like. Fetch some back logs for the fire tonight. There's plenty on the wood-heap. Leave 'em on the edge of the veranda till we want 'em. How d'you like your chops?"

"Lightly grilled."

Mr. Luton was about to serve dinner when Knocker Harris appeared at the back door and was invited to sit at table. Instead of the old dungarees, he was wearing a go-to-town reach-me-down suit badly in need of pressing. His brown eyes were twinkling, and he chewed energetically that he might swallow quickly the tobacco he had cupped into his mouth on arrival.

"Had a good day?" enquired Mr. Luton.

"Not so bad, like," replied Knocker Harris. "Did a bit of business. Said a few words here and there."

"Who did you see in town?"

"Oh, this one and that."

Mr. Luton chuckled, placed a plate of chops and mashed potatoes before his guests, and himself sat at the head of the table, stiff and proper as any proud patriarch. On his either side squatted a dog, and on the hearth sat the purring cat.

"Any luck?" asked Knocker Harris, gripping a chop bone in a knuckly hand to enjoy the last of the meat.

"A good bite," replied Bony. "Got away. I was half asleep and missed the strike."

"You gets that way sometimes, waiting. J'u have any callers?"

"Three."

"Ah!"

"The quack, the parson, and the policeman," interjected Mr. Luton.

"Is that so!" Knocker Harris was immensely pleased. "Well, I expected something, like. Soon's as I got to town, I seen the quack's car outside his surgery, and I says 'How d'you do' to the chemist standing in his doorway. Then I had a chin-wag with a couple of old 'uns on the seat outside the pub, and I sorta mentions we has a famous visitor out our way who knew Ben and seems to want to know a bit more, like. Then I went across the street and bought some pills off the chemist. I lets it drop to him about the visitor out here. Then in comes the quack to get something, and I leaves him being told about the visitor by the chemist. Seemed very interested by the noos.

"When I got back to the seat outside the pub, the old 'uns have gone in for their snifter, so I sits on the seat pretending to count me change, like. It happened that the newspaper bloke came out of the bar and, seeing me, he sits down and starts a yabber. 'How's the fish biting?' 'How's the country lookin'?'

So I told him we had a famous visitor what knew poor Ben and seemed like grieving 'cos he'd died so quick, like."

"Did you mention my name?" Bony asked, and Knocker Harris looked hurt.

"'Course not. You told me not to. I said what you told me. Said that our visitor was a detective. The paper bloke wanted to know your name, and I told him I just missed hearing John tell it. Anyway, he went off back to his paper to write it out, and I went for a dram of rum and had a word with the barman, like. He told me that Jukes would be leaving in his launch for his up-river house-boat, so I hunted a bit for Jukes and he said he'd be leavin' about three and I could take a ride with him.

"After that I mucked about talkin' to people. Trade's pretty bad and they ain't got much to do, like. Then I ambled down to the jetty and boarded Jukes's launch to wait for him to turn up. The policeman turned up 'fore he did, and he wanted to know about our visitor, what his name was and all that, like."

Knocker Harris returned his interest to the grilled chops, and Mr. Luton waited before saying:

"What d'you mean . . . all that?"

"Oh! Wanted to know why we had our visitor. He wanted to know what he'd come for, like. Wanted to know if he was a relation of yours. You know, all them kind of questions, and I'm dumber than usual. What time did he get out?"

"About four."

"Didn't waste much time, did he."

They ate in silence until Mr. Luton served baked apples with custard sauce. Then Knocker Harris said:

"The policeman would come in his car from the bridge. So would the quack. Which way did the parson come?"

"Down-river, following the path," replied Bony.

"Ah!"

Another period of silence before Mr. Luton asked:

"Something on your mind?"

"Yair," admitted Knocker Harris. "Been wonderin' who'd been poking around me camp, that's all. That ruddy nosey parson musta. Like his cheek. If I was to go mucking around up at the big house, they'd yell for the police, but they don't mind rooting through my camp when me back's turned, like. A quid for the rich and a kick in the stern for the poor. That's it all over. Wait till the local politician comes asking for me vote. I'll tell him. . . ."

"How do you know that the parson visited your camp?" interrupted Bony.

"Me dog told me when I got home. There isn't much to that dog, but he can talk. To me, anyhow. First off, he told me someone had been mooching around the joint."

Immediately the meal was over, Knocker Harris remembered he had to re-set his belled fish-line, and Mr. Luton told Bony it was a mere excuse to get out of the washing up. The two men completed this chore, and then the night had come and a roaring fire was lit in the lounge and they settled to gossip.

The conversation was adroitly kept away from Wickham's meteorological work, and centred upon the people who lived in his house. Yet it did seem that Mr. Luton's knowledge of them was scanty, and his opinions coincident with those of his old friend. And Wickham's opinion of those he housed appeared to be governed by the degree in which they interfered with his work.

"Who ran the estate?" asked Bony.

"Feller by name of Sinclair. He still manages it. Employs four men. Him and his wife lives at the back of the station, and the men live in a hut. Ben always said Sinclair made the place pay. Couldn't do aught else, what with the price rise of wool and fat lambs."

"Have you any idea of what Mount Marlo might be worth today?"

"Near enough," answered Bony's host. "Last year Ben was offered one-fifty thousand pounds, walk-out walk-in basis."

"Did he own much beside the property—investments, other property?"

"That I couldn't say," slowly replied Mr. Luton. "He did tell me he had some securities in that chest down below."

"Down below? The cellar you mentioned?"

"Yes. You want to look?"

"Certainly."

"All right. We'll go down. Know anything about locks?"

"One can do much with a piece of fencing wire. I remember seeing some by your back fence. I'll obtain . . ."

They looked sharply at each other. Outside, the dogs broke into warning barking. The man who knew them said:

"Someone coming. Another caller, could be."

Chapter Seven

RAYS OF LIGHT

THE garden gate snapped shut. Mr. Luton's eyes puckered expectantly. When footsteps sounded from the veranda, he began to smile, and he shouted:

"Come in and be damned."

The door was flung open to admit a young woman wearing a light raincoat and a kerchief tied round her hair. A man followed her. His belted coat emphasised physical strength and lent distinction to his carriage. He bowed stiffly.

"Why, Sunset!" exclaimed Mr. Luton, advancing to meet his visitors.

"I do hope I'm not damned, Mr. Luton," teasingly said the girl, and Bony liked her low, rich voice.

"Didn't know it was you. Didn't recognise your step on the veranda."

"You did recognise mine, I presume," stated the man, wryly smiling at Mr. Luton and attempting to include Bony. The dark eyes succeeded where the smile failed, accepting Bony's face, feature by feature, his hands, his feet.

"You . . . You are Inspectore Bonaparte, yes?"

"That's right," interjected Mr. Luton, saying to Bony: "Meet Doctor Linke. And this is Miss Jessica Lawrence."

'Sunset' Mr. Luton had called her. Her hair, her skin, her eyes, were of the sunset, and when she smiled Bony was unaccountably reminded of apples lying on meadow grass. Not to be out-pointed, he bowed, and a Frenchman would have envied him.

"We came down to gossip, Inspector," she said. "You don't mind?"

"To talk with you would be a privilege, Miss Lawrence," Bony gallantly replied. Then his hand was being crushed in a clamp, and he was faintly annoyed at not being quick enough to counter the clamp.

"I, indeed, am happy to meet you," said Dr. Linke, and because he smiled infectiously was forgiven the hand-grip. "As my Jessica said, we came to gossip, to speak of many things including the kings and . . . and what you say?"

"Cabbages," laughed the girl.

She removed the kerchief. Her hair was then a delight to behold. The man assisted her with her coat and Mr. Luton took it from him and indicated chairs. Bony noted that the cat had fled. Linke found a pipe and tobacco, and was unable to mask his interest in Bony and yet conceal the basis of his curiosity.

"You learned I was staying with Mr. Luton . . . from whom?" enquired Bony.

"At dinner to-night Mr. Weston mentioned the fact," replied the girl. "Afterwards, when we had left the house for a walk, Carl suggested that we call, Inspector. There's been something on his mind, and—well, here we are."

"That is so. Here we are," agreed Dr. Linke, beaming at them, his expressive blue eyes bright and his wide shoulders lifted. "We have talked, my Jessica and I, and we are not—how you say?—easy of mind. Incidents lately have indicated, slightly, a pattern, and patterns are the fire of the smoke. You understand?"

"Of course. Go on, Doctor."

"Forgive me if I seem to proceed cautiously, Inspectore. If I make error, please correct. Your purpose in being here?"

"I am visiting Mr. Luton for the fishing," replied Bony. "Mr. Luton and I are old friends who haven't met for many years. He heard I was in Adelaide, hence the invitation. I applied for leave of absence and obtained ten days."

"You are, naturally, a detective?"

"Yes, but not of the South Australian Police Department. I am a Queenslander."

"The pastor also said at dinner that you knew Mr. Wickham. True?"

"I did know him," calmly lied Napoleon Bonaparte, and added: "Years ago."

Dr. Linke leaned forward as though to emphasise his next remark.

"Could we agree, Inspectore Bonaparte, that Mr. Luton has put before you his thesis on the hoo-jahs?"

The pronunciation of 'hoo-jahs' brought a smile from his hearers and he caught its infection. That he was extremely earnest in striving to reach a goal was obvious, and Bony eased the road a little for him.

"Mr. Luton has explained his convictions, based on experience, concerning the effects of alcoholic poisoning. He has also put forward his conviction that Mr. Wickham did not die from alcoholic poisoning. He has proffered sound argument in support of his contentions. I am still keeping an open mind, Doctor."

"I thank you, Inspectore," Dr. Linke said, formally. "The incidents of which I spoke just now, seemingly to form a pattern, lead me to agree with Mr. Luton that Mr. Wickham could have been liquidated."

"You agree with me about the hoo-jahs!" exclaimed Mr. Luton, plainly delighted.

"I am—how d'you say?—being pushed to the belief, Mr. Luton." He frowned as though finding it difficult to choose words from the limited vocabulary at his command. "I want . . . I think . . ."

"Let me explain, Carl," the girl interrupted. "Inspector

Bonaparte, Carl, as you must know, is a New Australian. He came to Australia after the war, and he had to serve two years as an agricultural labourer, even though he is quite famous as a meteorologist. You know how it is; with all foreign medical men, scientists, professional men and such."

"I know how it is, Miss Lawrence, and how ridiculously stupid is the neglect in our country of their abilities."

"Well, Mr. Wickham contrived to have Dr. Linke assigned to his estate, and, once here, there was no intention of wasting Carl's gifts and knowledge on milking cows and grooming tractors. Last year, Carl was granted full Australian citizenship, and he naturally is a little nervous of attracting official notice by being, shall we say, associated with murder, to put it bluntly."

"Yes! Yes, my Jessica. That is how it is. You see, Inspectore Bonaparte?"

"I see," replied Bony. "Let me assist in clearing the fog for all of us. I am a foreigner in South Australia, on holiday, and not on official duty. How I spend my leave can be of no legal concern to anyone, provided I don't break the law. I don't know if you have in Germany what we call private detectives, and the Americans call private eyes, Doctor, but you may regard me as a temporary private eye." Bony chuckled. "I have on many occasions been strongly tempted to urge my superiors to journey to the nether regions and myself to carry on as a private eye. I would be fully occupied in winding up unsolved murders."

"In other words, Doctor, you can spill it," chortled Mr. Luton.

"I thank you, I thank you," energetically acknowledged Dr. Linke, addressing himself in turn to Mr. Luton, to Miss Lawrence and to Bony. Bony addressed himself to the girl.

"When those at dinner spoke of me, what was their attitude?"

"Mr. Weston mentioned you were with Mr. Luton, shortly after we sat down," was the reply. "He seemed cynically amused. Then Dr. Maltby said he had met you, and, further, that he had heard in town you were interested in the death of Mr. Wickham. Without speaking, something passed between him and Mrs. Parsloe, as though both followed the same thought and needed support from the other. It was seen, too, by Mr. Weston, who said: 'I am reminded, my dear Agatha, that this extraordinary person's namesake, the Emperor, often advised that when in doubt it is best to do nothing.'"

"That I do not comply with," argued Dr. Linke. "When doubt comes, it is best to do something. I have doubted and I have acted. I am here. I will tell you. Mr. Wickham was a very good friend to me, and to my Jessica. He was a fine man. He brought me here. He gave me work I love. Slowly, for you understand I have scientific training, he brought me to see there could be much in his line of research. I came to understand how valuable accurate long-range weather forecasts would be to agriculturists and to the world. And as we worked together, so I came to fear the hostile forces gathering to oppose him and halt his work."

"What is your situation now he is dead?" asked Bony.

"It is this, Inspectore. The day after the ashes were released, Mrs. Parsloe came to my office for, she said, an understanding. She wanted to know where her brother kept his papers, his data on his weather work. I told her it was there in the office safe. She opened the safe, and what she sought was not there. It was nowhere in the office.

"Then I told her the book must be somewhere. A thick notebook having green covers. I had myself seen it a thousand times. Her brother guarded the book. He would take it from the safe, consult it. Sometimes he would add data and ever return it to the safe before he left the office. So it was not there in the safe, and I went with Mrs. Parsloe to the house and we searched all about for that book and did not find it."

"Did no one have access to the safe other than Mr. Wickham?" Bony asked.

"No other person."

"There were two safes, Inspector," offered the girl. "Mr. Wickham's private safe, and the general office safe. As Carl has said, Mr. Wickham guarded that green notebook always. He told me it contained his tables and ultimate calculations, the factors controlling solar eruptions and other vital data which eliminated error."

"So," agreed Dr. Linke. "When the green notebook was not discovered, Mrs. Parsloe was angry. She said it must be somewhere and I was to find it. I believe that if my Jessica hadn't proved it was kept in the private safe, and we had no key, Mrs. Parsloe would have said I had stolen it. Because the next day I was visited by a policeman and another man."

"Yes, that was strange, Carl. Tell the Inspector about that," almost ordered the girl.

"They came, these two, at a quarter of noon," continued Dr. Linke. "The policeman was a sergeant of the police from Mount Gambier. The other man was, how you say? a civilian. He said he was of the Commonwealth Investigation Service. He had my dossier from the U.N.O. and from the Australian Immigration Department. He questioned me many times about my life in Germany, my political affiliations, everything. I had told everything before, to officer after officer; there was no more I could tell him. Then he questioned me about my life here at Mount Marlo and the work I had been doing for Mr. Wickham. They stayed at the quarters for lunch, and continued the interrogation till five o'clock.

"When they were gone, Mrs. Parsloe came. She told me she had to report the loss of the green notebook, and as I was her brother's chief assistant, and a German, she felt she must report me. I . . . I was angry. She said she was sorry. She said that the second assistant was to leave the next day, she had dismissed Mrs. Loxton, our housekeeper, and that I was to eat at the big house—which I do. For many hours that evening we all searched for that notebook, and the second assistant urged that the pastor and my Jessica search his luggage before he left. He made the pastor search his person, too. The next night the office was broken open and searched by burglars."

Dr. Linke almost glared at Bony. Mr. Luton bent forward and poked at a log. Bony's brows lifted a fraction.

"After I had examined everything, it was known that the burglars had taken nothing. It took us hours to restore order. They entered by the door and left that way. So they must have had a key to the front door of the office. None of the windows had been forced, d'you understand? And they had opened the safe, too."

"The private safe, Doctor?"

"That is so."

"Let us trace the key to that private safe. Do you know how Mrs. Parsloe came to have it?"

"No, Inspectore. I have thought. It must have been on the body when it was brought from Mr. Luton's house. When she came to the office that day, Mrs. Parsloe used the key, and she locked the safe again and took the key away."

"You told her of the burglary?"

"But naturally."

"What did the police do . . . say?"

"Do . . . say . . . nothing. Mrs. Parsloe would not send the report to the police."

"They decided that the publicity would be unwelcome," said Miss Lawrence. "The family, I mean. They held conference. As the burglars hadn't stolen anything, they agreed to do nothing about it."

"Curious," murmured Bony. "What have you been doing, Doctor, since Mr. Wickham died?"

"Seeking to work through to his achieved objective by the examination and study of the data, what we have. Mrs. Parsloe had told me she does not want me to leave Mount Marlo." Dr. Linke braced his powerful shoulders. "I will not go, Inspectore. There is something . . . what you say? . . . funny going on. It began weeks ago. On July 3. When two men came to call on Mr. Wickham.

"They came in a fine car. From my desk I could see the car drive to the front door of the big house. I saw one man go to the front door and ring, and the maid came and pointed to the office. The man entered again into the car and they drove to the office door.

"The men came in and asked for Mr. Wickham. The second assistant asked the man his purpose and the man said he wished to speak private business with Mr. Wickham. The second assistant went to Mr. Wickham, and returned to inform the man Mr. Wickham would see him, if he stated his business. The man told the assistant he had a mission to place before Mr. Wickham, and the assistant enquired his name. The man said 'Smith'.

"You see, by then I had summed this man. His name was not Smith. It was not even Smidt or Smudburg. He wore Australian clothes, but he had been going to an alien barber, possibly a New Australian whose name few Australians could speak. I didn't address him. You understand why? We unfortunates of the world have learned caution. The second assistant escorted him to Mr. Wickham's office at the far end of the building, and then reported to me: 'Speaks English all right, but doesn't look it.' And although he spoke correct English, it was too correct, and his haircut was a . . . revelation."

"How long was he with Mr. Wickham?" Bony asked.

"About one hour." Dr. Linke applied a match to his pipe with studied deliberation. "Ten days after that, on July 13, Mr. Wickham had a strange call from the Commonwealth Bank. He wasn't in the office when it came. He went to the bank in Cowdry that night at ten o'clock."

They watched the expression of pleasure grow on the brown face and light the deep blue eyes of Inspector Bonaparte as he said:

"You know, Dr. Linke, I find your conversation decidedly captivating."

Chapter Eight

TEMPTATION UNDER FOOT

"WHAT I have told you, Inspectore, is a bare citation of events, and purposely not stated in chronological order, meaning to gain your attention, and, I hope, understanding," continued Dr. Linke, speaking slowly and as though repeating a previously composed address. "Permit me to go to the beginning.

"You understand my life here in Australia has been good. I have no complaint. I am, what you say, a free man in the mind. I can work hard at what I want to perform, and I have not to say: 'Heil Hitler,' or 'Bravo, Mr. Menzies,' at noon each day. Mr. Wickham, always he treated me with respect, and when we did not agree, he did not say: 'You get out! I sack you.'

"Our life was very good. I respect Mr. Wickham. His mind was free of orthodoxy and he proved what he knew. And then he would ask: 'What is proof?' For what often in the past have proved to be true, had proved to be a lie in the present.

"He asked that I work along certain lines of investigation, so to leave him free to continue along other lines. He asked for my results. He was entitled to them. He was paying my salary, and he was being a very good friend. It was not for me to demand of him the results he was getting. And of his own work he told me very little.

"So, then, all of us were very happy to be with Mr. Wickham. We were sad to see him worried, and many times he was worried. Sometimes he would tell us. Sometimes he would—what you say?—bottle it up. Many visitors came for him. Some were meteorologists. And the newspaper correspondents. And the members of the board for Primary Producers. But the first visitors I suspected were bad persons were the two who came to the office on July three.

"The man who talked to Mr. Wickham, with the office door closed was—how shall I say?—perfume . . . o-oder . . . oderous. . . ."

"In Australia we'd say he stank," rumbled Mr. Luton and Dr. Linke smiled his gratitude.

"That's it. The man stank. He betrayed his . . . his . . ."

"Stink," assisted Mr. Luton.

"Carl means that the man's appearance, his face, hair, eyes, everything gave him away," Jessica Lawrence contributed.

"Ah! Yes, it gave him away. To me it gave him away," went on the doctor. "He was from those persons who have become termites. He stink, no, stank, of those who are without a name because they have so many names they have forgotten their born name. And he had a shoulder pistol. The car driver also had one. The car driver never spoke but once, when he came in to lunch, and then he foolishly tried to make us think he was an Irishman.

"Two, three days after they had gone, Mr. Wickham said something to me that might relate to those men. He said: 'Linke, d'you think wars are started when the season is thought to be propitious for the aggressor? ' I told him that I thought it not a coincidence that the two World Wars began after the European harvest had been gathered. Then he said: 'If a Hitler knew for fact that all over Europe 1960 would be a famine year, followed by another famine year, would he stock his granaries in the years '58 and '59 and start his war in '60?' Then he asked: 'Can you imagine the value of long-range accurate weather forecasting to a would-be world conqueror?'

I replied that History tells much about victories and defeats caused by unpredictable weather conditions. He asked, not because he did not know. He wanted my agreement. So we agreed that accurate long-range weather forecasting would be a tremendous weapon.

"I remember Mr. Wickham looking at me a long time and thinking, so that his eyes were seeing strange and terrible pictures. After much time, he said to me: 'It is comforting, Linke, to know we are not living near the Iron Curtain.'

"He would say no more, Inspectore, and he did not ever talk direct about the visit of two Eastern Europeans. Then, on July 13 was that telephone call. I recognised the caller's voice. It was the manager at the Commonwealth Bank in Cowdry. I hide my money in that bank. He has helped me. He arranged for me to be a member of the Tennis Club. So I know his voice. He asked to speak with Mr. Wickham. It was ten minutes after eleven o'clock in the morning. So it was that Mr. Wickham was away with the estate manager. I said if I could give Mr. Wickham a message, and the caller said no, no, he would ring again. Then, as is polite, I enquired his name, and the caller was so silent.

"Mr. Wickham did not return until a minute before dinner. I saw him enter the house, saw Jackson, the driver, put the car in the garage. We had arranged some important work together that evening, and I waited until he came to the office to inform him of the call from Cowdry. He did not come to the office until after nine o'clock, and then to inform me we would work together another time as he had the engagement. Yesterday I spoke with Jackson, the chauffeur."

Dr. Linke paused in what was a narrative to light his pipe, and possibly to highlight the climax. "What next occurred was that the manager rang once more when he knew Mr. Wickham would be at dinner, and he rang the House. My Jessica remembers Mr. Wickham was called to the telephone from dinner that night. He was two hours after dinner in his study, and then must have instructed Jackson to take him to Cowdry. He told Jackson not to speak of this journey, and Jackson spoke to me only because Mr. Wickham died. The car stopped at the private entrance to the Commonwealth Bank. It was then ten o'clock, and Mr. Wickham was with the manager for nearly one hour. When Mr. Wickham came from the bankman's private door, two men came with him. The two men spoke a little moment with Mr. Wickham, and then walked away. Mr. Wickham entered the car, and Jackson brought him home."

Dr. Linke having ceased talking, Jessica Lawrence rose to her feet, saying:

"I'm going to the kitchen, Mr. Luton, to make tea and sandwiches. I can't see any relationship between the visit of those foreign men and the visit of Mr. Wickham to the Commonwealth Bank."

"He didn't bank with the Commonwealth, Sunset," stated Mr. Luton. "I know that for a fact. And why go there at ten at night? If the manager wanted him to play cribbage or something, he wouldn't have been so mysterious on the phone."

"The only relationship I can see is that both occurrences are extremely odd. Now, where is the sandwich filling, Mr. Luton?"

"Better show you," replied the old man, and together they left for the kitchen.

"Did he say anything to Jackson during the drive home?" Bony asked the Doctor.

"He did not say one word. Jackson said he spoke twice to him, and there was no reply. I did not see him after he returned. The next morning he seemed nothing unusual."

"It would appear, Doctor, that Mr. Wickham did not visit the bank manager to play cards or to enjoy a social evening.

Both the time and the period of time are against it. Was Jackson able to describe the men who emerged with Mr. Wickham?"

"It is for that I asked Jackson, Inspectore. He said he had noted the two who had called at the office, and the two with Mr. Wickham at the bank were not the same. He heard them say good-night to Mr. Wickham, and they were not aliens."

"Perhaps Mr. Wickham kept his secrets as well as securities at the bank."

"No," replied Dr. Linke, a huge hand waving triumphantly. "I asked Mrs. Parsloe and she informed me she had gone to the Commonwealth Bank and the other two banks to enquire what they held for Mr. Wickham. They held nothing at all. And the lawyer had nothing, not even the will."

"Does Mrs. Parsloe know that her brother paid that visit to the bank manager?"

"I did not tell her. Jackson did not tell her. We did not because Mr. Wickham had instructed Jackson not to say."

"Did you happen to record the number of the car which brought the two men to the office?"

"No. But Jackson did so. It was X 10007. A Humber."

"I must become acquainted with Mr. Jackson. Did Mr. Wickham ever say, even hint, that he might present his life's work to a Government . . . any Government?"

"I cannot be precise," replied Linke. "I believe that Mr. Wickham tried much time ago to assist the Australian Government."

"I might be able to answer that one," Jessica said from the kitchen doorway. "Five years ago Mr. Wickham did approach Canberra. The outcome was that he was rebuffed on the ground that his methods were unorthodox in the view of meteorological experts. He told me that he would not again approach the Commonwealth Government. He spoke bitterly, and had every cause to do so."

Mr. Luton nudged the girl, and she turned to take from him a tray on which were plates and a larger plate of meat sandwiches. He followed her, carrying another tray bearing tea cups and tea.

"Ben got no change from the Commonwealth Government," he said, his eyes small and hard. "He never said why, but I know why. If the Gov'ment had accepted Ben's methods of long-range forecastin' all the duds in the Meteorological Departments would be out of work, and they'd all turn agin' the Gov'ment at the next election."

"It's true, and that's Australia all over," was the support he received from Jessica Lawrence. "You can't do anything, get anywhere, in this country unless you belong to a trade union. It doesn't matter how clever you are, unless the powers that be say 'Bless you, my brain child.' Mr. Wickham was an outsider, so he couldn't possibly know anything about weather science. There are fully qualified doctors working as labourers because they qualified in Europe and won't be accepted by the local medical union. Carl has been a qualified meteorologist for fifteen years, and they'd put him to work ploughing or milking cows."

Doctor Linke held up a hand, saying:

"Please, my Jessica. You ought not to speak so of the Government, of the leaders of this Australia."

"I will, Carl. I can and I will," the girl flashed at him.

"Same here," shouted Mr. Luton, pouring the tea on the tray instead of into a cup. "To hell with the Gov'ment, the loafing, lazy, money-grabbing bas . . . ."

"Now, now!" interposed Bony, laughingly, "you must not unduly shock Dr. Linke, who hasn't been long enough in the country to appreciate that one of our remaining freedoms is to gibe at the antics of our multiple rulers."

Mr. Luton chuckled; Jessica squeezed her sweetheart's arm, and Bony led the way to less contentious subjects. He felt that he was knowing Ben Wickham much more than hitherto and that Wickham must have been a great man to have inspired loyalty in such contrasting people.

As the girl and Linke were leaving, she squeezed the hand of Mr. Luton, and thanked him warmly for his hospitality, and he looked down upon her from his great height and chuckled.

"Fine young woman," he said when again seated with Bony. "I like that German more than I did. Some of 'em must have had a rough time."

"What he told us was significant," Bony said. "There is one point, however, which isn't as sharp as others. One day Mrs. Parsloe opens the private safe and does not find the secret notebook, and the next day the Investigation man arrives to put Linke through the mill. The period is too short between the time Mrs. Parsloe reported Linke and the time the Commonwealth I.S. man arrived. I must find out if he has an office at Cowdry, or was staying at Cowdry. And why."

"Think he could have burgled the office for Ben's books and things?" asked Mr. Luton. He smiled. "It would be funny if he did, 'cos I've an idea."

"Many ideas are productive of great results, Mr. Luton."

"Can you pick locks?"

"I am a professional," replied Bony gravely.

"That don't tell me much, but I'll pass it. Down below there's a chest what Ben kept things in. After we decided on that last bender, he went down there with some papers in a leather case. Might be we could take a look."

This time Bony smiled broadly. "I saw a piece of wire just outside the kitchen door. As you suggest, we will look at once."

He brought the wire when Mr. Luton was locking the front door. Then he made sure that the window blind was drawn that there was no possibility of anyone looking into the living-room-kitchen from without. He pushed the table to one side, and carefully rolled the linoleum so that it would not crack or crease.

"A long time ago, the Parsloe woman came and found me and Ben on a bender," he said. "We'd got a supply of whisky from the pub in Cowdry, and she heard about it. So we dug the hole, as I told you, and carried the mullock down the garden so's no one would know. Ben had a friend up in Adelaide, and the friend has a son who has a car and an outsize caravan. So every year when the fishing is good, the friend and his son come down with a load of grog to keep us stocked up."

Mr. Luton set a match to the wick of an oil-lamp. He lifted a trap-door to disclose a flight of wood steps flanked by a handrail. He went ahead carrying the lamp, and a moment later Bony stood in the cellar and began to chuckle.

"What d'you think of her?" asked Mr. Luton, having set the lamp on a bar of polished red-wood. Behind the bar the shelves were packed with bottles of spirits. In front of the bar were two cuspidors and two wood box seats. There were veritable stacks of cased spirits along one side of the cellar, which was as large as the living-room and the sitting-room combined.

"Are all those cases full?" Bony asked.

"Well, me and Ben never had no use for empty cases."

Bony sat on the pile of two which served as a seat at the bar. He noticed that none of the shelved bottles had been opened, and the proud Mr. Luton guessed the thought and said:

"We used to spend a lot of time down here, before Knocker called pretty late one night and we had to rush up top and straighten things quick enough to stop him getting suspicious. After that we didn't use the place as a pub, just kept her as a store. Just as well, too, because the steps got awkward as time went on, and then there was always the lamp."

"Harris doesn't know about this cellar?"

"That's right, Inspector. No one knows. Only me and you."

"And Ben's friend and the friend's son?"

"They don't know, either. When they brought the supplies we got 'em to stack it all in the sitting-room, and out in the shed. Brought it down here ourselves."

"And how long has this been going on?"

Mr. Luton chortled, and was frank enough.

"Eleven year back I was sort of retired on a small place I had on the Darling, and Ben came there and wanted me to come and live near him. Said he owned a nice little cottage where I'd be comfortable and he could come and have a drink without being blackguarded by his relations. So I sold out up north and came here. Now he's dead I think I'll go back up north. They always say that once you've been on the Darling River you're bound to go back to die on her. Ah, now! Ben's box."

Mr. Luton pulled down a stack of whisky to disclose a long cedarwood chest having a heavy brass lock and two heavy brass clasps, and, under the minute, Bony had the lid raised. There were several hard-board, loose-leaf files, a large envelope unsealed, and a green-covered notebook.

Chapter Nine

JUST A COUNTRY TOWN

TEN o'clock the next morning found Bony and Mr. Luton on the high road to Cowdry. It was Friday, market-day, and both intended to shop. The sun was masked by scudding cloud racing eastward, and the air was cold with the acrid, scentless tang of drought. But a good day for walking.

"I intend to interview the manager of the Commonwealth Bank," Bony said when they were nearing the town, at a pace that Mr. Luton thought too slow. "Do you happen to know the staff at the bank?"

"I know 'em by sight, but not all of 'em by name," replied the ageless man. "Manager's name is McGillycuddy. There's two clerks. One is Craig and I think the other's called McKenzie. The cashier's name is Kirkdale, and a young brat of an office boy who don't do much but read comics. Then there's a couple of young flips."

"Why is it that our national banking institution is overloaded with Scotchmen, and the Customs Department is snowed under with Irishmen?" asked Bony, and his walking companion chuckled and replied, evading the question.

"Now, now, no sectarianism."

"I was merely being conversational," Bony observed with slight asperity, and again Mr. Luton chuckled.

"I'm careful because underneath Cowdry there's a lot of it, the sort of sectarianism which don't always apply to religion. Out a bit from town there's a settlement of small market-gardeners what is crammed with Italians. There's some in Cowdry who hates them, and some they hate, with reason. So the Scotties run the banks, the Irish run the Gov'ment Departments, the Italians run the market gardens, and the Australians chew tobacco and lean up against veranda posts. If only all these ruddy lunatics would forget their grandfathers, the country would be worth livin' in."

"I agree, Mr. Luton. How is Cowdry off for Communists?"

"There's a local branch, so says Knocker Harris, who thinks he's a comrade. The chemist is the worshipful master. Then there's the Masons, the Buffaloes, and the Rechabites. Knocker has belonged to all of 'em except the Masons, who wouldn't have him."

"Quite a town," Bony said as they rounded a bend and came in sight of it.

"Nine pubs, racecourse, two bowling clubs, golf club, tennis clubs, and a two-up school back from the wharf a bit on Sundays."

"Think I could hire a motor-boat for the week?"

"Out of season, but you might. I know a man who has one with a trusty engine."

"Would be better than walking back. By the way, that seat outside a hotel mentioned by Harris. From it would you be able to keep the Commonwealth Bank under observation?"

"Easy."

"Where is the Post Office?"

"Opposite the bank."

"Excellent, Mr. Luton. I want you to sit on that seat, watch me enter the bank, watch the bank till I come out and until I join you again, which might not be for half an hour, and make a note of any member of the bank staff who might leave the bank, and where he goes. Clear?"

Mr. Luton nodded happily. They came to Main Street,

fairly wide and lined with the usual shop and office buildings. Bony estimated the town population at something like two thousand. It had the conventional stone soldier blowing his bugle, the horse-troughs where no horses ever again would drink, and the usual posts supporting the usual shop verandas, with the usual people leaning against them even though it was only a quarter to eleven in the morning.

The Commonwealth Bank was of sandstone that needed washing or painting, and having parked Mr. Luton on the hotel seat, Bony entered. He was confronted by a long counter supporting much brass grille work, and to an unengaged cashier presented his card and asked to see the manager.

"I'll see if the manager is free," the cashier said, the burr very faint. He nodded to a point behind Bony. "Take a seat over there, please."

Bony turned to observe the seat, a hard bench against the wall. It seemed almost that the cashier suspected a hold-up, that he hated anyone to pause too close to his cage. Bony turned back to the cashier, his eyes now glacial.

"Inform the manager that I'm a busy man, without delay."

The civil servant opened his mouth, shut it as though it ought to be shut, and departed. Bony leaned elegantly against the counter and rolled a cigarette, watched by the cashier in the next cage, who betrayed anger that this customer didn't swiftly obey the order to withdraw to the bench and wait till he was called. When the cashier returned, Bony's brows rose to a supercilious question mark.

"The manager will see you. That door."

The cashier pointed to a stained door off the main hall, and Bony sauntered to it, opened it without knocking. The man seated beyond a large table desk didn't look up from his writing until Bony sank into the chair placed for the bank's clients.

"Detective-Inspector Bonaparte? What can we do for you?"

The voice was low and hard and also, like the cashier's, just touched with a burr.

"Are you Mr. McGillycuddy?"

"Yes."

"I am hoping for co-operation, Mr. McGillycuddy. Did the late Mr. Ben Wickham have an account here?"

"Mr. Wickham . . . Mr. Ben Wickham . . . an account here? No, Inspector."

"Did he lodge securities with this bank?"

"No, Inspector. What's on your mind?"

"The bank, therefore, did not have any official interest in the late Mr. Wickham's affairs?"

"That is so."

Bony produced his pocket-book bearing his identification card.

"I am not an officer of the South Australian Department, as you will see, Mr. McGillycuddy. You need feel no obligation to answer my questions or give the information I desire. I have recently completed an assignment with the South Australian Police Department, and doubtless could obtain a further seconding from my Department if necessary."

"Of course, Inspector." The manager was now suavely affable. "The precise nature of your official position at the moment need not concern us."

"I thank you," drawled Bony, and produced his tobacco pouch and papers. The manufacture of the terrible cigarette fascinated Mr. McGillycuddy, and when burning tobacco threads fell to his blue carpet, he restrained a shudder.

"I am prosecuting a line of enquiry into the activities of the late Mr. Wickham," Bony went on, "and I have learned that on the night of July 13th he paid a visit to this bank, following a conversation on the telephone you had with him early in the evening. I would be vitally assisted did you inform me of the reason for that visit."

"Mr. Wickham did not come here, Inspector! He was never one of our clients, as I admitted a moment ago."

"Oh! A social visit, perhaps."

"No. I did not know Mr. Wickham well enough for him to visit me in private hours."

"Well, well! I find it disturbing to have doubt cast on the veracity of my informants."

Their eyes clashed. The manager's gaze didn't waver, nor did the expression of polite interest wane.

"Obviously, Inspector, you have been misinformed. Mr. Wickham did not call on me at any time."

"Too bad." Bony pretended to be vexed and seemed in no hurry to depart. "After Mr. Wickham died, were you ever asked if he had lodged securities with you?"

"Yes, as a matter of fact, his sister called one morning saying they were unable to locate some important documents and asking if we had them. I told her we held nothing belonging to her late brother. Is it . . . are you interested in those missing documents?"

"Partly, Mr. McGillycuddy, partly. Mr. Wickham appears to have been lax in matters not immediately connected with his work. Well, I won't keep you longer. Thank you."

"Anything, Inspector, that we can do to assist you." The manager came from behind his desk and accompanied his visitor to the door. They shook hands, and Bony stepped into the main hall and heard the door close behind him.

Crossing to the bench he sat with several clients, and with some deliberation withdrew a notebook from his breast pocket and proceeded to pencil notes in a shorthand he could not decipher, nor could his close neighbours on the bench. There were then no clients actually being attended to by the cashiers. The cashier who had taken his card to the manager left his cage and passed in the direction of the manager's office. Covertly watched by the second cashier, Bony continued with his meaningless notes. A number was called and a client rose from the bench and walked to the grille of the second cashier, who pushed money and a bank-book under the grille to her.

The first cashier was absent a full three minutes, and he had been back in his cage a minute when Bony casually returned the notebook to his breast pocket, rose and sauntered out.

At the kerb lounged First Constable Gibley. Gibley was in plain clothes, and was apparently astonished to see Napoleon Bonaparte make his exit from the Commonwealth Bank.

"Hullo! Mornin', Inspector! How did you get along with the Reverend yesterday afternoon?"

"He annoyed me," the smiling Bony told the policeman. "Cast his line within a yard of mine and instantly hooked a sizeable bream. And I'd been there for hours."

Gibley's chuckle was more a rumble deep in his hard stomach.

"You can't beat the Church," he said. "In for the day?"

"Yes, a few things I want. A road map of the locality. Where is the bookshop?"

"Just along the street. I'm going that way. What d'you think of Cowdry?"

"A sturdy little town. Orderly?"

"No crime. A few drunks on Saturdays and a fight or two at the football. No place for a feller wanting to keep in training. Still, we can't all go up like you've done."

They came to the bookshop, and the policeman entered with Bony. Bony did not want the road map, but he bought one and a couple of magazines. Again on the sidewalk, he said:

"Is there a foreign element in this town?"

Gibley frowned for a fleeting split-second.

"Can't say there is," he replied. "Italians out at Doubie's Creek. They keep close, work hard, and don't often go to market in the brawl line. Any reason for asking?"

"I am always interested in the composition of a community. By the way, where is the Police Station?"

"Farther up the street, and then down a side street. Good house. The kids are well schooled, and the climate is healthy."

"You must have hurried to reach the bank when they telephoned you I was there?"

"Yes. Had to move. They wanted a check-up on you." The big man brought his gaze back from the road to the slim man at his side. "What the . . . Did they tell you they phoned?"

"Oh, no," drawled Bony. "No, they didn't tell me, Gibley. It just happens I am a mind reader . . . sometimes."

"Damn! I sort of slipped, didn't I, Inspector? Well, I got office work to do. Be seeing you again, I hope. The wife's pretty handy with the teapot, any time you like to call."

"Thanks. I'll remember that."

The policeman crossed the road to take a side street to his station, and Bony strolled on until he found a café where he lingered over an ice-cream he didn't want. From the café he walked back along Main Street, on the Post Office side, went into a butcher's shop and purchased five pounds of the best steak. He was now sure that Constable Gibley had seen him enter the café, had watched him enter the butcher's shop, and continued to watch as he entered the Post Office, where he despatched a telegram to the Officer in Charge of the Traffic Branch, Adelaide, asking for the owner of car numbered X 10007.

Constable Gibley was lounging in a shop doorway when he gained the street and sauntered on. He could see Mr. Luton grimly on duty. Crossing the road, he put down his parcels on the seat, and asked:

"Who is the most talkative barber in this town?"

"That one," replied Mr. Luton, pointing. "Self-winding, like them new-fashioned clocks."

Bony nodded and found the barber without a customer. The man had a talker's chin. Also a high-pitched voice. During the first fifteen seconds he had greeted Bony, discussed the weather, tried out the races of the previous Saturday, and was branching into fishing. By this time Bony was tied with a sheet and at his mercy. He managed to get in:

"Ben Wickham wasn't wrong in his drought forecast, was he?"

"Luck, sir. Just flamin' luck. And the mugs take him for true. Greatest disaster that ever happened to Orstralia, that fortune-telling, star-gazing crook. The low-down on the weather! He says that next year the drought is gonna move up into Queensland again. And what'll happen? All the fool cockies won't fallow and sow, won't take on hands, won't buy nothing. Okay! Okay! Good luck to the cockies. But no matter what, there's no guarantee there'll be a drought. The rains'll come as usual and the cockies won't have no fallow, no sowing done, no crops. And millions of people starving over in Asia. Thousands starving here in Orstralia. Depression. That's what it means. Why, even my business has gone down more'n fifty per cent this year. Good job old Wickham did die orf. We don't want his sort in Orstralia. No good for business."

"Many people come down here for the fishing?" Bony edged in.

"Useta be a number of regulars. This year hardly any. No money. They say trade is terrible bad in Adelaide. People . . ."

"The policeman ought to have a quiet time."

"Nothin' much for him to do. Blokes haven't got the dough to get blind and kick up rusty. Gibley! Time he got moved on. Nose is too long. Thank you, sir. That'll be three and six."

Bony left the chair and surveyed his hair-cut which he found passable. He said, while searching for small money:

"Many strangers in town?"

"Strangers! Look, I don't think there's more'n three, the town's that dead. I can count 'em on one hand. One, a la-de-da what's been stayin' with the manager over at the Commonwealth. Two what's living in a caravan and doing some fishin'. Don't like them. Foreigners of some sort. Don't know what. Then there's a feller what rented a holiday shack for a month as from last week. Cripes! We're lookin' up, sir. You make number five stranger. Where you staying, if I might ask?"

"With Mr. Luton, out of town on the river."

"Oh, Luton! Fine old-timer, he is. Not many of his sort left. Good old battler. Sooner call a spade a bloody shovel than a trowel. See you again."

Bony crossed the street and joined Mr. Luton, and the old man said, importantly:

"You'd been in the bank five minutes when Gibley arrived in a hurry and stopped outside like he'd suddenly remembered he had nothing to do and no place to go. A minute after you came out, the bank office-boy went over to the Post Office with two telegrams. Either that or one message took two pages to write on."

"Anything else?"

"Nothing except that Gibley's been following you around. He's eyeing us now from inside the paper shop."

Bony was delighted and looked it. He said:

"How often have you baited for bream and caught a kingfish? Let us have a drink."

Chapter Ten

EXPERIENCE POINTS A FINGER

THE afternoon was cold and blustery, and Bony employed the first part of it at Mr. Luton's wood-heap, splitting billets for the stove and axeing logs for the lounge fire. Mr. Luton did not approve, but Bony wanted exercise, and the labour did produce an idea. Into a tin he dropped the witchety grubs which the splitting disclosed, juicy fat grubs about the size of a man's thumb.

It was here that Knocker Harris found him, and, up-ending a log, he sat and relaxed preparatory to a gossip.

"You doin' a bit of yakker," he remarked on the obvious. "Bit of work don't do nobody any 'arm, like. Have a good time in town?"

"Quite," replied Bony, leaning on the axe. "Met the policeman. Seems all right."

"Yair. Seems," snorted Knocker. "Good at pinchin' drunks, and hoeing into the Italians when they kick up a dust. Sooner fish than earn his wages, though." Mr. Harris spat. "Gonna put me and John into an Old Man's Home! That's what he thinks."

Bony chopped, watched shrewdly by Knocker, who presently said:

"You walk both ways or get a lift?"

"Walked. We tried to hire a boat, but none are available."

"Been tryin' to get John to buy one, but he don't take to the idea, like. Anyway, I've caught kingfish on me night line, so the yarn of havin' to troll for 'em don't play poker with me. You find out what was give to Ben?"

"Haven't really tried. By the way, you saw him when he was dead?"

"Yair. About ten minutes after John found him konked out in the sitting-room."

"How did he look?"

"Look? Calm like. Coulda been asleep, but he wasn't."

"Have you ever seen a man dead of the horrors?" Bony asked, conversationally.

"No. Seen a bloke once pretty crook on drinkin' home-brewed spud juice and metho. He was a beaut. Black hair and a ziff what hid all his face exceptin' his eyes. Did he perform! You oughta seen him." The quiet drawling voice held no trace of humour, and not much of interest, till he said: "You know, what John calls the horrors ain't real horrors, like. They had sense enough, them two, to go on the cure, like, before they got the dinkum sort of horrors. All they had was seein' things what they could flick off their ears or their hair, like. They didn't do no prancin' around, you know, like climbing up the roof or up a tree. They never yelled and screamed like some I knew in the old days. Only time they got excited was when they flogged the trees for bullocks. You oughta seen 'em. Characters!"

"You never joined them?"

"No, Inspector, I never could. I can't take it, like. The booze plays hell with me ulcers. One rum is my limit when I goes to town, and only then 'cos I got to be sociable, like."

There seemed nothing of value to be gained from Knocker Harris, and Bony became bored. Relief was given by the noise of an approaching car, which aroused the dogs to frenzy.

"Could be the flamin' quack," surmised Knocker. "Don't you take no lip from him."

A minute later there appeared round the side of the house a woman whose face resembled that of a horse, and whose stocky figure was made ridiculous by the tight brown trousers she was wearing. Her voice was harsh, and she was engaged in what is known as talking-down—in this instance, Mr. Luton.

"The quack's old bitch," inelegantly announced Knocker.

"Well, I certainly hope so, Luton," the lady was saying. "As the doctor has so often told you, a man of your age ought not to take alcohol save medicinally, and then only sparingly." Mr. Luton began to speak and was wiped off the slate. "We have been greatly worried about you, Luton. This isolation is tragic, tragic. It's no use arguing. You'll simply have to give up this place and live where you can be properly cared for. Oh!"

"This is Mrs. Maltby, the doctor's wife," boomed Mr. Luton, the lid of his left eye half-masted. "Inspector Bonaparte, Mrs. Maltby."

"So you are Inspector Bonaparte, are you?" queried the lady. "Wonders will never cease. Before leaving town I called at the Post Office, and the postmaster asked me to bring a telegram for you."

"That is kind of you," Bony said, unsmilingly.

"No. I intended talking to Luton on my way back. Er . . . we have been thinking you might have called at the house. Mrs. Parsloe rather wants to speak to you. Some afternoon about four. Now I must be off. Good-bye, Inspector."

Bony lowered his head politely, and the woman strode back to the gate with Mr. Luton and the accompanying dogs as escort. Knocker said, as though hoping that Mrs. Maltby would hear:

"What d'you know?"

Bony chopped wood, hoping there were no more Mrs. Maltbys to be encountered during his career. There was only one way of dealing with such women, the way an aborigine deals with his impertinent wife, but that was not for Inspector Napoleon Bonaparte. Knocker Harris's suggested treatment shocked even Bony. He repeated the suggestion for the reclamation of Mrs. Maltby to the returning Mr. Luton, and was sternly ordered to 'cut that out, and come in for tea.' Unabashed, Knocker followed Mr. Luton to the kitchen, and Bony followed more slowly while reading the message:

REGISTERED IN THE NAME OF KLAVICH. STOP. CHIEF CLERK TO HUNGARIAN CONSUL ADELAIDE. WHAT YOU DOING AT COWDRY? REGARDS. TILLET.

After several cups of tea, Bony strolled along the river-bank as far as the bridge spanning the highway. For some time he leaned against the stone parapet watching the fish jumping for flies, and the larger fish chasing others. He noted with interest the peculiarity of this river, the banks of which were not of earth and shelving, but of precipitous limestone going straight down to the depths. Scrub and tall trees grew right to the edge of these faces of the great cleft which had admitted the sea.

From the bridge he walked to the highway almost to the line of pine trees providing the wind-break for Mount Marlo, and then turned off the road to bisect the grazing paddocks where there was no grazing and no stock. He came to a path barely discernible which appeared to come from opposite the gates to Mount Marlo, and which he followed to the back fence of Mr. Luton's garden, and he wondered if that was the path made by the late Ben Wickham.

After dinner, when they sat smoking over coffee, he said:

"The telegram Mrs. Maltby brought was from the Traffic Branch in Adelaide. They say that the car used by those foreigners to call on Wickham is owned by a staff member of the Hungarian Consulate. Are you still sure that Wickham never mentioned them to you?"

"I am," replied Luton, calmly. "Nor did he say anything to me about why he called at the bank after hours. Mind you, that was like Ben, not to say anything to me. Exceptin' to moan now and then about his sister and the Maltbys, he never talked of his private business, and he had to be pretty full before he'd talk about his work. He did talk about the flaming stars, but not often about his weather-forecastin'."

"So that when you did meet, you discussed the river, the fishing, and the past?"

"That's so. You see, Ben was a gentleman. He never deliberately talked over my head, as the saying goes. He'd arrive here, unload his moans about what happened up at the house, and after a bit we'd both go back over the years and talk about old times."

"I suppose that when he became sufficiently sober to return to his house, he was feeling despondent?"

"No. He used to tell me we'd had a hell of a fine time and that he felt he'd had a brain wash and was ready to get on with his job."

"Did he express an opinion of Dr. Linke?"

"Seemed to like him. Said he was first-rate and keen. Never said anything against him, excepting . . ."

"Excepting?"

"Excepting that Linke sometimes jawed him for coming here for a bender."

"He was bitter about the Government persistently refusing to take his work seriously, wasn't he?"

"Too true he was." Mr. Luton's eyes widened and blazed. "While our people are jeering at him, and our weather men are calling him an outsider, the Russians step in. They did, didn't they? The Hungarians are Russians, aren't they?"

As Mr. Luton demanded agreement, Bony conceded the

thought. Other thoughts he did not express. He said, instead:

"Have you ever seen a man die in delirium tremens?"

"No. But I've seen a man who died of the hoo-jahs."

"Tell me about it."

"It was a terrible long time back. I must of been about twenty or so, and I was working up in Queensland, droving cattle. Open country, you understand. The year was bad, and my job was to ride ahead and scout for water for the cattle.

"The Government had just sunk a bore called Number Eight, and I met a couple of prospectors who told me it was gushing good and that the water was drinkable. They said an old bloke was in charge of the plant which hadn't been moved on, and they reckoned by this time he'd have gone bush as he'd been on the booze and was raging around when they left.

"Anyway, I went on to take a look at this bore, and see what feed there was for the cattle. I found it all right. And a bit of a shed near the dismantled gear. I knew what had happened before I went inside. The old feller was dead in a corner, and I'm game to bet there was fifty empty Pink-Eye brandy bottles. He hadn't been dead long. The day before, I reckoned. Looked bloody awful."

"Describe him, please."

"Hell! What for? He was dead of the hoo-jahs. Lying on the floor, and the place stinking of Pink-Eye. Part of a bottle still in his hand. Had it by the neck and back a bit like he was fighting the demons off."

"Do you remember the expression on the dead man's face?" persisted Bony.

"I won't ever forget it, Inspector. Never made no difference to me, though. Still, I sort of knew when to stop. He didn't."

"Describe the expression on the dead man's face," Bony continued to persist.

"His mouth was open like he was yelling when he perished.

Blood had poured from it. He'd been chased round and round the shed, for you could see his tracks what made a road all round. And he'd run inside towards the end, to escape the things that were chasing him, and they caught up with him in the corner. He was looking at them, seeing them when he died."

"When you found Ben Wickham dead, did he remind you of that man at the bore?"

"He certainly did not. The feller at the bore died when he was awake. Ben died in his sleep."

"Died in his sleep!" echoed Bony.

"Yes. He was lying peaceful, like he slept, when I found him."

"His eyes were closed?"

"Partly so. I kept 'em closed proper, with a florin apiece. That's why I say he died of something given to him; not from the hoo-jahs."

"Were the coins on the eyes when the doctor came?"

Mr. Luton was triumphant.

"Course not. I took 'em off when I heard the car."

Chapter Eleven

THE SQUIRE'S CHEST

WHEN they should have gone to bed, they went down into the cellar, Bony carrying the lamp, leaving the table and floor-covering in the living-room ready for quick replacement in the event of interruption.

At this second visit, Bony could not resist the impulse to chuckle at the mental picture of two wily 'hard doers' determined to maintain freedom against the onslaught of relations and outsiders. Additional to the neat stacks of spirits, there were a dozen cases of beer, and on a special shelf he had not previously noticed, because it was in a corner opposite the bar counter, he espied six bottles of Drambuie evenly spaced, obviously by reverent hands.

"Quite a plant, eh?" remarked Mr. Luton. "Whisky there in that pile. Brandy over there. Rum right behind you, and the gin over here. We'd sense enough to be careful of the oil-lamp, and arranged the stock so we could find the right bottles in the dark. Once we camped down here all night, with the trap-door down. Air got a bit foul with the lamp lit, so we turned it out, and afterwards I ran a shaft to come up inside the wood-shed just behind the wash-copper. Could camp here a month with the lamp lit now."

"Who planned it?" asked Bony, more to keep Mr. Luton occupied while he examined the place.

"It sort of grew from the years gone by. At the end of roaring hot days when we'd unyoke the bullocks and was drinkin' tea and too tired to eat, we'd tell each other what we'd do when we made our fortunes. We agreed we'd build a shack beside a nice cool river where the grass was always green, and where the sunlight was green, too, because it fell through bright-green tree leaves. And we agreed we'd build a private pub at the back of the shack, and stock her to the roof. We'd have a bar counter, and ice-boxes and things, and we'd drink from the best crystal glasses when we felt like it, and tin pint pannikins when we felt like that. The crystal's under the counter there, and the tin pannikins. Only difference we made to our pub was to sink her underground. D'you think . . . Would you like to wet her?"

Bony refrained from looking at Mr. Luton. He knew what it was to be exhausted by a never-ending hot day on outback tracks, to the point of being unable to undertake the chore of cooking a meal. He knew what it was to crave with a poignant longing to feel iced liquor sliding down his gummed-up throat, and to feast his eyes on cool water lazing along under the moss-green branches of overhanging trees.

The invitation sprang from pride in having a dream made reality, the humility of spirit that life had been kind to make the dream come true, when reality never came to thousands of others who dreamed the same dream.

"It would be a pleasure to see you behind that bar, Mr. Luton."

Mr. Luton's smile was reminiscent. Lifting the counter-flap, he passed inside and, with the rows of shelved bottles at his back, gravely asked Bony what he would have.

"Whisky, with soda if you have it."

This was a place where you couldn't miss. Mr. Luton produced a seltzergene bottle and filled it with water. He fitted a cartridge to the bottle and smiled at Bony without speaking. There was a case on the floor, and this he had to open with hammer and chisel, that the show bottles on the shelves would remain intact. He set up a bottle of Scotch, and from under the counter brought up two remarkably fine crystal goblets. They poured their own drinks.

Bony made another complete survey of the dream come true. He raised his glass, and over it saw Mr. Luton's raised glass, and his bright hazel eyes above it. He bowed, and drank.

Presently, Bony turned back to the cedarwood chest he had not re-locked with his piece of wire. He returned to the bar with the parchment envelope marked 'WILL'.

"This, obviously, is your friend's missing will," he said. "As you see, the envelope isn't sealed. I would like to read it for possible light it may throw on Ben Wickham's life which he did not reveal even to you."

"Go ahead."

Bony read, and thoughtfully returned the will to the envelope.

"The major part of the estate, apparently large, is bequeathed to his sister, Mrs. Parsloe," he said. "He willed twenty thousand pounds to Mrs. Maltby, ten thousand each to her husband and Jessica Lawrence, and to you he left this property . . . house, land, and, in his words, what's under it. You are to receive also twenty thousand pounds. You have been appointed the sole executor. The executor to present all else in the chest to Dr. Linke."

Mr. Luton was frowning.

"I didn't want the money, Inspector. I told him so."

"Wickham made other provisions," Bony went on. "He left a thousand pounds each to Mrs. Loxton, the chauffeur, and Knocker Harris. There is one peculiar clause or provision in the will. The beneficiaries are divided into major and minor participants. If any of the major beneficiaries contest the will, and the legal points governing this are most explicit, the entire estate is to pass to Dr. Linke. Tell me, when Wickham said he intended leaving you twenty thousand, did he say, or even hint, that he had informed the others of his intention concerning them?"

"Yes," replied Mr. Luton. "Said he had told them what he had done in his latest will. Excepting one thing. He didn't tell 'em who was to have his weather records and papers and things. I think I can see why he put in that bit sayin' if any of them contested the will Linke was to get the lot. One or other, according to Ben, might argue the point about leaving the weather secrets to Linke."

"What of Mrs. Loxton, the car driver Jackson, and Knocker Harris? D'you know if he told them?"

"Ben didn't mention them."

"The will doesn't state who drew up the document. Do you know who the solicitors are?"

"Parker & Parker, in Cowdry, as far as I know. Ben said that the present Parker's father was his father's law man. Eh! Don't the Reverend Weston get anything?"

"Not mentioned."

"He'll snort. What'll we do with the will?"

"Put it back in the squire's old chest."

"All right! But . . ."

"You have been trying hard to convince me that Ben Wickham was poisoned in this very house, Mr. Luton. You knew about that cedarwood chest, and that Ben Wickham added papers to it as late as the day he came to join you on that last bender. You could have a key to that chest, or have opened it as easily as I did with wire. You could thus have gained access to the will, have learned its provisions, learned that you inherit twenty thousand pounds and this property, including 'what is under the house'.

"You could have murdered Ben Wickham. None but yourself had such opportunities. That you have tried to convince me, that you have convinced Harris, that you tried to convince Dr. Maltby and the policeman that Wickham did not die as the result of alcoholic poisoning, would amount to very little, because the body no longer exists. All that you know. Nothing can be proved against you, and this you must know also. But the facts that you had easy access to the will, that the testator died under extraordinary circumstances in your own house, would make you a very strong suspect with the police and most especially with the relatives. You understand all that?"

"I didn't kill Ben," Luton said, quietly.

"I would be the most disillusioned man of this century should I become convinced that you had," Bony murmured. "So, until I can produce a very much stronger suspect than you, and thus save you from much annoyance, the will shall remain in the chest. Agreed?"

"Whatever you say."

"Be advised. Henceforth, do not put forward the assertion that Wickham was poisoned, not to anyone."

Mr. Luton seemed a trifle less willing to agree, but did so. Bony glanced at his wrist-watch. He pointed out that it was close to midnight, and persuaded Mr. Luton to go to bed and leave him for an hour or so to delve among the records in the chest. To this the old man readily agreed, and departed without a glance at the whisky bottle.

Bony sat on the cases beside the bar counter, and automatically rolled a cigarette and applied a match. On only one point was he convinced, and that was Mr. Luton's innocence of murder. But there was the opportunity for someone else to have murdered Wickham, the time of that opportunity being between four in the morning when Luton visited his friend to give him the dose of 'medicine', and six twenty-five when Luton was wakened by hearing Wickham laughing. A time period of approximately an hour and a half. Someone could have entered the front room where Wickham was being tortured by the hoo-jahs and offered him a drink containing poison. Wickham must have known who that someone was, trusted him—or her—and, not as strong-willed as Luton, have succumbed to the temptation to accept the drink.

Who? Any person mentioned in the will? The foreigners who appeared, at least, to have begun negotiations for Wickham's weather secrets; the office burglars, even the person or persons who had met Wickham in the private rooms of the bank manager; even a hired assassin paid by those powerful interests opposed to Wickham, fantastic though this thought might seem to be?

The 'who' was of less importance than the 'why', if the dead man had been poisoned. Mr. Luton did have both motive and opportunity. Then again, Dr. Maltby, Mrs. Maltby, Jessica Lawrence, Mrs. Parsloe, had many thousands of pounds' worth of motive, while the ex-housekeeper, the chauffeur, Knocker Harris, all had motive worth a thousand pounds. There was no beginning. There was nobody to begin with. There was nothing that a man could get his teeth into.

Bony shuddered and abruptly went to the chest and fell to real work.

The green notebook baffled him from cover to cover. He could not understand the diagrams nor the terms used to explain them. 'Baric surfaces', 'synoptic codes', baffled him, and the algebraic problems led him nowhere.

The files, however, did interest him. There were seven of them, one for each of the last seven years, and apparently they contained correspondence which Wickham had carefully excluded from his secretary. The letters were written from America, from France and Germany, from Finland and Italy. They contained offers of financial support, ranging from a high Government appointment at Washington to the sum of one million pounds from a man signing himself Edward Tilly, and giving an address in Lisbon.

There were newspaper cuttings either praising Wickham or condemning him, and it could not but be noted that encouragement came chiefly from the United States and vilification from Australia. Only on the last file, and during the last six months of Wickham's life, was recognition grudgingly conceded by professional meteorologists and any interest taken in his achievements by the various Australian Governments.

If ever there was a prophet who had received no honour in his own country, and no support in his efforts to improve the lot of agriculturists, and therefore of the world, it was the late Benjamin Wickham. Bony was sickened by the petty jealousy in human hearts, and by the lack of imagination in men of high estate. He experienced relief when Mr. Luton descended with a huge jug of coffee and a dish piled high with buttered toast.

"Thought it time you had some shut-eye," Mr. Luton said, faintly disapproving. "Coffee and brandy will make you look for bed."

The tray with the coffee and toast he placed on the bar counter, and from the pocket of his dressing gown he extracted the brandy bottle in current use.

"You should not have risen so early," Bony admonished him.

"I didn't go to bed. I sat up afore the fire."

"Oh! Why?"

"Been doing a spot of thinkin'. You know, I was a damn fool to put those coins on Ben's eyelids."

"I have been wondering why you did it."

"Me, too. Could have been several reasons. I remember thinkin' that Ben would like having his eyes closed properly. Then when the car was coming with the quack, I took the coins off, so's the quack wouldn't say I interfered. After we talked about men dying in the hoo-jahs, I come to see that my puttin' them coins on the eyes stopped the quack believin' my idea about him being murdered."

Bony drank the spiced coffee with appreciation. He said:

"You could not have deceived a pathologist, however. We know little of post-mortem effects. Wickham could have died through collapse of the heart caused by the action of alcohol, and not necessarily the action of alcohol on the brain. He might well have fallen into a coma. I rather think that if he died when in a coma his eyes would be as you described them."

"Then you don't believe he was given something?"

"I am admitting neither to belief nor disbelief. You tempted me to come here for the fishing. Then you captured my interest with your remarkable theories concerning the effects of alcohol. Then Doctor Linke furthered my interest by events concerning Wickham during the few weeks prior to his death. From these events stem many things. Result, Mr. Luton? The result is that I continue to probe until I am satisfied Ben Wickham was, or was not, murdered."

Chapter Twelve

A TRADE IN INFORMATION

REFRESHED by a 'spot of shut-eye', they breakfasted late and remained at table as they smoked. Bony, as usual, was well groomed, and his host was wearing a rough tweed suit.

"What was Ben Wickham's opinion on cremation, d'you know?" Bony asked.

"Didn't ask him," was the reply. "He never talked about it that I recall."

"Were his parents cremated?"

"I know that one, Inspector. They were buried in the cemetery at Cowdry."

"Why, then, was Wickham's body cremated? He expressed no such wish in the will." Mr. Luton evaded comment, and Bony went on, "Do you think, if Benjamin Wickham held a decisive view of the manner in which his body should be disposed of, that he would have discussed the matter with you?"

"Yes, I think he would," replied Luton. "But he didn't talk of it, and neither did I."

"Then we must assume that the subject of the disposal of the dead was not one of interest to him; that he never spoke of it to his relatives and friends. His parents had not been cremated. From whom did the suggestion of cremation originally come? I should like to know. Death is the profound finality of life; cremation is the finality of death. We may study the bones of a man dead many thousands of years; we cannot study the dust of a man scattered to the four winds. I shall ponder these truths while taking your dogs for a walk."

Mr. Luton watched Bony pass through the wicket gate, preceded by the dogs, who were infinitely more keen on hunting than walking. His strong jaw was set to a hardness and his eyes thoughtful. He was still thoughtful when he went to the rear and fed the hens, and returned to wash the dishes and straighten the house, and, later, to carry three empty beer bottles to the river and toss them in. The habit of years stood by him. The empties he had filled with water that they would not float.

A boy came shortly after eleven with a telegram for Bony, payment of a special rate having ensured its delivery. The Electricity Department's meter reader came just after twelve, and Mr. Luton paid the account with a cheque. To Mr. Luton, long accustomed to a peaceful retreat, the morning was unusually crowded, and was lighted by the return of Bony, who suggested they split a bottle of beer.

The glasses were filled, when Mr. Luton remembered the telegram.

"Ah!" breathed Bony, gazing upon the flimsy, "I've been expecting that. It will be a message from my Chief at the C.I.B. in Brisbane instructing me to report at once. I have received many such telegrams, and most I have ignored. Then comes a follow-on message from the Chief Commissioner's secretary ordering me to report at once, or else. This form of blackmail being unsuccessful, another telegram arrives, suspending me from duty, and unless I report by a certain date I shall be sacked."

"That brings you to book," smiled Mr. Luton.

"On the contrary. I report when it suits me, and it suits me only when I have finalised an investigation. So I discuss the situation with my Chief Commissioner, who damns and blasts my eyes and swears I'm not a policeman's bootlace. I have to point out that, despite this relative position, I do bring home the bacon. So all is forgiven."

"I can quite believe it," Mr. Luton said, seriously.

Bony opened the telegram, and read aloud:

"FROM SUPERINTENDENT LINTON, C.I.B. BRISBANE. REPORT AT EARLIEST. THIS INSTRUCTION OF TOP IMPORTANCE. ADD MY PERSONAL ENTREATY YOU COMPLY WITHOUT DELAY."

Dropping the flimsy to the table, he drank while regarding his host over the glass, as he had done down below.

"Not the usual wording," he said. "Slightly ambiguous, the ambiguity being the additional personal note from Linton. Good man, Linton. We all like him, though he isn't prone to 'additives', a word now favoured by oil companies advertising petrol. Normally, 'report back or be damned'; in this instance, 'add my personal entreaty you comply without delay.' And so, Mr. Luton, as someone once said: 'The game's afoot.'"

Mr. Luton could not, of course, understand the basis of his guest's obvious satisfaction, and naturally could not grasp the real significance of that telegraphed order. He knew that Bony had applied for and had been granted ten days' leave of absence from duty, but did not see the point that, the leave period being granted, only a reason vitally important would have dictated its cancellation.

He was not perturbed when Bony abruptly withdrew to the front veranda, there to meditate until called for lunch. During lunch Bony spoke but seldom, so preoccupied was he, and immediately after lunch he went out to the garden without offering assistance with the washing-up. It was three o'clock when Bony reappeared to say that the Reverend Weston was fishing from the bank, and that he had a score to settle with him. And:

"Afternoon, Padre. Any luck?"

Light grey eyes were turned upon Bony, and the quick smile did nothing to soften the ever-present hint of harsh intolerance.

"Ah! Good afternoon. No, they are not biting to-day."

"Do you mind if I cast beside you?"

"Go right ahead. Let your neighbour do unto you what you did unto him."

Old clothes and weathered boots failed to detract from this man's grimly powerful personality. He examined Bony as the latter baited a hook with a bunch of garden worms. The long brown fingers fumbled with the task, and so the parson turned his attention to his own gear. That gave Bony the chance to bait with witchety grubs.

Before those grubs had descended three feet they were devoured by a fast-moving kingfish. The water swirled. The tip of Bony's rod flashed downward.

A kingfish is a different proposition from a gentlemanly trout. There are no 'by your leaves' in his make-up, and he has much in common with Australian politicians and Australian thugs, who invariably mix it, boots and all. Bony was determined to land this fish, and without damage to Mr. Luton's rod, and the Reverend Weston quickly admitted that he knew how to handle this ruthless fighter.

It occupied Bony eleven minutes to bring the fish to the gaff expertly wielded by Mr. Weston, whose sportsmanship was adequately proved. Afterwards they sat on the log seat and estimated the weight of the catch as being about fourteen pounds. That subject disposed of, it was time for a cigarette. Then they tried again, with worms, and nothing happened, and Mr. Weston said he really would have to employ someone or other to prepare the boat for trolling.

These two men found much in common. They were both insatiably curious. The minister was the less patient.

"Would you be offended if I asked you one or two candidly personal questions?" he asked.

"Not at all, provided they don't touch my income-tax returns. I suggest that we trade a little. It could be that we stand either side a fence."

"Agreed. We'll trade. You open the negotiations."

"What was the basis of Ben Wickham's friendship with John Luton?"

"Alcohol. His father was a solid drinker, and he lived long. Ben took after his father, but he didn't have his father's rigid social code." Weston smiled when he added: "Nor did he have his father's capacity and staying power."

"Thank you, Padre. I have two more," Bony said.

"Good. Shoot them."

"At whose instigation was Wickham's body cremated?"

"Difficult. I think it was I who first suggested it. There is much to be argued in favour of cremation, æsthetically chiefly. I recall that the suggestion was opposed by Mrs. Parsloe, and supported by Dr. Maltby and his wife. Mrs. Parsloe surrendered when Maltby further suggested the dispersal of the ashes over Mount Marlo, as a fitting gesture to a famous man."

"Again, thank you. My third question: Is Dr. Maltby well off?"

"I can best answer that by saying that Maltby and his wife are worried by the non-location of Wickham's will, under which, Wickham once told them, they were to receive substantial sums."

"Would you permit a fourth question?"

"Certainly," assented the Rev. Weston, brows uplifted to narrow forehead.

"When Luton asserted that Wickham died of a cause not due to alcohol, why was a post-mortem not insisted on?"

Weston chuckled, and the humour in his eyes seemed to be genuine.

"It was obvious, even to Maltby, that the cause of Wickham's death was the effect of too much alcohol on his weak heart. Luton could produce neither proof nor logic in support of his astonishing assertions. I think I see what you are driving at, Bonaparte. The feeble-minded might be led to indulge in a whispering campaign, but that couldn't touch the family. Anything more?"

"No," replied Bony, smiling. "It's now your turn."

"Very well. How did you manage to rise so high in your Police Department? I am not being impertinent, I do assure you. You must have met many obstacles, extraordinary hurdles, and I sense a story far more irresistible than that of errand boy to millionaire."

"My beginning was subordinate to that of the errand boy," replied Bony. "I was found beneath a sandalwood tree, found in the arms of my mother, who had been clubbed to death for breaking a law. Subsequently, the matron of the Mission Station to which I was taken and reared found me eating the pages of Abbotts's *Life of Napoleon Bonaparte.* The matron possessed a peculiar sense of humour. The result—my name. Despite the humour, she was a great woman. Aware of the burden of birth I would always have to carry, she built for me the foundations of my career. My entry to the Queensland Police Department came about after I had won my M.A. at the Brisbane University, and my progress in the Department has been due to the fortunate fact that the Commissioner abhors failure in anyone, and has managed to evade dropping dead from rage-induced apoplexy long enough to ensure that I received just recognition. You see, I have never failed to finalise an investigation."

"You must find that most gratifying," dryly remarked Mr. Weston, and the undertone was not unnoticed by Bonaparte.

"I must not fail, and that is not gratification of vanity. You may fail and try again. Another's failure will be accepted without comment, and little effect on his career. To yet another, failure will have no adverse effect on his mind or his career, for he will take it as temporary. But I must not fail, ever."

Mr. Weston was not unintelligent.

"Tell me more," he urged, "of your career."

"That Mission Station matron began it," Bony went on. "She gave me all her affection and, too, she gained mine. She began my training before I could crawl, began the building of this misnamed man of two races. She inculcated in me beliefs and ambitions which were to become the driving forces of my life; and with these forces I have had to contend against pre-natal influences inherited from my aboriginal mother. She instilled into my mind the ability to see and evaluate my own limitations, and enough wisdom to detour, as it were. She taught me to fear nothing of the living, to fear no one other than myself. She didn't think of it, I suppose, because she didn't teach me not to fear the dead."

"And you really feel yourself omnipotent to—er—finalise your present investigation?"

Mr. Weston found himself drawn to meet the blue eyes of the man who turned slowly to look at him. It was then that Mr. Weston realised that his ideas of half-castes were somehow just so much tosh. It was then that he first realised that the circumstances of a man's birth are no obstacle, save to the snob. He heard a voice which seemed to have no association with the mind beyond those extraordinary eyes.

"My present investigation, Padre?"

"Well, er . . . I thought . . . I thought you might have credited old Luton's crazy theories with a modicum of truth. There could be a basis of truth in them, don't you think?"

"What do you think, Padre?"

Mr. Weston felt like a small boy caught out in some deceit. Abruptly, he regretted having been so superior, of having thought of himself as being a pinnacle high above a half-caste. He was angry now, because he suspected he had been subtly encouraged to tumble into a trap. He had to answer that question; and truthfully.

"I think there might be something in what the old boy says."

"Mr. Luton has had a wide experience of delirium tremens," reminded Bony. "Proof of his assertion that each type of spirituous liquor will produce its distinctive demons, is, however, not forthcoming. Were you referring to Mr. Luton's assertion that Ben Wickham did not die of alcoholic poisoning?"

"If we admit that Mr. Luton is right on the first, then he could be right on his second claim," allowed Mr. Weston, mopping his forehead with a red silk handkerchief, and obviously relieved that Bony was gazing outward over the river.

"There are, I understand, many people made happy by his death."

"That is so, Inspector Bonaparte."

"Do you think that among them are those living locally?"

"I could admit only to the possibility."

"When did you first come to think there could be something in Mr. Luton's theories?"

Mr. Weston hesitated.

"It was some time after Ben's body had been cremated. I am sure of that."

Bony said suavely: "Should I begin an investigation relative to the death of Ben Wickham, be sure that I shall continue until I prove to myself, at least, that he was murdered or that he was not murdered. Meanwhile, I am enjoying my stay with my old friend."

"Of course! Of course! Then am I to understand that you

are not investigating the circumstances surrounding the demise of my late friend?"

"You are to understand precisely what appeals to you most."

"Ah! You do right to chide me, Inspector. Pray accept my questioning as from an interested party. Perhaps Mr. Luton has told you of my position in the house up yonder. I have for long years been very close to both poor Ben Wickham and his sister, Mrs. Parsloe."

"He did mention you," Bony replied with a chuckle. "He told me of your concern for his health after I had informed him how you had caught a fish from under my own hook. It was then I told him I would balance the scales. Acknowledge that I have now. The secret? I'll give it to you. Witchety grubs are first-class bait. You'll find them if you split firewood."

Mr. Weston stood with Bony and smiled. Gone was the unease, and healed were the wounds to his vanity, for he was now in the presence of a merely ordinary man, and a likeable one. It was long after he left Bony on the river-bank that he remembered being led into a trap, and suffered a sneaking fear that he was to be lured into another.

Bony watched his tall and angular figure trudging along the track to the main road, and when the parson had disappeared he sat again on the tree-trunk and again rolled a cigarette. Casually he said twice, the second time loudly:

"The enemy has retreated. You may come out, Mr. Harris."

Knocker Harris emerged from the hollow log to rise stiffly to his feet, and with a thankful sigh to sit beside the fisherman.

"Beaut, ain't he?" he said, nodding at the kingfish. "Nearer fourteen than thirteen pounds."

"Why were you holed up under my favourite seat?"

"Well, it's like so," defended Knocker. "I'm on me way to visit John and you, see? I'm drawin' nigh when I sees the

Reverence castin' down-river a bit, like. I sees I can't side-step without him seeing me if he looks my way. So I acts the abo. When he does look up-river, I'm a fence-post. When he looks somewhere else, I moves forward to this log. Only cover for me is inside, like. Then his reverence comes along right beside here, and I know he's here 'cos the dogs barked."

"They didn't bark when you came?"

"No, of course not." Mr. Harris chuckled while splitting open a cigarette for the tobacco, which he tossed into his mouth. "Got no time for him, Inspector. Nasty bit of work. What's the use of parsons, I'd like to know? Only bludging on the people. Never does no work. Parisites, I calls 'em. Always sticking their dirty noses into other people's bis'ness, like. Gonna put me and old John into a home, says he. What a ruddy hope! He get any change outer you?"

"You heard what we said," Bony said, coldly.

"That I didn't. Wished I could of. The hole into the log's a bit small, like, and it was sort of blocked with me feet. How did you know I was in there?"

"I could smell you."

Chapter Thirteen

THE RECALL

"FUNNY how the Reverend sort of got to like this part of the river lately," remarked Knocker Harris. "You know, before Ben konked out, me and John had some peace, like. But not since."

"Mr. Weston doesn't often fish here?" prompted Bony.

"No. First time he came here fishing was the other afternoon. Come to pump you, like. Ain't to be trusted further'n you could belt with one hand. Landed over at the house one time when Ben and John was coming out of the hoo-jahs, and what he said to them you'd never read about. And them that crook their eyes was fixed like marbles in a bottle, like."

"They were, doubtless, rather ill."

"Ill! You wouldn't know 'em. Corpses they was, livin' corpses. See that kingy's eyes? They had eyes like that when they was soberin', like. Dammit, they had mouths like that, too. Sort of saggin' open. I'd better gut this fish for John."

Knocker Harris slid forward to kneel beside the fish and proceeded to scale it and remove its innards on to a sheet of bark, as he said, to give to the chooks. He was obeying still the commands of his mother and father—"Waste not, want not".

"They were truly sick when recovering?" persisted Bony.

"Sick!" echoed Knocker Harris, as though the question was an aspersion upon his friends. "You wouldn't know 'em, as I told you."

"There is, you think, something in what John Luton says about the effects of the hoo-jahs being in accordance with the grog?"

"Course there is. I know. I've seen them fellers often enough when they was having the hoo-jahs. Last time, it was knockin' hoo-jahs off their ears and shoulders, like. Time before, they was knockin' them off their chests and knees. That was rum, I think. Knoo a bloke once who used to have the hoo-jahs on metho with a dash of battery acid." Knocker turned from his task to laugh without restraint. "Once, when I seen him in the horrors, you could have got a thousand quid for him from a waxworks joint. He was properly stiff with horror, hair and all, like."

Knocker took the fish to the river to clean, leaving Bony with the picture of two near-lunatics being nursed by one who, unless of simple mind, could not have borne the load with such patience. The picture gave place to another, of saltbush plain and mulga forest, and two dust-grimed, sweating men striding beside groaning bullocks hauling a veritable mountain on wheels. The visions were part of a greater which made psychological sense.

He heard the car turn off the highway and shouted the fact to Knocker Harris. Harris appeared up the steep sandstone bank, taxed by the fish he managed to keep from dragging on the ground. Nodding to Bony, he hurried to the house, yet had to pass the car, which beat him to the gate. Constable Gibley spoke to him, clearly about the fish, and Bony was thrusting hooks into safety corks when the policeman said at his elbow:

"My boss at Mount Gambier rang up about you, Inspector. I'm to inform you that Headquarters, Adelaide, telephoned the following:

" 'Request Inspector Bonaparte to obey instruction received

by telegram from his Department, so that personal relationship with Adelaide officers can be maintained on friendly footing.' "

"Too bad, Gibley," purred Bony. "Just when I am catching a nice fish or two. When did you inform Adelaide I was holidaying here?"

"I didn't, sir. I did check up on you with Mount Gambier. According to the book."

"Quite a little mystery, isn't it? I am granted leave, and then am peremptorily ordered back to duty. It would almost appear that my presence here is distinctly inconvenient to someone. Would you know who it is?"

"No, sir. I'm only a senior constable."

"And I, Gibley, am only an inspector. All right! I'll go quietly. Inform Mount Gambier that I'll be leaving for Murray Bridge by coach in the morning, and will board tomorrow night's express for Melbourne. You might reserve my coach seat on your return to Cowdry."

Gibley looked relieved.

Next morning when Mr. Luton walked with Bony to the highway he was distinctly depressed, and as they waited at the bridge he asked:

"D'you think you'll be coming back?"

"Some day, I hope," replied Bony. "Soon, perhaps. Whatever has actuated my chiefs in this matter of recall must be of a most unusual character. That is the reason why, in this instance, I am obeying orders. Well, here comes the bus. I have the address of Ben Wickham's friend in Adelaide, and I may communicate with him, and present certain facts. Doubtless he will call on you. Thank you for those most pleasant few days under your roof. Should you ever come to Brisbane, I shall be hurt if you don't look me up. So, *au revoir*, Mr. Luton, and all the best."

Mr. Luton long remembered the flashing smile illuminating the brown face and the blue eyes, and Bony remembered the brilliant background of trees and white bridge behind the tall, erect figure flanked by the two dogs.

*   *   *   *   *

Superintendent Boase, Officer in Charge, Criminal Investigation Branch, S. A. Police Department, was tall and rangy, grey and close to sixty. Of him there was nothing remarkable save that his grey hair stood up, and his grey moustache stood out. When Bony entered his office, the corners of his mouth indicated what the rest of his face wasn't permitted to do—the smile of welcome.

"Hullo, Bony! How come?"

"Just before leaving Adelaide I decided to run down to Cowdry to spend a few days with an old friend, as I had obtained ten days' leave. No one here knew of my intention, and I managed to secure a seat in a tourist bus going to Mount Gambier. At Mount Gambier, I spoke to Sergeant Maskell, whom I had met several years ago. It was a personal, not an official, contact, you understand. Told Maskell I was going on to Cowdry for some fishing. On my way up to-day I saw Maskell again, and he assured me he did not, because there was no reason to, report that I was with my friend but a mile or so from Cowdry. Prior to my telegram to Traffic Branch about a car, did you know I was staying near Cowdry?"

"Didn't even know you sent an 'Information please' to Traffic. First I knew of your being down there was day before yesterday when the Chief rang me to check when you left for Brisbane."

"Would you mind ringing Traffic and asking Tillet what action he took about me, other than supplying information about a car?"

"Not at all."

"Ask him if he reported my presence at Cowdry to the higher-ups."

Boase turned to his telephone, and on replacing the instrument, said:

"Tillet says he didn't mention to anyone your being at Cowdry. Said he had no cause to do so. Thought you were on normal duty. What is this?"

"Yesterday I received a telegram from my immediate superior, Linton, ordering me to report at once. Later yesterday the local constable at Cowdry came to tell me that his Divisional H.Q. had telephoned him to pass a message from Adelaide which is a follow-on to the telegram direct to me. If you know nothing, it would seem that action is being taken on a high level."

"Certainly seems so. But what's it all about?"

"What I want to ascertain is: who informed Brisbane I was in Cowdry? Tillet says he's out. You say you are out. Mount Gambier was straight enough in saying they had not reported my presence there to Adelaide. Will you find out from your high-ups how they learned I was at Cowdry?"

"Sinclair would know. I'll trot along and X-ray him." Superintendent Boase tried to stare Bony down, and, not for the first time, was beaten to it. "You know, occasionally you're the most exasperating feller. You are not pinching anything off my territory, are you?"

"I am merely doing some psychological research work, which I believe might be of ultimate value to the world."

Boase sighed at such recalcitrance. He was away ten minutes. On being seated again behind his desk, he loaded a pipe and applied a match, and then studied Bony as he might a fingerprint.

"The high-ups didn't know you were in Cowdry, and didn't give a damn where you were until they received a hot message from Brisbane asking them to shift you out of South Australia at the double. Someone in Cowdry has put your pot on. What've you been doing?"

Bony was about to continue prevarication when Boase began to nod his head portentously. He said:

"You on to another angle of the smuggling racket, eh? Got something of the kind up your sleeve, and think you'll try to put one over poor silly me. And someone down there with plenty of standing got on to you and blew the gaff to your Department."

"There could be something in what you suspect," slowly admitted Bony, delighted with this gift road of escape. "However, it's a little far-fetched, as my wife would say. That summons from Brisbane cannot be side-stepped, though, and I'll have to report back. I'll compile a memo covering my psychological research work which you may find useful, and will post it from Sydney."

"The subject of your memo wouldn't be the death of Ben Wickham?"

"How could it be?" Bony mildly enquired. "I understand that you permitted the body to be cremated and the ashes scattered over the dead man's estate."

"True enough. Had to. Couldn't allow the body to explode with booze fumes after it was buried deep in a respectable cemetery."

"Then why mention Ben Wickham?"

"Interesting bloke, that's all." Boase again smiled only with the corners of his mouth. "I suppose the real truth is that you were playing the wag and enjoying a nice spot of sport with the kingfish. I've done it myself. Sometimes it don't come off, and then you have to run around your pals to find out who the blasted pimp is. If you ever do find the darling who put you away, let me know. I'll fix him. We policemen have to stick together."

"Which is why I came to you."

"Wise guy. You might do the same for me one day."

"I would not miss the opportunity." Bony rose to go. "Thank you, Boase. See you again sometime."

They shook hands, both satisfied, both aware he was not believed by the other. Almost casually, Superintendent Boase asked:

"When will you be leaving Adelaide?"

"By to-night's express. I'll fly north from Melbourne. I'll let you know who pimped on me, and you might arrange something one dark night."

"You come up all the way by road coach?" asked Boase, idly fingering a document.

"Yes. On arrival in the city, I parked my case and found a café where I loitered over a pot of tea and a newspaper. After leaving the café, I strolled up King William Street and . . ."

"Cut. No point," interrupted Boase. "Asked because I was thinkin' of something else. What about dinner at the Railway Dining Rooms before your train leaves? Meet you there in an hour."

Bony gladly agreed, and they were given an alcove table where they could talk. After the entrée, Boase said:

"You know, Bony, you're not hard to work with, although you never work to the book. There have been times when I envy you your independence. I am not alone in that, either. You got more pals here than you think. Sinclair's one of them. Being private secretary to our Chief Commissioner, he's as near the hub as anyone can be. Yet he knows nothing outside that communication from your own Chief, and he told me he feels there's a lot he could be told by his own boss."

"Did his boss issue the instruction to Mount Gambier that made Gibley call on me?"

"Yes."

"D'you know Senior Constable Gibley?" asked Bony.

"Met him a couple of times. Bit of a stay-put, apparently."

"Clean slate?"

"Far as I know. Come off it, Bony. What are you up to down there?"

"I'll tell you. I went there for the fishing. I stayed with an old character named John Luton. He interested me in the various effects of alcohol on the human brain. In modern parlance, I think he has something. Have you heard anything about that?"

"No. Tell."

Bony related Mr. Luton's convictions, which included that covering his belief in the cause of Ben Wickham's death. When done, Boase was thoughtful. He asked:

"You do much digging?"

"No."

"Couldn't have been in Gibley's report to Mount Gambier. Would have come through to us, otherwise. Still, kind of cranky idea I'd hesitate to pass on when I was a constable. What gives it significance is the possibility that from Luton's ideas on grog and your interest in his ideas sprang that something which brought about your recall to Brisbane. Must be someone down there so important that if you don't get back to Brisbane like a bat out of a Nullarbor Cave, you'll be chucked out of the Department with not the faintest hope of being reinstated."

"It does seem that someone at Cowdry fears . . . me."

"Sure enough," agreed Boase. "I'll keep it in mind. Let me know if you should find out what it's all about, will you?"

Bony concurred.

"These are funny times, as you'll agree," Boase said, seriously. "Sort of complex to what they were before the war. They talk about the cold war as though it is something going on millions of miles away. I know of at least two cold wars going on here in Adelaide, and not between the Russians and us, either. Yes, I'll keep this Cowdry business in mind. Time to go. I have an order about you. Have to see you off the State premises."

"Indeed!" politely murmured Bony.

"Yes. Nothing personal. I asked for a good companion. Nice-looking and smart. She'll accompany you as far as Serviceton."

The policewoman was all that Boase said of her. She was wearing a tailored suit, and Bony was presented to her on the platform. They sat together in the first-class compartment, and at Serviceton she expressed regret that she had to leave the train and catch the incoming express back to Adelaide. Serviceton is just outside the South Australian border, and the Melbourne–Adelaide expresses pass a few miles beyond this point.

Chapter Fourteen

MR. LUTON'S PANACEA

IT had been a hard day for Mr. Luton. For him the bottom of the craft of life had been badly holed, and the buoyancy of the previous days was gone. He had come to place strong faith in D.-I. Bonaparte, faith based on personal liking and respect for superior intelligence. Not by the flicker of an eyelash had he betrayed the blow to his faith given by Bony's defection following the boasts bearing up what had appeared to be superb independence of the Boss.

If you lose faith in someone, you find faith in yourself badly shaken, and that was the feeling from which Mr. Luton suffered during this hard day of Bony's departure.

Knocker Harris failed to cheer him. In fact, Knocker Harris was this day a little boring because he was inclined to condemn D.-I. Bonaparte merely through feeling that Mr. Luton was condemning him. When Knocker Harris broached the subject of Mr. Luton's loneliness, Mr. Luton snapped him short, knowing the suggestion which would be bound to follow. Knocker's affection for Mr. Luton was that of the weak for the strong, and sometimes the strong is wearied by the ingredient of adulation.

What irritated Mr. Luton more was Knocker's opposition to the occasional benders. The opposition wasn't expressed in plain words, and the excuse was Knocker's ulcers, which forbade him to join in the riot, when actually it was just plain wowserism, in the view of Mr. Luton.

Hang it, if a man can't have a drink without being criticised, it was just too bad. Mr. Luton stared savagely at Knocker Harris and told him he didn't need nursing, that he was still able to feed himself, and quite capable of telling people like Knocker Harris to get to hell out of it.

That was the way it went this afternoon of the day Bony left for Adelaide. Mr. Luton took from the cupboard the part-filled bottle of whisky, poured half a tumbler of the spirit and drank it neat, right in front of Knocker Harris.

Knocker looked solemn and sighed loudly. He produced a cigarette and popped it into his mouth, paper and all, and the manner in which his jaws chewed further irritated Mr. Luton.

"You had better get back to your own camp," growled Mr. Luton. "Be dark in an hour, and I got chores to do."

Knocker accepted the hint, gazed disapprovingly at the bottle, and departed. Mr. Luton thereupon had a real snort, which emptied the bottle. He walked without a trace of faltering to the sitting-room, and proceeded to dismantle the stretcher used by D.-I. Bonaparte, placing the blankets in a cupboard, the sheets in the wash-tub in the adjacent laundry, and the stretcher on a wall-rack in his own room. Then he re-laid the fire on the open hearth, took wheat to the penned fowls, and fed and chained the dogs to their abodes at the bottom of the garden.

Rain scatted on the corrugated-iron roof, just to mock the drought. The wind was rising. The day passed out in a painful swoon, and Mr. Luton drew the blinds with care, locked both front and back doors, and prepared his dinner of cold fish and hot tea.

Untold millions of men would have revelled in Mr. Luton's situation. The stove burned warmly. The light shed brilliance on the clothed table bearing the dish of cold fish flanked by cut lemons. The doors were shut, barring out from this castle the night and the wind. And in the basement was that of such allure as to bring old Omar Khayyam leaping from his dusty grave.

Yet material comforts alone do not achieve the acme of content. Mr. Luton had come to value home comforts, but not above the value and importance of friendships. Friendship is like a tree—the slower it grows the stronger the weft and the longer the life.

To pluck a man off a pub wood-heap, cart him off from the scene of his fall and nurse him back to sanity used not to be an uncommon act. There was little of the 'do good-ers' about these Samaritans—just plain insurance taken out against the day when they, too, might lie with the dingbats on a pub wood-heap. Friendship is not formed thus, but is formed between men who experience together hardships, trials, and victories. The icy winds of winter sweeping day and night across saltbush plains, and the torrid heat of summer within a mulga forest, will unite men or send them tearing madly out to a salubrious city. Because young Benjamin Wickham joined John Luton in the job of moving tons of goods with a string of bullocks, nothing could break a friendship thus cemented.

"Excepting death."

Which was what Mr. Luton was thinking as he ate his dinner, sitting stiffly upright in the Windsor chair with table manners of long ago.

The rain stopped scatting on the roof. It had to, because Ben had said it wouldn't rain enough to fill an egg-cup off an acre catchment of claypan. Having dined, Mr. Luton cleared the table, washed the dishes and strode to the front sitting-room fire. He sat in this favourite easy chair listening to the seven o'clock news, but this evening even the items about the Cold War failed to arouse his usual contemptuous snort. But when the silky tones of the announcer introduced the news reviewer, he did snort:

"Not here you don't, you ruddy echo."

The growing fire drove him back, so that he couldn't touch the fender with his slippered feet. And then his eyes rose slowly, to rest their gaze on the bullock yoke.

With axe and adze, chisel and glass-paper he had fashioned that yoke and fitted it on the neck of the finest bullock that ever lived. It had been a hefty steer, and no man could say what breed he was. Awkward, unreliable, rebellious when yoked into the middle of the team. Awkwardness gave place to sure and deliberate movement, and very early in its career Mr. Luton found it unnecessary to use his whip.

Eventually, Squirt was promoted to lead bullock on the off-side, the key position in the team, because as the off-side leader he was partially shielded from the driver by the near-sider. No matter where Mr. Luton was along the line of twenty-six or twenty-eight animals in pairs, as long as his voice reached Squirt, this magnificent leader instantly obeyed. Team bullocks are quite intelligent in the hands of an intelligent driver, and Squirt was a king among bullocks.

A grand old feller, Squirt. Sell him! No. When Mr. Luton sold the team after Ben had left to take up his inheritance, he kept Squirt in a pub stable and yard for a month, and then took him to his grazing property, where both could enjoy comparative retirement from those endless tracks flowing from mirage to mirage.

With the place went equipment, among which was a heavy two-wheel dray. When Mr. Luton needed firewood, he would take the huge whip to the home paddock gate and crack it. Within minutes Squirt would appear, and Mr. Luton would yoke him between the shafts of the dray and set forth for a load of dry timber. He would drive the old bullock between standing trees, leaving but an inch or two clearance to the wheel-hubs. He would command Squirt to 'come here' or to 'gee-off', and the animal actually appeared to delight in obeying. Often he would look back over a shoulder, at first Mr.

Luton thought, at himself. It occurred to him that Squirt was looking back for the long-vanished team mates, and so he pretended the team mates were behind Squirt, and put on the performance of old days. The shouted profanity, the masterly conjunction of adjectives, and the strings of most improper nouns brought the ghosts of all the dead 'artists' of the tracks crowding around Mr. Luton with admiration. And Squirt would actually pretend he was straining his insides to haul the dray from a non-existent bog.

He died of old age. Mr. Luton spent four days digging a grave and burying him, like a kid mourning a car-slain pup.

A man has to love something. What is love? You tell me.

Ben turned up, an older Ben, a Ben more assured of his own strength, the same old fighting Ben created by Mr. Luton from a Ben who was disillusioned and soured. Ben wanted a mate—that's all. Ben was having a rough time down at Mount Marlo, what with a sister who never ceased her efforts to reform him, and the professional meteorologists who had never ceased to scorn his work, in press, in conference, in private homes and clubs and bars.

A snort! A bender! The hoo-jahs! Rub the bottle! The genie! Take us back twenty years! The glare of the sun! The dust of the track! The smell of the bullocks! The atomic reports of the whips! The muscles under the hides of men and beasts rippling with power!

Thus passed the evening of this day. About eleven, Mr. Luton went to bed, having wound his pocket watch, filled his pipe, and set a glass of water on the bedside table. When he woke and snapped on the light, it was shortly after one o'clock. He drank the water and set a match to his pipe and lay with the bedclothes tucked under his chin and one hand gripping the pipe-bowl.

It appeared that the heeler at the bottom of the garden couldn't sleep either. Now and then he would emit a short yelp as though tormented by a flea, because he couldn't be hungry, and he needn't be cold if he stayed inside his kennel.

Having smoked the pipe of peace, Mr. Luton snapped off the light and tried for sleep. It was very quiet without, save for the occasional bark of the dog, added to, at long intervals, by the barking of the other. Marauding fox, thought Mr. Luton. Well, the hens were locked up safely enough.

An hour passed and still Mr. Luton was awake. Leaving the bed, he dragged on a dressing-gown and raised the window blind. Outside, the garden with the laundry and the wood-shed and distant hen-house were stilled by the moon, as were the trunks of the trees beyond the garden.

Mr. Luton broke abruptly into positive action. He switched off the bedroom light and passed to the living-room, where he re-kindled the stove cinders with brushwood. He dragged the table aside and went down under, taking no light, and presently came up with an unopened case marked 'Rum'.

Re-closing the trap, replacing the linoleum, and pulling the table back to its normal position, he opened the case with a steel implement like a jemmy, and having a claw which easily ripped wood lightly nailed. Without haste, Mr. Luton poured rum into a tin pint pannikin, and added a few drops of water.

While this first deep-noser was establishing contact, he removed the sheaths from the remaining eleven bottles, placed the bottles in the cupboard beside the stove and the straw he pushed into the stove. Two drinks later, he smashed the case into kindling wood, and tidily placed it in a small box kept handy for the purpose.

The tide in the bottle was down two-thirds when he went to the back door, intending to shout at the irritating dog. The moon was low. No cloud marred the radiant night.

He did not shout at the dog. Instead, he closed the door and took another drink, a real snort this time, and walked, steadily and surely, to the sitting-room. He took down from the wall one of his beloved whips, passed out to the front veranda and along the cinder path to the gate in the wicket fence, the whip slanted over a shoulder, the long belly and long leather lash trailing on the ground.

No bullock driver ever appeared to the stars and the sleepy birds as this one did. Mr. Luton, arrayed in dressing-gown and slippers, white hair ruffled, white moustache bristling, walked with his old-time slouch towards the line of great trees near the river-bank. He paused to survey these trees. Then he spoke:

"Now, Ben, first thing you got to remember is that bullocks can't hear too well if they don't want to. Another is, bullocks don't understand polite language. If you say to 'em: 'Git-up there!' they think it's a cat purring. Now watch and listen to me."

Mr. Luton whistled—one long-drawn note. "Smokey! Red! Pieface! You loafing get from a Tory-bred snivelling bloody runt. Come here, Squirt! Bit more! Come here, Squirt! Red! You . . ."

Mr. Luton's by no means palsied arms lifted the whip off his shoulder, and slowly proceeded to whirl in a circle above his head the heavy leather, reaching some eighteen feet. His tall body swayed to gain momentum, and suddenly tautened, swung slightly backward to halt the whip handle. The leather flowed away like a living anaconda, flowed to the very tip of the lash with a deafening report.

"That'll do! Whey! Whoa-back!" The driver turned slightly to his rear. "Get the knack of it, Ben? The voice is more important than the whip-crack. You never hit a beast if he don't deserve it. Remember that bullocks is a bit sensitive. If you mooch along thinking of the last pub, the bullocks will likely enough fall down dreaming of the last time it rained and brought up the pigweed. If you put guts and energy into your driving, them bullocks will put energy into their hauling. And you got to steady 'em and get 'em all hauling together. I'll show you how to get 'em excited, to pull through this here sand-bog."

Again the whistle for the leaders to pull ahead and straighten the haul-chain right back to the pole. Again the command to "Lean into it!" Again the stream of invective, this time directed to Lumpy, whose ancestors had been most careless. The whip swung round, faster and faster, the report sharper and louder than that of a discharged shot-gun, and the driver swaying, his feet wide, his shoulders almost bursting the seams of his dressing-gown, shouting and swearing, cajoling, threatening.

"What!" he yelled. "You'd stop the wagon dead in the middle of a sand-bog, would you?" Mr. Luton pranced up and down the line of trees. The whip touched one, slashed another, hissed at a third. One minute of pandemonium passed, a second had almost sped when Mr. Luton dropped the whip and pressed both hands to his chest.

"I'm gettin' on, Ben. You know that, don't you? Can't cut capers like we used to, but, by hell, you and me could still make bullocks shift thirty-forty tons on a tabletop. Getting old, all right. Dropped me flamin' whip. Have to put another cracker on her sometime. We'd better go on over to the house for another snort."

Shouldering the whip, Mr. Luton walked across the clearing to the front fence. And the trees nodded and began to chew their cud, and old Squirt turned his great head with the sawn-off horns to watch his master depart.

Mr. Luton closed the wicket gate, walked strongly along the cinder path, stepped lightly up to the veranda and entered his house. Closing the front door, he proceeded to replace the whip on the wall nails.

When he turned to make for the door to the living-room, he saw two men who seemed to be emptying the cupboard of his hoard of rum. He made no effort to reduce the sound of his movements, and the two men went on with their task. On entering the kitchen he roared:

"What in hell d'you think you're up to?"

Neither man spoke. One looked at the other; the second man nodded. The first casually approached Mr. Luton, his face without expression, his eyes expressionless. He punched him on the chin, and, as Mr. Luton was trying to recover his balance, snatched an automatic from a shoulder-holster and laid the butt against Mr. Luton's temple. As the victim was collapsing to the floor the man hit him again.

Chapter Fifteen

BOOTS AND ALL

MR. LUTON discovered himself lying on the living-room floor. That was after he had accustomed his eyes to the direct rays of the ceiling light. Pain hammered at him, and swift anger burned. The clock on the mantel took shape, and he remembered that the time was of more importance than the cause of his discomfort.

Twenty-three minutes after four o'clock.

A voice said: "Get up."

The toe of a shoe pounded against Mr. Luton's ribs, and he scrambled over to draw up his knees and with effort at last managed to stand. A chair was jammed against the backs of his legs, and he sat, the chair against the wall so that he faced the back door, with the sitting-room to his left. One man was decidedly foreign, the other less so. One was tall and slim, wearing a dark suit under his unbuttoned overcoat, and the other was smaller and wore his overcoat with the collar turned up. Their heads were round, large. The hair of both was dark and grew far back above foreheads narrower than the width of the face. Their eyes were dark and small, and appeared prominent in faces almost devoid of colour.

The tall man seemed to be the leader. He sat at the table, opened a suitcase, produced a length of light sash cord and tossed it to the smaller man, who proceeded to bind Mr. Luton's hands. Mr. Luton kicked him in the ankle, forgetting he was wearing slippers. The blow failed to produce a wince, and the binding continued.

"Keep your feet still," ordered the man quietly.

Mr. Luton rebelled, and the heel of a shoe was stamped on his toes. Expertly and swiftly, Mr. Luton's feet were bound to the chair-legs and his tied wrists bound to the chair-back. The man then stepped back, carefully gauged distance, and viciously kicked Mr. Luton's right knee-cap. With the same methodical approach, he kicked Mr. Luton's left knee-cap.

You have to hand it to these people. They can deal it out without heat, without even the faintest visible hint of malice.

Mr. Luton craved to be sick, such was the pain. Fire consumed him and icy-cold sweat drenched him. And deep down was born a fury that he couldn't take it, that he was too old, that he was weak when once he had been strong.

"Luton," said the man seated at the table. "I require information. You have that information. You were dear friend to Benjamin Wickham. You drank together. You have tales to tell. Wickham told you about his work with the weather. He told you about his papers. I want them. Where are they?"

"Don't know," growled the old man.

"Mr. Wickham had a secret book, a book with green covers. Where is it?"

"Go to hell."

The slim man nodded, and the other once again took careful aim and kicked Mr. Luton's right knee-cap. Only the cords kept the victim from falling off the chair. Blood from a temple was flowing slowly down his lined cheek and staining redly his white moustache.

"Tell," commanded the tall man.

Mr. Luton was mute. His eyes were glazed. The man at the table sighed with resignation, and took from the case a hypodermic syringe and a capsule.

"No more assault, Paul. Too old to stand it," he said calmly. "He might not know of that we want. This drug will prove it. Rip the sleeve."

The shorter man produced a clasp knife, opened it and advanced to Mr. Luton. His approach was casual. In neither face had there been any evidence of sadism, but the complete lack of emotion was more horrible than the depraved leer of a devil. He expertly ripped the sleeve of the dressing-gown, and was about to insert the point of the knife in the sleeve of the pyjama coat, when there was a loud report and, for the first time this night, emotion did register on the white face.

The knife clattered to the floor, and blood spurted from the hand which had held it.

The ensuing silence lasted for precisely five seconds. Neither man moved a fraction of an inch, save their eyes, which jerked to right and left. Then a third man was in the room, standing just inside the doorway to the sitting-room.

"Will one or both of you gentlemen kindly grant me the excuse to kill?" mildly enquired Bony.

Two pairs of dark eyes glittered. That was all. No movement; no sound save the regular beat of water dripping from a tap—blood dripping to the floor.

"If I sound melodramatic it is to be regretted, gentlemen," Bony purred. "Doubtless you have heard of me, and doubtless, too, knowing that I am a police officer you gamble on a police officer made weak by Anglo-Saxon laws and regulations. In that you are mistaken. In Australian parlance, I am one out of the box. I have at the moment no inhibitions. I have a hunger, gentlemen, a craving to kill. This Western civilisation, which you hold in such contempt, is the only brake to my lust."

"I'm bleeding to death," snarled the man with the wounded hand, his eyes like agates, his upper lip lifted with pain and hatred.

"Of mere passing interest," murmured Bony, and Mr. Luton felt astonishment at the altered face of his recent guest. There was no doubt, too, that the others noted the blazing blue eyes, the flash of white teeth, the expression of unutterable loathing. The lips trembled; the cheeks twitched; but the eyes never flickered, and the automatic never wavered a hair's breadth.

No one watching that automatic, and that brown face, could have an inkling of what was really going on in Bony's mind. They would know nothing of the battle being waged, on the one hand by his aboriginal instincts, and on the other by the training imposed on him by what is named 'Western civilisation'. There is pardon for killing under intense provocation; there is none for cruelty inflicted on the helpless.

"You with the hand! March to your left for the towel on the wall rack. Use the towel to bind the hand. I shall be waiting for the excuse to kill, after I put a bullet through your other hand."

This human jungle monster couldn't take it. He was genuinely on the verge of fainting as he staggered to the wall and snatched the towel,

"Stay there facing the wall," commanded Bony. "You at the table, stand!"

The slim man stood, eyes never moving from the blazing eyes holding him like a fascinated rabbit.

"Retrieve that knife and cut Mr. Luton free."

The slim man bent to pick up the knife. The other spun about and leaped. The automatic roared and blood spurted from his left hand as he stood dazedly looking down at it. The slim man had straightened swiftly, to be frozen into stone by the barrel of the gun emitting a faint trail of blue smoke.

"There will be no more fancy shooting, gentlemen," Bony warned. "You! Back to your wall. You! Pick up the knife and cut those cords. Ah! Nice sharp knife. Used, I suppose, to cut throats." The cords fell away from Mr. Luton's ankles and wrists, and he lurched to his feet and stood glowering down at the slim man. "Your double-barrel shot-gun, Mr.

Luton," interposed Bony. "Number One shot if you have it."

The old man padded away to the bedroom.

"Who are you?" suavely asked the slim man, eyes frantically trying to lock the blue eyes so that they would not take in his companion. Not that the companion was in good enough shape to start anything.

"You know who I am. You thought I was crawling back to my superiors and therefore you had a free hand here. And I know you. If you and your superiors were to use your minnow brains more and be less addicted to raw brutality, you would be more worthy of my attention. Certainly you would not have made that stupid mistake of calling on Mr. Wickham in a car belonging to the Hungarian Consulate; or commit the childish error of scorning our Australian barbers. Mind you, they are no artists. However, I suggest that you forward my advice to your masters luxuriating in that place of intrigue and treason named Canberra. What drug were you going to administer to Mr. Luton?"

" A soporific."

"What drug? Or am I to accept your refusal to answer as the excuse for which I am waiting?"

"Sodium pentothal."

"Its action?"

"Eliminates will-power and induces the craving to sleep."

"And you keep the victim awake by torture until he gives?"

"Yes."

"And you wine and dine with the staff members of embassies, consulates? Well, there is this to be said for the Australian black-fellow—he *is* particular with whom he sleeps. Thank you, Mr. Luton. A hammerless gun! Are you sure the safety catch is off?"

"You can leave it to me."

"I hope I can leave it to you to pull a trigger without the slightest hesitation?"

"Only one, Inspector? I never fire singles."

"Now then, you two! Face the wall. A little farther back, Mr. Luton, that a swinging arm cannot knock your barrel aside. At the slightest excuse, shoot for a kidney, either side the spine. You take the left specimen while I attend to the right."

The pistol barrel was jammed hard into the spine of the slim man, and a chest pushed him hard against the wall so that he was unable to twist round with any degree of freedom. An arm wound about him, and a brown hand plucked the automatic from the shoulder holster. He was also relieved of a pocket wallet, and his clothes were efficiently searched for secondary arms.

There were fewer risks with the wounded man, and the search produced a sap as well as an automatic, and an implement that looked like a fountain-pen, in addition to a pocket wallet.

"Turn about. Sit there."

They sat on chairs against the wall. Mr. Luton covered them with the shot-gun while Bony went through the wallets. Save for treasury notes, there was nothing—not even a card bearing a name; not even a driver's licence.

"How did you come here? By car?"

"I . . . we forget," answered the slim man.

"I will tell you," Bony said. "You came up-river by boat. The boat is moored to the bank yonder. You are living in a caravan down near Cowdry. Daylight will be here in an hour. You should be back in your caravan before daylight."

"What is this?" asked Mr. Luton.

"A timely observation, Mr. Luton. It will occupy us at least two hours in setting this house to rights. Let us say five shillings an hour. They will pay you ten shillings, and depart."

"Depart!" echoed Mr. Luton. "Let them go?"

"Well, we don't want them living with us, do we?"

"Living with us! Hell, no."

"Very well. We must speed them on their way. If day should come and find us associating with them, what would the neighbours say?" Bony extracted a ten-shilling note, brand new, and the wallets he put into the case. The syringe and capsule case he put aside with the fountain-pen which fired a potassium bullet. "Now, gentlemen, you may depart. Return to your boss and tell him you have made a muck of things. Your boss will then understand that you have been attempting to bail up real Australians, who do not play the game according to cloak-and-dagger rules."

White faces, expressionless, terrible faces of human automatons! Backs stiff, they marched out into the setting moonlight, round the house and through the wicket gate, and so across the clearing to the hired boat they had moored at the river-bank. Mr. Luton and Bony watched the boat slowly move down-stream till it was out of sight.

They went back to the house, where Bony proceeded to light the stove, and Mr. Luton to replace cupboard débris from the floor. Then he saw Bony looking down at the treasury note on the table.

"Burn it," he said.

"Oh, no," replied Bony. "This note, just issued by a bank, will tell us if these birds came from Adelaide or Canberra."

Mr. Luton paused in his work, a bottle of rum in the crook of one arm, another held in the opposite hand. There was no doubting the admiration in his voice when he said:

"You're a ruddy corker."

"I am not," denied Bony. "In fact, I am now feeling reaction. Pour drinks—long ones. I was never more frightened in my life."

"Frightened!" exploded Mr. Luton. "Frightened!"

"Yes, frightened. If those fellows had given me the excuse

to shoot them dead, I would never have forgiven myself."

"The dirty bastards," snarled Mr. Luton, filling pint pannikins with rum.

"I agree. The dirty bastards. . . ."

Bony lifted the pannikin to his lips. Mr. Luton said nothing when he noted how the brown hand was shaking.

Chapter Sixteen

A PROMISING PUPIL

MR. LUTON was rubbing an embrocation into his bruised and swollen knees, while Bony was busy at the stove cooking breakfast and watching the coffee-pot.

"Getting old, blast it," growled Mr. Luton. "Old age is a curse. Can't take a bit of stoush any more, and can't deal it out."

"Strong-smelling embrocation you have there," remarked Bony.

"A good one Knocker Harris invented. Half eucalyptus and half camphorated oil with a dash of some of the herbs he's got in his bit of a garden." Mr. Luton chuckled. "Knew a feller who suffered from rheumatism. He'd heard that pure emu oil was good for it. So he got an emu and boiled him down and drew off about a pint of pure oil. Before he come to use it, his son came on it and oiled his saddle and bridle with it. Next day all the leather was like spongy paper and finished."

"Did he ever try it for the rheumatism?" questioned Bony.

"So they say," replied Mr. Luton, now whistling through his remaining teeth like a man grooming a horse. "Terrible penetrating stuff, emu oil in the pure. It cured his rheumatism overnight, but it rotted his leg bones to sponge inside a week." A moment later he asked, off-handedly:

"D'you think those ponging foreign bastards will come again?"

"I hope not, but they may."

The old man stood, making a wry face, and he said furiously:

"Look! Forty years back I'd have pulled their ears off and mixed their rabbit brains together. What do you reckon this country's coming to?"

"Your question would indicate that Australia is proceeding from one point to another, Mr. Luton. Instead, it has already arrived. You have been extremely fortunate, and I, to a lesser degree, by having lived in an era when human behaviour was influenced by a code inspired by the world's rulers. Since the world's rulers have become schemers and scientific thugs, what can be expected of us, the ruled, the scum? Don't let it worry you. Good and evil are relative."

"Could be right. That bacon smells good. How did you get back here?"

"Train and car."

"When you left, did you intend coming back?"

"Yes. What about your hands? Breakfast is ready."

Mr. Luton unrolled the legs of his pyjamas and hobbled to the wash-bench.

"Knees any easier?" asked Bony.

"Much. Take a lot to damage 'em properly. But that ape knew just where to kick."

"He and his kind have, of course, plenty of practice. I am serving you three eggs. We have to eat. When Gibley told me the other afternoon I was to report to my Department, or else! it was necessary to determine how strong were those persons who were made nervous by my presence here. I did that by going to Adelaide, and I assessed the strength of the opposition when the S.A. Police Department went to the extraordinary limit of having me conducted out of their State. I am convinced they were motivated by a Power outside their State and outside the Constitution.

"Those thugs knew I left by bus yesterday morning. It is

certain that it was they who broke into the office at Mount Marlo. And that they are the foreigners in whom Constable Gibley expressed interest. Their actions, I believe, have nothing to do with my recall and the extraordinary behaviour of the S.A. Police Department.

"Anyway, before reporting to the C.I.B., Adelaide, I rang Mr. Wickham's friend who, with his son, supplied the necessary transport for stocking the bar down below. It was arranged that he would have his car just outside Serviceton when the Melbourne train pulled in. The police escort being instructed to leave me at Serviceton, I was saved the bother of evading her, and was happy about that, because she was a joy to look at, and intelligent."

"Wait a bit!" implored Mr. Luton. "She . . . she . . . she! Police escort a she?"

"Yes. Policewoman. Chosen, I think, to reduce to the least possible minimum any rancour I might feel toward the S.A. Police. Anyway, we arrived at the bridge just when you were exploding your whip. The young fellow who drove thought the reports were those of guns, and only with difficulty did I prevail on him to leave it to me, and also to leave me at the bridge and return to Adelaide.

"We arrived when you were addressing a bullock called 'Red'. Accept my sincere compliments on your linguistic artistry! We heard plainly all the adjectives in their magnificent sequence. However, in the midst of our enchantment, your performance ceased, and on arrival I found that you must have gone in for a gargle. The front door was open, and I heard voices. I regret that I did not arrive two minutes earlier.

"We are left with several items. Those thugs were indifferent to what was occupying you at this time, being confident they would quickly find what they were looking for. They thought there was no danger of interruption from you, and, because of the hour, no interruption from anyone else. Hence the open door. They knew what they were looking for—that green-covered book. And they knew of Wickham's friendship with you, and of his visits here."

"Think they would have found the cellar?" asked Mr. Luton.

"They would be experts in tearing a house to pieces."

"What was wrong in handing 'em over to Gibley? They can't do such things in Australia."

Bony shrugged. "Remember the story about the great king who visited Australia and committed a murder? To have handed those trained sadists over to Gibley might have resulted in ringing down the curtain before the end of the drama."

"All right. Leave 'em. What about the Melbourne police? Wouldn't they check up on the train and find you wasn't on it?"

"Without doubt. My disappearance will send many people into a dither. Which is why, like Brer Rabbit, I am going to burrow deep."

"You going to hole up? Where?"

"In your pub down under."

Mr. Luton evinced swift contentment. Bony said:

"Time flies, as a thousand million people have said before me. We must sleep, unfortunately. Now please listen carefully to what I say, while I clear the table and wash up. You will be the custodian, and there will probably be many visitors."

An hour later, Bony surveyed his sanctuary, after hearing the trap-door shut and Mr. Luton replacing the floor-covering.

The stock had been slightly rearranged. The stretcher bed was set up against one damp wall, and a couple of gin cases served as a bedside table. The oil-lamp burned on the bar counter, and there was a primus stove on which to boil water for tea.

At three places a series of one-inch auger holes had been

bored, to provide Bony with listening points. He could thus hear what was said at the front door, within the lounge, and inside the living-room. If Mr. Luton wished to converse with him, he would have only to lie on the floor at one of these points and emit a mild version of his bullock team whistle down the auger holes. Stacked spirits provided mounting steps to the listening vents.

It was a quarter to seven when Bony turned in. It was four minutes after two when he woke. Like the cellar, the house above was still.

Bony lit the oil-lamp. He put on his several spare pairs of socks and a large blanket dressing-gown belonging to old Luton, and started the primus.

About three o'clock he heard, very faintly, the dogs barking, and a moment later, the distant thud of Mr. Luton's feet on his bedroom floor. The thudding eventually changed to the padding of comfortable slippers.

When someone knocked on the front door, Bony climbed the steps of brandy cases to sit on the topmost, when his head touched the perforated flooring. He could hear his host crossing the sitting-room, heard the door open, and Senior Constable Gibley say:

"Day-ee! What! You on the booze again?"

"Do I look like it?" snapped Mr. Luton.

"Yes."

"Well, I'm not, Senior, and I'd take it kindly if you minded your own business. I had a bad night, as you seem to be interested, and if a man of my age can't sleep when he likes and get up when he likes, then it's time the atom bomb blew up the likes of you. What is it?"

"Now, now, no sparks, Luton. Keep your hair on. I only called for a chinwag, anyway. You goin' to ask me in?"

"Don't see why. Still, if you want to waste the taxpayers' money. . . ."

They moved back into the kitchen and the door was closed. Bony descended from his brandy steps and mounted the gin steps which brought him beneath the kitchen dresser. He was in time to hear Mr. Luton following his instructions.

"Cup of coffee or tea? I'm going to light the stove."

"Whatever's handiest," accepted Gibley. "Anyone been around this morning?"

"How in hell should I know? You woke me. Lumbago kept me up all night and I didn't get off to sleep till after daybreak."

"All right! All right! Of course the dogs would warn you if anyone had come around. They make enough noise."

"They would of woke me, I suppose," admitted Mr. Luton. The sound of case wood crackling in the stove reached Bony. Gibley said:

"How long do you intend living on here now old Wickham's dead?"

"Just as long as it suits, Gibley. Anyone putting up an argument?"

"You're a source of worry, that's all. I don't like old blokes living alone. It's not safe. Anything could happen and they'd perish before anyone woke up to them being ill. That goes for Knocker Harris, too, although he's a different case. If he caught himself alight or fell into the river there wouldn't be much to it. You got any relations or anything?"

"You know, Gibley, up in the back of Noo South, in my time, there were towns called 'police-controlled'. The police in 'em could do pretty well what they liked, especially with swagmen and old pensioners camped on the river near-by. Would you like to know something?"

"I like learning, Luton. Make that tea strong."

"It'll be strong enough to twitch your appendix. What you don't know and what the quack don't know is that this house and the land along the river right to the highway belongs to me. You can tell Maltby that. And you can tell him, as well as yourself, that I'm the boss of this bit of country. Ben being murdered don't leave me defenceless."

"Well now, you don't say!" Gibley said slowly. "How come? They haven't found Ben's will yet, have they?"

"Nobody don't need to. So neither you nor Maltby can shift me. Like to learn some more?"

"Yair. I'm in the mood. Where's the sugar?"

"When I came here to live I'd sold a fairish bit of property up in Noo South when the price of land and stock was going up on the wool boom. So I got a lot of money to spend on advertising and such like, and I got a friend or two who knows how to do it. If you or Maltby interferes with Knocker, I'll give you and the quack such a advertising that your ears will burn right off your skulls."

"I'm not saying I was going to interfere with Knocker or you," countered Gibley. "All I'm saying is that you both give me a lot of worry, both living alone, and with no one living close to give a hand if needed."

"Very thoughtful of you, Gibley," Luton came back. "Pity you talk so much to the quack. He's not good for you."

"To hell with Dr. Maltby!" exploded the policeman. "I was only thinking of your welfare and my responsibility if anything happened to you. Wouldn't be so bad if you lived together. Why don't you put Knocker up here? He'd be happy to doss in with the chooks."

"So you been talking to Knocker, eh?"

"I have not—not on this subject. How did you come to know Inspector Bonaparte?"

"He told you."

"I know, but I've forgotten."

"You come out from town, but you didn't think to pick up my bread from the baker, did you?"

"I did. It's in the car. When did you say you met Bonaparte in the old days?"

"Up on my place out from Wilcannia. He was making for Bourke and stayed the night. That was the first time I met him. When don't matter, and how often don't matter, either."

"Seems to be a smart sort of caste, by all accounts. They wanted him back in Brisbane in a mighty hurry. What did he think of your cranky idea of Ben Wickham being murdered when he had the jim-jams?"

"Said he'd think about it."

"Didn't take to the idea, eh?"

"I don't think he did," answered the old man, and Bony congratulated him silently on his astuteness. "Blast it! What's the matter with them dogs? Someone else must be coming. Don't I ever have any peace?"

"Let 'em come, Luton. I'll have another cup of that appendix-twitcher."

Without going to his porch auger-holes, Bony could hear the car approaching and stop at the wicket gate. The dogs maintained their warning right until someone knocked on the front door.

"I'll see who it is," decided Gibley.

Bony heard the door being opened.

"Why! Hullo, Sergeant."

"The wife told us you were making out this way, Gibley. We're wanting a few words with Mr. Luton. May we come in?" Two men crossed the threshold. "Good-day, Mr. Luton. This is Superintendent Boase down from Adelaide. What, you drinking tea, Gibley?"

Mr. Luton acknowledged the introduction to Boase, and gave to Bony that he already knew Sergeant Maskell, stationed at Mount Gambier. Mr. Luton suggested that someone bring extra chairs from the lounge, and that he'd made a fresh pot of tea. The Mount Gambier sergeant told Gibley he could get along, and Mr. Luton reminded him to leave the bread.

The talk was thin until after Gibley drove away. Superintendent Boase expressed the wish to have a home like this, beside a river like this, and the Mount Gambier policeman asked how the fish were biting, and did Mr. Luton think that Knocker Harris had a fish he could take back to his poor wife and starving children. Mr. Luton said he had about five pounds of kingfish he could have and welcome. After that, Superintendent Boase got to work.

Chapter Seventeen

ACCORDING TO THE BOOK?

NO man rises to the position of chief of a criminal investigation branch of a State Police Department merely for the manner in which he combs his hair. Superintendent Boase had well earned his promotion. Adept in dealing with the criminal mind, as well as minds not so tabulated, he was now at some disadvantage by never having met a Mr. Luton. He began correctly, continued easily, never suspecting that Bony was right under his feet.

"I've come down from Adelaide, Mr. Luton, about a matter you could say is no damn business of mine," he said. "I'm referring to the recent visit of Inspector Bonaparte, who has been a personal friend of mine for several years."

Boase expected Mr. Luton to spring to defence by silently waiting for more, but Mr. Luton's eyes smiled.

"Bonaparte's an old friend of mine, too." He chuckled. "My father was a doer. He used to tell me: 'Us Lutons don't discuss our friends with the police, 'cos we never know what our friends have been up to the night before.'"

Having a sense of humour, Boase didn't find it hard to laugh.

"I'm sure our mutual friend Bonaparte hasn't been up to anything illegal," he assured Mr. Luton, and asked the sergeant to pass the scones. "Matter of fact, he called on me yesterday on his way east to Melbourne and Brisbane. Spoke warmly of you, and about his few days' fishing down here. I don't know what's behind the sudden recall to Brisbane, but he hinted at a spot of trouble. You know how it is with us policemen. One in trouble: all others help out. Did you happen to invite him down to stay?"

"Yes. About fourteen years ago."

"He just turned up? You didn't actually expect him?"

"I did and I didn't. He wrote askin' how the fish were running, and I wrote back that a couple of million were in the river waitin' to be hooked. As for him being in a spot of trouble, don't you worry. Inspector Bonaparte came out of the Back Country, like me, and we don't pull our forelocks to any jumped-up boss. He didn't go back to Brisbane because his boss ordered him to. He went back to find out what it was all about, to tell his boss to mind his blood pressure, and come back here to finish off his fishing."

"I know how he felt about it, Mr. Luton. We all have a job to hold down, and he has a wife and several fine boys to think of."

"His wife came out of the Back Country, too," Mr. Luton countered, the smile again in his eyes. "Likely enough, she'd kick his backside if he pulled his forelock on her behalf. And his boys would hold him while she did it. Us people from the Back Country can always look after ourselves. How long have you been in Australia?"

Superintendent Boase was secretly jolted by this question, but he claimed Australian origin. The old man pressed home the attack, deceptively mild of face and voice.

"Then you ought to know, Mr. Boase, that trouble to Bonaparte is like a lovely colleen to an Irishman. My mother came out of County Clare when they was chasin' English landlords into the Atlantic. So you get two of a kind."

Boase politely agreed with Mr. Luton, beginning to realise that he wasn't going to arrive very fast on an easy over-drive. The old man sat regally upright in his chair at the table, his expression being of bland benignity. He came again.

"Did you happen to mention to Bonaparte that theory of yours about Ben Wickham dying of something other than alcohol?"

"I have an idea that Constable Gibley did," replied Mr. Luton.

"Did he now?" Boase was rocked by this falsehood for which the Recording Angel placed a mark against Bony's name. "What did Bonaparte think of it?"

"Said he thought it was good enough to have his scribe put it into a book what's to be called 'Kidding the Bloody Police'."

"Did he, indeed!"

Boase searched for, and failed to see, the slightest trace of mockery in the hazel eyes or in the vibrant voice. Mr. Luton continued, furthering the impression that he accepted these visitors with natural bonhomie:

"My father used to say: 'If you can't get a man to bite on sugar, try a lemon. If he bites on either, he's unreliable.' There's Dr. Maltby. Knows everything—perhaps. Don't like me. So I tried him with the sugar of this yarn about different effects of the hoo-jahs, and there's no need to offer him a lemon. I tried Gibley, and he didn't get to the lemon, either. Bonaparte didn't even take the sugar. I'd have been surprised if he had."

"Don't you know it's wrong to make such a statement to a policeman?" asked Boase, abruptly severe.

"I know this much, Mr. Boase. When a statement like that is made just after a man dies, it's wrong for a quack to sign a death certificate before opening him up, and more wrong for the police to allow the body to be cremated."

Boase frowned, and Mr. Luton knew he had him, and inwardly was jumping with glee.

"That, of course, was Bonaparte's views, eh?"

"Tramp on it, it's mine!" Mr. Luton roared with such vehemence that the two men were stunned. "Like all the city la-de-dahs, you think us Outbackers are a lot of morons. You think we're all comics what the papers draw. Look, my old man couldn't read nor write, but he could make better whisky out of spuds than ever came out of Scotland. Another cup of tea? Plenty in the pot."

This sting without a tail nettled Superintendent Boase. He shifted gears back to low.

"I understand that Bonaparte called on the Commonwealth Bank in Cowdry. D'you know why?"

"Yes. Didn't the manager tell you?"

"I haven't gone into it that far. Why did Bonaparte go there?"

"Because I asked him. We walked to Cowdry one day as he wanted a hair-cut. On the way, I asked him if he'd call at the Commonwealth and find out if old Ben had left his will there. That's all."

"Why are you interested in Wickham's will?"

"I'm interested to the tune of twenty thousand quid. Ben told me he had put it in. No will—I don't get the twenty thousand. No will's been found yet."

"Lucky man, if it is found," observed the Mount Gambier sergeant. "What I could do! I'd retire to this river and buy a rip-snorter of a cabin cruiser and a cosy house. Was Bonaparte in a good mood when he left?"

"Yes and no," replied Mr. Luton. "He was annoyed because you sent Gibley to tell him to go home. Said it was no ruddy business for the South Aus. Police. Said he'd speak his mind to his own high-up-ers, and wished he had memorised my bullocky language. I didn't blame him. This is a free country, or was before Federation."

'High-up-ers!' 'Morons!' 'Forelock!' Boase thought he could trace friend Bonaparte all round Australia on those words. His mind was now easy. There could be nothing in this ancient's idea that Wickham had been poisoned, too little anyway, to send Bony on the warpath. Good job that. Anything of that kind made public, there would be a hundred or so 'Please explains why permission for cremation.' Damn Wickham. He'd been a continuous source of annoyance to official Australia. To Luton he said:

"Bonaparte get any fish?"

"Eight or nine kingies," replied the old man. "That's what made him wild. Having a good time down here, and they couldn't let him alone for five minutes, but had to send for him. I told him: 'Don't you take it, Bony.' What do they expect? Expect a man to chase murderers in his sleep?"

"Perhaps. . . ."

"You running a racket down here?" blasted Mr. Luton. "Don't think it likely, though. But someone could be runnin' one, and got frightened 'cos they thought Bony might find out. Or did they want him to round up them bodgie-widgies? Anyhow, there's one man left in this country who can milk a goat, and that they're going to find out when Bony gets home."

"Good luck to him," said the Mount Gambier man, "and, by the way, my wife and kids really would appreciate that fish."

"They shall have it, Sergeant. I'll go get it."

The old man padded away to the outside meat-house. Sergeant Maskell observed, thoughtfully:

"Doesn't sound as though Inspector Bonaparte said anything to him about his nosing around in Cowdry. Think the yarn about going to the bank for the will was true?"

"Could be," slowly admitted Boase. "Bonaparte would do anything. Slippery devil, but I like him. What's your opinion of Gibley?"

"Good enough policeman. Knows the book. But I still don't get that bank angle. We ask the manager why he rang Gibley immediately Bonaparte left him, why he asked Gibley to look him over. The manager fidgets, and asks us to tell him why he shouldn't be suspicious of a man with a name like that claiming to be a police inspector."

"Seemed on edge because we'd looked in," agreed Boase. "I've a pretty good ear for clocks."

"Meaning, Super?"

"Meaning that when a man don't tick properly, I know it."

The slop-slop of slippered feet told Bony that Mr. Luton was returning with the fish. He heard Sergeant Maskell warmly thanking their host for the gift, and a minute later the sound of their departing car reached him, whereupon Mr. Luton closed and locked the front door. Bony crossed to the brandy steps, to hear Mr. Luton whisper through the auger-holes:

"They're gone. You hear 'em?"

"Every word, Mr. Luton."

"How did I go?"

"Magnificently," replied Bony.

"You want anything?"

"No. I'll come up for dinner after dark, if that will suit you."

"Do me. I'll be on the watch, and have dinner ready by half-past six."

Bony descended the brandy steps and perched on the rum cases against the bar counter. Absently he rolled a cigarette and smoked, going over every word Boase had said, seeking beyond the words. He knew Boase was curious as to why he had come to Cowdry. Boase had not found out why he had called at the bank, because the manager wouldn't tell, and had invented an explanation for calling Gibley. The suspicion that the telegram despatched by the manager, that day he had called at the bank, concerned himself became a conviction. Only through that bank manager had his superiors known he was at Cowdry.

The wording of the telegram of recall was not in character

with those who sent it, and to arrive at this knowledge one had to go back to their actions in the past.

First: Bony had been promoted to Detective-Inspector because of special abilities, and for special investigations. He was not to be employed on city crimes, where, obviously, his talents would be wasted. He was to be employed on special assignments in the Outback and outer urban areas. And his services were to be available to other Australian States should they be asked for. That was the original intention when the appointment was granted, and it remained so, with only an occasional exception.

The appointment was made some twenty years before by the Chief Commissioner of the Queensland Police Department, when Bony was a young man recently graduated from a training depot, and with a reputation which began some considerable time before he entered the depot.

At the time, the Chief Commissioner, Colonel Spendor, was himself a new broom. A strict disciplinarian, he was given to choleric ranting and abuse of his officers and his secretary. Yet all his threats were merely blah, and all his decisions were just, and all his officers and the secretary remained through the years his most loyal junior colleagues.

Of them, Bony was the most difficult. These are not the times when a police officer can be a Javert. If he does not apprehend a criminal within what is assumed to be a reasonable period, he may be put to another investigation and another officer assigned to his unfinished labours. Or he may be taken off his investigation, which is left in cold storage.

What to do, therefore, with a born Javert? What to do with a responsible senior officer who, when once put on a trail begun by a killer, will not leave it when a Chief of the C.I.B. orders him back, and when he is so instructed by the Chief Commissioner himself?

In the Army, a court-martial. In the Civil Service, a

cupboard job where the delinquent can rust in his own stupidity. But not with Colonel Spendor.

Second: there was almost a routine in these recalls sent to Inspector Bonaparte. An order to return to headquarters issued by the C.I.B. failing, a direct order from Colonel Spendor would be despatched. This also failing, Colonel Spendor would rant and rave, and send yet another telegram giving a date when pay would cease if, etc., etc. This, too, being ignored, the final telegram would sack Bony from the Police Department.

Thus the routine. Silly in itself, as no police officer may be sacked unless on the advice of the Police Disciplinary Board, directed by the Chief Secretary.

At the conclusion of every such routine, Bonaparte would report to his immediate superior, and would be 'carpeted' before Colonel Spendor. Colonel Spendor would go through his act, unique in itself, and venomously pardon him, after being informed that the culprit had successfully concluded the investigation to which he had been assigned, invariably a homicide, and usually one on which other officers had fallen flat on their faces.

How can you sack a man who never fails to bring home the pork?

Those earlier orders were off the record.

Only this last recall order was according to the book. But why the haste to have him leave his 'spot of fishing'?

Why was action taken to prevent him from yet again thumbing his nose at the 'higher-ups'?

Chapter Eighteen

THE FINAL STRAW

THE wind was blowing direct from the South Pole and, to counter it, the fire in Mr. Luton's sitting-room was leaping up the chimney.

Before the fire lounged Mr. Luton and his guest, both arrayed in pyjamas and dressing-gowns, the one smoking a pipe, the other inhaling from something vaguely resembling a cigarette.

Adventure had come again to Mr. Luton's days; contentment seeped into his mind as the fire warmed his body.

"What's the next load we pick up?" he asked in the manner of the teamster. "Police? Foreigners? Ben's relations?"

"Police, probably," lazily answered Bony. "By now the hounds will know I did not arrive in Melbourne. . . ."

"Hounds! Don't like the word, Inspector. Makes me think of a fox, and you the fox, or Brer Rabbit, like you said."

"I'm sure Brer Rabbit never had a more comfortable burrow. And all the adventures Brer Rabbit had with Brer Fox and Mr. Man were not so interesting as our encounter with Mr. Badger. You see, the police will be rushing here and there questioning people about me, wearing themselves out, while I snugly relax."

"But what the hell are they after you for?" demanded Mr. Luton.

"They haven't yet explained," Bony replied. "Meanwhile,

I have ideas, one of which is gaining prominence. Shall I tell you a story?"

Mr. Luton nodded, and wiggled his toes in his carpet slippers.

"Once upon a time," Bony began, "there was a great and mighty king, wearied by his courtiers, had writer's cramp through signing so many documents, and longed to bestir neighbouring kings and presidents.

"This great king wasn't English or Australian. He believed that, when dissatisfied, the only possible counter was to do something about it. And so he decided he would travel to far countries and start something.

"In the course of his world tour, he came to Australia, where the courtiers and the officials grovelled before him, and all the people were told to gather and give him cheers.

"This kind of reception, however pleasing to the grovellers and the common herd, bored him so much that he determined to find his own amusement. So one dark and stormy night he made a rope of his bed-sheets and slid to the ground and stole away unseen, as all the guards were in the canteen and betting on who would receive the coveted medals."

Mr. Luton's pipe had gone out, and he had forgotten to wiggle his toes. Bony lit another alleged cigarette and began the next instalment.

"All this, of course, happened in Australia, actually the country into which stepped Alice through the Looking-Glass. Once the great king had eluded the stuffed shirts, he wanted to sing and dance—and did. People looked at him and wondered, because it was hours after the six o'clock pub-shut, and how, thus, could he be drunk?

"Still controlled by this mood of abandonment, he came to the end of a dark street, when a woman appeared and said: 'Hi ya, sailor! Looking for a sweetheart?' Now the famous king had never before been addressed with such democratic forthrightness, but this he minded less than being asked if he were looking for a sweetheart. Not since the age of two, when his nurse had asked him what he was looking for under the bed, had he had to look for anything such as a pair of socks, a two-shilling piece, or a sweetheart.

"He drew himself up to his full majestic height and told her all this, but all she said was 'Your sort couldn't find anything.'

"For the first time in his life, he forgot he was a king who could do no wrong—and did it. He took the woman's scrawny, unwashed neck into his hands, and strangled her. And he was still at it, when young Constable Napoleon Bonaparte chipped in with: 'What's all this?'

"Hearing this gruff voice, the great and famous king thought he would have a try at another neck, and, for the first time in his life, didn't get what he asked for . . . or did he? When he recovered from his astonishment, he found himself in the local police station. The Chief Commissioner was bathing his bruises, a superintendent was replacing a broken shoe-lace, and five inspectors were offering him sweetmeats. Only Constable Napoleon Bonaparte was chewing his finger-nails. With brilliant secrecy, attended by the entire police force excepting Constable N. B., the great and famous king was returned safely to the bosoms of the stuffed shirts.

"'How dare you assault His Majesty?' demanded the Chief Commissioner. 'Had to, sir, to make him loose his fingers from the dead woman's throat.' The Chief Commissioner was crying, such was his horror at this act of *lèse-majesté*, and as all his under-strappers waited for him to pronounce a hundred years' hard labour for the offender, up spoke Constable N. B., saying: 'I've made out the charge sheet, sir, naming His Majesty, and indicting him of having feloniously slain one, to wit, May Jones, of Albion Mews, a known street-walker aged forty years and five months.'

"The Chief Commissioner fainted. The superintendent rushed for the whisky, and all the inspectors rushed Constable N. B. to the nearest cell, the cell next to the morgue, where, on a cosy slab, lay the remains of the tragic victim of royal disdain.

"Next day the unfortunate constable was taken from durance vile to the presence of the Chief Secretary, who said: 'Now, my man, listen—or else! When on duty last night, you came on two men attacking a third man. You rescued the third man from the thugs and took him to the police station for medical examination, and there it was discovered that the victim of assault was none other than His Majesty, King Wonky of Martonia. It happened that His Majesty, feeling slightly depressed after his uproarious welcome by the populace, decided to leave Mansion House and take a stroll. His Majesty now wishes to bestow on you the Order of Mug-Wumps, twenty-fourth grade. And, Constable Bonaparte, the Australian Government has decided to relieve you of paying income taxes for ten years. O.K.?'

"Now, the young constable, being altruistic, reminded the Chief Secretary that a corpse lay on the cute slab in the morgue, and no matter what expert morticians could do to it, the proof was plain that the woman had been properly strangled. The Chief Secretary said: 'So what?' The Chief Commissioner said: 'So what?' So said the superintendent and all the inspectors. And they said 'So what?' so often that the promising young constable retired from the Police Department and set up as a 'private eye'. And everyone lived happily ever after. . . . Why worry about a mere corpse?"

Mr. Luton pondered for precisely two and a half seconds, and then burst out with:

"So what?"

"Ah! There you have it, Mr. Luton. I will interpret the facts. Constable Bonaparte was prevented from doing his full duty. Inspector Bonaparte must be prevented from doing his duty here in the vicinity of Mount Marlo."

One of the charming attributes of the aged is that they are neither avidly curious nor impatient to ask questions. Mr. Luton remained passively interested. He had seen the broadly outlined picture Bony had painted and knew that Bony would complete the picture soon, for Bony was pensive, and the cigarette threatening to burn his fingers was proof of it.

They were both startled in like manner by the abrupt barking of the dogs. Against the inner stillness of the mind beat the wind about the eaves and the branches of the trees. The clock in the adjacent room whirred, struck nine deep notes, and when the last note was softly fleeing there came the rush of feet up the steps and across the veranda, and urgent knocking on the door. The men rose; Bony to move into the dark interior of the living-room, Mr. Luton to deal with the caller.

"Mr. Luton!" cried Jessica Lawrence. "I . . ."

"Why, Sunset! Come in! Come in!" The girl almost ran into this haven. She was wearing a light coat buttoned to the chin, a beret charmingly counteracting the wide eyes and panting breath.

"Anyone with you?" asked Mr. Luton, holding the door a fraction from closing.

"No. No, I came alone. Dr. Linke . . . Carl . . . has gone away. I . . . I've been running. I was being followed."

"Sit you down, Sunset." Mr. Luton closed the door and shot the inside bolt. Bony entered, and the girl went to him and gripped him by the arms.

"You here, Inspector! I heard you had left, gone back to Brisbane."

"Rumour is often humour, Miss Lawrence." He pushed her gently into a fireside chair. "Take it easy. All my friends call me 'Bony'. I hope you will so honour me. Never believe that Bony deserts his friends."

"Cup of tea, Sunset? Coffee if you like. Brandy in the coffee, too," suggested Mr. Luton.

"Whatever . . . Thank you."

The old man hurried to the stove and the dresser for cups and saucers. As the girl seemed unable to decide, he chose coffee, with brandy, for all three.

"Cigarette?" offered Bony. "Shall I make one for you? I'm not an expert, but . . ."

"Thank you. I have some here. Oh! I'm so glad to see you."

"Nice of you. Dr. Linke . . . you said he went away. Where has he gone?"

"I don't know. They came for him this afternoon."

"Your cigarette is out. Relax!" Bony smiled at her, and that helped defeat hysteria. "Mr. Luton won't be long with the . . . I'll wager it'll be coffee with a kick in it."

Mr. Luton came in a few minutes later to find the girl less agitated and Bony studiously not looking at her. There was no doubt about that coffee.

"Coffee," remarked Mr. Luton, accepting his cue, "is never worth drinking if there is only a drop or two of brandy in it."

"So!" murmured Bony. "You don't just drip the brandy into it?"

"You insult coffee and brandy by mating them too carelessly," observed Mr. Luton, and then flushed because he might have drawn the wrong analogy. "You pour brandy into coffee. Drops reminds me of medicine."

"Thank you, Bony, and you, Mr. Luton. I'm better now." Jessica Lawrence spoke firmly. "But I was followed, and I did run in a panic."

"Tell us about that first, Jessica."

"I decided I must contact you somehow, and I thought Mr. Luton would tell me how. About Carl. So I left the house without telling anyone. The moon is bright, but the clouds are racing and there's plenty of moon shadow. I came to the highway all right and chose it down to the bridge, instead of taking the path across the paddocks, because it's a good night for walking. Then, when half-way to the bridge, I had a sort of feeling, and I looked back and saw a man on the road.

"I hurried along, and he seemed to hurry too. I don't know what made me do it, but I stopped and looked at him. He was about a hundred yards away. He stopped too. I called out and asked him who he was. He didn't answer, and I walked back to see him more clearly. And he went back too. When I turned and came on, he turned and followed me again.

"I came to the turn-off at the bridge and followed the track to this cottage, and the man stopped at the bridge and lit a cigarette. I thought, I'm all right now, and I walked the track beside the trees and came to the patch of scrub. As I was passing the scrub, suddenly I saw another man. He was standing behind a bush, but I could see his head above the top of the bush. He was very still. It was then that I took to my heels and bolted, coward that I am."

"Sure that the man behind the bush wasn't the man who followed you down the highway?" Bony asked.

"Positive. There must have been two of them."

"Could you describe them?"

"Well, the man who followed me on the road seemed to be tall. He was wearing a raincoat and . . ."

"Pardon. A raincoat! Could you distinguish the coat?"

"No. It was the shape of the man that told me he was wearing a belted coat. The other one, the one behind the bush, was shorter, I think. Not much taller than I am. Both wore hats."

"Could you hear the man walking on the hard road?"

"Yes."

"Anything peculiar in the sound of his footsteps?"

"Well, yes, there was. The sounds didn't come evenly. I know! He was slightly lame."

"Anything more about them?"

"No, Bony."

"Tell us about Dr. Linke."

"I was in the office when Carl came in from the recording instruments. It would be about a quarter to three. He . . . he threw a kiss to me and went to his desk to transfer the readings to the graph charts. A little after three I put the kettle on the stove and we had afternoon tea as usual about half-past three. I'm afraid we loitered."

"Loitering can be very pleasant, Jessica. Go on, please."

"I am telling you this because it was much later when I realised I ought to have noticed the time. So it must have been after four o'clock when a car drove up to the office and Carl went to see who it was.

"I heard voices. Carl's was raised in protest. Then he came in, followed by that man who came to question him when . . . you know, the Commonwealth Investigation man. There was another man with them. Carl said he had to go away for a day or two, and the two men went with him to his room.

"I peeped through the front door at the car. It looked like a police car, but I took the number. There was a man in the driver's seat, and I think I've seen him before. Then the two other men and Carl came along the side of the office. Carl was carrying his suitcase. I watched them get into the car and drive away. . . ."

"The man who accompanied the Commonwealth Investigation fellow—was he tall and large, with stiff greying hair and a stiff grey moustache?" Bony asked.

"Yes. Yes, he had hair and moustache like that."

Bony chuckled, and said:

"The iron *is* growing hot. That would be Superintendent Boase. As a lady character I once met would say: 'Well, I never!' Dr. Linke carted off for questioning! Mysterious men trailing his fiancée! Inspector Bonaparte unwarrantably ordered home from the front line! 'Well, I never.' So I shall now handle this situation in the best traditions of the private eye. A snort of Bourbon, brother, while I check my shooter. I'll soon fix those guys. Nothin' to it."

Chapter Nineteen

A FINE NIGHT

'PRIVATE EYE' NAPOLEON BONAPARTE went below to dress, and emerged in dark clothes, a black silk scarf displacing the white collar, and wearing black canvas shoes.

He sipped a second cup of coffee minus the brandy, smiled at Jessica Lawrence, and rolled a cigarette while waiting for Mr. Luton. A moment later, Mr. Luton came in with a double-barrelled shot-gun and a box of cartridges. He had switched off the light in the kitchen-living-room and closed the door.

"I shall be gone less than an hour," Bony told them. "On my return, I shall announce myself before you admit me. That point clear?"

Mr. Luton nodded, and loaded the shot-gun.

"Under no circumstances will you open the door to anyone save me, no matter if the person is known to you by his voice, and no matter what he says, such as 'Police here,' or 'Open in the name of the Law!' You will not so much as answer him. Clear?"

Mr. Luton snapped the breech shut and again nodded.

"I want both of you to sit quietly in this room and do nothing until you hear my voice. Should anyone begin to break in, make no effort to dissuade him. Let him gain entry, and then point your gun at him. You will be very nervous by then, and the gun will go off. Guns go off without triggers being pulled, in most criminal cases. Guns are always blameworthy;

the criminal never. Your gun will go off; you will be blameless. But see to it that, at the precise moment your gun is discharged, it points in the true direction."

"You mean that, Bony?" exclaimed Jessica Lawrence.

"Absolutely. Mr. Luton is still suffering from damage to his knees. Now listen, Mr. Luton."

The plan of exit being unfolded, Mr. Luton accompanied Bony to the living-room, closing the door to the sitting-room behind them. The living-room was then in total darkness. The inside bolt and the lock on the back door having been oiled, neither the bolt nor the key made noticeable noise and, inch by inch, Bony drew the door inward, slowly letting inside the comparatively bright moonlight.

With the door half-opened, he stood listening. The wind was still strong. The clouds continued to race across the moon, so that one minute he could see the kennels at the bottom of the garden, and at the next could barely distinguish the door of the meat-house.

The two dogs were standing, and only slightly moving. As it was cold, they should have been inside their kennels. They were not at peace, and they were not alarmed. They were merely suspicious. There were no sounds from the day-loving birds, who were obviously asleep, and when a night-loving owl fluttered above the bordering trees, the picture was complete, and its meaning plain.

There was no one in the vicinity of the house.

Outside, Bony paused to hear the soft snip of the bolt being shot home. The key he didn't hear being turned by Mr. Luton, who would then cross the dark living-room to enter the illumined sitting-room where waited the girl. Thus no silhouettes.

When the moon was masked, Bony walked the garden path to the kennels. The dogs saw him coming, wagged tails, refrained from barking, and contented themselves with wingeing their pleasure. He made a fuss of them, gave each a sweet biscuit, and climbed the rear fence to gain the trees and scrub which, either side of the house, formed a wide border to the river.

Here the moonlight was appreciably reduced. He turned up-river, and roughly followed a line parallel with the path to Knocker Harris's camp. Progress was slow, for the bush was thick and spiny, and progress had to be silent.

Eventually he saw the light, a mere pin-hole in the dark canvas. He paused to glance at his watch. Four minutes to ten. Finally he could see the edges of the aperture through which the light was coming, and even then he could not see the outlines of Knocker's house. He did hear voices. Knocker entertained a visitor.

There were so many holes and cracks in Knocker's abode that to eavesdrop would be easy, were it not for the midget Australian terrier. Bony was not that anxious to overhear what was being discussed, but he did want to see the visitor.

Arriving at the edge of 'the lawn', he refrained from stepping on to it, in view of Knocker's snares—not that he was fearful of tripping over one, but because he could not re-set it exactly as Knocker had done. Skirting the lawn, he noted that the wind was from him to the hut as he crossed the path. Six yards farther on was the river-bank, the rough landing-stage, and the contrivance of fish-line and bullock-bell.

The midget dog was still passive inside the hut. No bird voiced an alarm outside it. Bony pulled in the line, removed the bait, tossed it back and vigorously rang the bell. He skipped into the bush. The birds woke and complained. The little dog in the hut frantically yapped. The door opened and out rushed the dog, followed by Knocker, carrying the pressure lamp, and another man wearing a belted overcoat.

The visitor was tall, inclined to be stout, and was plainly

excited. Though the moonlight fell strongly on him, Bony could not identify him. He hurried after Harris, who hurried after the dog, who raced to the belled fish-line.

"No go! Fish got away." There was a hint of anger in Knocker's voice. The man said:

"Pity. It might have been a beaut."

"Took me bait, anyhow," grumbled the hermit. "Must have been only playin' with it, like. I thought the bell didn't ring like she oughter."

"Tough luck," sympathised the stranger.

"Yair," agreed Knocker, re-baiting the hook, and, standing, swung the lead well out into the stream. The dog yapped its disappointment, and, when Knocker began to move back to the hut, ran on ahead. The stranger said:

"Oh, well, I'll get along. I'll do what I told you. Be here at eight for the bait. You'd rather the meat and things instead of money?"

"Yair. I don't want no arguments with the blasted Council."

"Wise fellow. Well, see you to-morrow."

"So long. Left your car at the bridge, you said?"

"Yes."

"Find your way back to the clearing?"

"That'll be right. Good-night!"

The stranger was able to find his way, without doubt, and obviously this was not his first visit to Knocker Harris. Bony followed him without difficulty. He eventually reached the clearing in front of Mr. Luton's house, having then received Bony's 'pass' for bushcraft, although he still had much to learn.

Casually the stranger crossed the clearing, unaware of the object behind him, which flitted in the deeper shadows cast by Mr. Luton's 'bullock team'. He skirted the track and had proceeded about a dozen yards when a man spoke to him and he halted to merge with the close-set scrub where Jessica Lawrence had seen a man standing.

Bony moved, on hands and knees, until he was within four feet of the two men now seated on a fallen tree-trunk.

"Damn cold waiting here. Do any good?"

"I'm not clear yet," replied the stranger. "Got a deal of background on old Wickham and Luton. They were certainly close buddies."

"Pretty thick, eh?"

"Thick as thieves are supposed to be. We could be right about that missing data. Old Wickham could have planted it with Luton, and Luton could be lying doggo. That girl left yet?"

"No, else I wouldn't be here."

"Tellin' the old boy how her sweetie was nabbed, I bet."

"Most likely."

"What do we do about her when she does come out?"

"As I told you," replied the stranger whose face Bony had seen.

"I don't much like it," objected his companion.

"I like it more since I pumped old Harris. That girl's sweet on Linke. She and Linke have been visiting Luton before old Wickham jumped off, and since. Those two were closest to Wickham. We know that. So we do as planned. We bail her up if she's alone, and we deal with old Luton if he's with her. We tell her we know enough about Linke to have him put away. If she answers a few questions we forget what we know about Linke. No rough stuff—not much."

Silence between them until the stranger said it was after ten-thirty.

"Wish she'd hurry up and come out."

"So do I," agreed the other. "But we sit here if we wait till daybreak."

Bony moved away, finally to walk noiselessly by the track

towards the bridge. He was both perturbed and gratified by these developments, even though this last pair of conspirators could not be so clearly labelled as the first. But there was the parked car, and much can be learned from a car.

It was standing well off the highway, on the far side, under gums beyond a space cleared for material when the road was being re-surfaced. It occupied Bony three minutes to be assured no one was sitting in it, or exercising cold legs in its vicinity. It was registered in Victoria, a Buick sedan of 1952 vintage, dark grey and lovely in the moonlight. There was nothing about it to indicate anything but a private car.

Bony automatically noted the registration, the size and make of the tyres, the fine leather of the upholstery. As he sat behind the wheel, the distance of the pedals suggested that the man who had visited Knocker Harris was its driver. The open dash-box beside the wheel contained a notebook, a pencil, pressure gauge, and, luckily—for every successful policeman has to be lucky, an envelope containing a garage account. The bill had been posted to Mr. S. V. Marsh, 32 Myall Avenue, Toorak, a fashionable Melbourne suburb when on the right side of the tram-lines.

The glove-box held a silver box of cigarettes, supporting the view that Mr. Marsh was a wealthy man. But wealth is deceptive. Many persons spring from wages to comparative affluence—a minor point.

Bony hated even the thought, but he found the tool compartment and took from the roll of canvas an adjustable spanner. The roll he returned to the compartment. The door he carefully closed, and was careful, too, that the door of the glove-box was shut.

The winter winds, even the recent imitation shower, had failed to dampen the tree débris, which Bony gathered with his feet and made a pile of, at the rear of the car. He pushed more débris under the front end. Then he loosened the drainage plug of the petrol tank and kicked débris under the rear end.

Motionless, he listened, watching and waiting for the next cloud to weaken the moonlight. Save for the wind, nothing disturbed. The cloud came. He struck a match. There was not sufficient petrol spilled to make an explosion, but enough to cause him to run for cover.

Bony flitted across the highway, under the trees, and through the light scrub bordering the track to Mr. Luton's house. When midway, he stopped. As he looked back, the glare rose bright between the tree-trunks and enamelled deep orange the foliage of the trees about the bridge.

There was nothing stealthy in the movements of the intending waylayers of a charming girl. Bony watched them, walking fast, so concerned as to be speechless.

Bony's flittering became a fast run. He knocked at the back door of the cottage, paused, then called:

"All set, Mr. Luton. The dogs are asleep and well fed."

The door opened and Bony slipped into the lightless sitting-room.

"Now, Jessica, we go. I will escort you home."

"Everything all Sir Garno?" asked Mr. Luton.

"A slight mishap near the bridge, that's all," replied Bony. "Lie low and don't open up till I return. Ready, Jessica?"

Outside the door, Bony apologised when he took her hand and hurried her along the path. The dogs were excited and he spoke to quieten them. They had cause to be excited. The girl saw the reason as she was being assisted through the wire fence at the bottom of the garden.

When in the open paddock and following the faint path over the drought-smitten earth, she referred to it.

"The fire?" exclaimed Bony innocently. "Ah, yes! A careless smoker dropped a lighted match. People will never learn. You can conduct 'Safety First' campaigns till you're blue in the face, and they won't learn. Heard a statesman once talking on the radio, urging listeners to 'put out that match'. One moron talking to a million. Of course he was a moron. They all are. Every year they warn the people about dropping lighted matches, especially when near tree débris and petrol and that kind of combustible. If the statesmen had any intelligence, they would prohibit the manufacture and sale of matches, and make everyone buy a lighter. People don't drop cigarette lighters. They're too expensive."

"May I say something?" the girl asked, breathlessly.

"By all means. I am all attention."

"You are hurrying too fast. And talking too much. And not telling the truth."

"My apologies, Jessica. Permit me to ease your mind. Dr. Linke will be all right; he will be allowed to return to his work here, and to you, even if I have to blackmail the Prime Minister."

At the fence skirting the highway, Bony bade no talking while he listened. Across the road stood the open gateway to Mount Marlo. The only sound was the wind in the pine trees. No footsteps on the road. Only the ruddy glare of the fire down by the bridge.

They sped across the road to the open gates and walked along the daffodil-bordered driveway.

"Please tell me about the fire, Bony."

Believing that the girl would worry unduly, he said:

"A secret. Between us. Those men you saw were waiting for you to leave Mr. Luton's cottage. They intended to frighten you with threats to force you to give information. So while you were waiting with Mr. Luton, I fired their car to create a diversion while I was being honoured as your escort. Will you accept an order from me?"

"Yes."

"I order you not to leave Mount Marlo at any time alone, until I say so. In the morning, as early as possible, I want you to send a phonogram. You can use the office phone? Without being overheard?"

"I'll manage that."

"Here is the message, addressed to a young lady in Melbourne, to ask her to contact you at the earliest possible moment. When she does, be very guarded. Say that I am in urgent need of her assistance at Mr. Luton's cottage, near Cowdry. Refer to me only as her Murray River friend. Clear?"

"Quite," replied Jessica, accepting the written message and slipping it into a coat pocket. Impulsively, she squeezed Bony's arm. "I can't tell you how grateful I am. You will do your best about Carl, won't you?"

"I have said so, Jessica. Now you run for the door. I'll watch."

He waited until he saw the door close behind her, then raced back to Mr. Luton.

Chapter Twenty

BONY LISTENS TO RADIO PLAY

"DID the dogs bark?" Bony asked when Mr. Luton had admitted him and they were again in the sitting-room.

"No, exceptin' once when one of 'em yapped as if a flea bit him without knocking."

Bony related the incidents of the evening, believing Mr. Luton should be prepared for possible future developments, and the old man frowned at the story of Knocker Harris's visitor, and chuckled when hearing of the 'accident' to the car.

"First," Bony went on, "nothing of our knowledge to Harris when he comes again. You must wait for what he gives or won't give about that car driver. Ostensibly, the man went to Harris to arrange for the delivery of fishing bait to-morrow, but actually to obtain information about your relationship with Ben Wickham. Which indicates that the centre of interest in Wickham's papers has moved to this house of yours. Those two foreigners were first to make that move: these last two fellows are coming round to it. We may assume that the last two are not associated with the first two."

"The two to-night? They foreigners?" Mr. Luton put forward.

"Not from their accent. The driver of the car need not be the owner, but the owner's name is Marsh. The garage account is for general servicing, not repairs. Now to see what is in the notebook."

Study of the notebook occupied five minutes.

"The driver, if not the actual owner, could be a commercial traveller," Bony said, slowly. "This is a record, almost in diary form, of expenditure on petrol and oil, hotel expenses, meals, roughly jotted down, possibly for transference to a swindle sheet at the end of the day. It begins in April, 1953, continues through to four days ago, when petrol was purchased in Cowdry. Between dates, the driver visited Adelaide, Melbourne, where he probably lives, then Canberra, back to Melbourne, Sydney, and so on. If he is a commercial traveller, then his territory covers three States and the Australian Capital Territory. The car being a Buick, his firm must be a wealthy one, or he could be the head of a small but prosperous firm. He could be a Government servant. Getting in deep, are we not?"

"We're left with some dark horses, eh?"

"No show, Mr. Luton, if we adopt the racecourse for the sea. Time is my bet. I am ever an admirer of Time, for Time has been my greatest ally. Now, there is another matter. Those records and the green notebook in the chest could be located I am uneasy, and we should do something about it. Have you any suggestions for a better hiding-place?"

"Don't know. Have to think. The pub's secret enough, isn't it?"

"I fear not," Bony said. "If the house was searched by experts, they would quickly find the trap-door. We must use imagination. Let us assume that you are an habitual drunk. That you were married to a very suspicious woman who does not approve of the cursed drink, and will, on sight of a bottle, empty it down the sink. Where would you plant your bottle?"

"In a hole under the perches in the fowl-house," promptly answered Mr. Luton.

"I anticipated your selection," Bony said smilingly. "Your hiding-place would not be a hundred per cent proof against a suspicious wife, but it ought to trick a change-daily boy. We'll do the job right now."

Mr. Luton was ready and eager. It occupied them almost an hour, for work had to be done without light, without disturbing the hens and their lord roosting on the perches, and replacing the over-lay exactly as formerly. The hole was not large, because Bony finally decided to leave the annual records in the chest, burying only the notebook, the will, the smaller book taken from the car, inside a biscuit tin.

Afterwards they ate a light supper, drank a hot toddy and retired, all doors locked and windows bolted, the loaded shotgun on Mr. Luton's bedside table, and the furniture and floor-covering in the kitchen-living-room so arranged as to permit Bony easy egress if essential.

Both slept in undisturbed peace.

At nine o'clock Mr. Luton took a breakfast tray down to his guest, who planned to spend the day on further study of the records in the chest. He then proceeded with the chores of the day: freeing the dogs, tidying the house, doing a little digging and sowing peas and transplanting early cabbage.

Shortly after ten, Senior Constable Gibley called, knocking on the front door, when Bony mounted the brandy steps.

"What! You again!" Mr. Luton said sharply.

"Me again, Luton," agreed the policeman. "How's the kettle? Boiling?"

"Damnation!" roared the old man. "You think I can supply the whole ruddy police force with cups of tea, and tea the price it is?"

"No. Actually, I brought you a pound of tea. Sergeant Maskell gave me the doings to buy it for you. Sends it with his compliments and thanks for the fish you gave him. Now you goin' to ask me in?"

"I've never yet refused a man a drink of tea or a bite to eat. Come on through. S'long as you don't ask fool questions, or make silly threats, you're welcome. What d'you come for?"

"I just told you," replied Gibley, easing himself into a kitchen chair.

"Now, now! That's only the jemmy that edges open the bank safe. Better let it out, or you won't enjoy the cakes I baked a couple of hours back."

"Well, as a matter of fact, I came to ask if you happened to fire the car down at the bridge."

Mr. Luton looked stunned, and waited.

"Seems that two men who've rented a holiday shack in Cowdry left their car at the bridge to do some night fishin'. Went down-river a bit, and while waiting for a bite, the glare told 'em about the car goin' up. What do you know?"

"What do I know?" roared Mr. Luton. "What do . . . Why, next thing you'll be accusing me of murder!"

"Do that, too, if your yarn about those hoo-jahs was true," counter-attacked the policeman. Mr. Luton was cut off from emphatic protest by his table guest. "Now, don't get so hotted up, Luton. Here am I being quite matey, and you almost make me believe you dislike me. Didn't you see the glare over the trees?"

"I certainly didn't, Gibley. On a cold and blustery night I don't go outside lookin' at the stars and things. I bide quiet afore my own fireside without wantin' to warm me hands at other people's fires. You telling me someone fired the car?"

"No, just a bit of fun," admitted Gibley. "They must have left a cigarette butt under a cushion or something. Must have been a good blaze. Burned the ground all round for yards out."

"Serves 'em right for fishin' at night. Why don't they work instead of loafin' around on holidays this time of year. Maybe they're them foreigners you was lookin' for."

"No, not them. These fellers come from Melbourne. Car owner's name is Marsh. I got them clear enough. There's another thing. Your pal Inspector Bonaparte's disappeared."

"Oh!" sneered Mr. Luton. "Was he bound and gagged in the car?"

"Not so funny, Luton. He was last seen at Serviceton, aboard the Melbourne train. He come back here?"

Mr. Luton turned sarcastic.

"No. Could be camped with old Knocker Harris. You seen him?"

Gibley ignored that.

"Mind me looking round here?"

"What for? Bonaparte?"

"That's right."

"I'm easy, Gibley. You've come through the sitting-room. He wasn't there. This is the living-room. He isn't here. There's my bedroom, over there. Take a look under the bed and in the wardrobe. There's no other rooms. Outside is the wood-shed and the meat-house. He might be in the meat-safe. Down the garden a bit is the fowl-house, and a bit further is the dog-kennels. Could be in one of them."

"Could be out in the scrub, where he went when you heard me coming," added Gibley.

"You got a warrant for him?" asked Luton with unfeigned astonishment.

"No, of course not. Just got to locate him, that's all. Hear anything about the office up at the big house being broken into?"

"No. By heck, things are livening up, aren't they?"

"You wouldn't know who's doing the livening up, would you?"

"Look! I been livin' here for years, and all I ask for is peace. Now I hope you'll take the hint."

Senior Constable Gibley smiled sourly, and strode from the house. He remembered to thank Mr. Luton for the tea and cakes when half-way to the front gate.

He had acted under orders which his superiors and he himself believed barely concerned them. He was satisfied that the destruction of the car was accidental, and satisfied concerning the identity of the driver and his companion. There had been ample time to check the relevant details with the police in Melbourne. As for the disappearance of Inspector Bonaparte from the Melbourne express, he had complied with what verged on a routine police broadcast.

With this Bony was also satisfied. What did concern him was that his disappearance had been broadcast. Officially he was a wanted man. And so far, as he had warned Jessica Lawrence to keep his whereabouts secret, only Mr. Luton knew he was in this cellar.

He heard voices at the rear of the house, and slipped down the brandy steps and climbed the gin steps in time to overhear Knocker Harris saying:

"Properly burnt out, like. They was to come in at my jetty this morning for bait-fish, but I suppose the fire sort of upset 'em. I seen Gibley comin'. So he didn't see me."

"How did those fellers find you?" asked Mr. Luton. "They come up-river?"

"No. Come to my place by car last night. Leastways one of 'em did. The other stayed in the car. That's what I don't get. How did the car catch afire? Gibley tell you?"

"No. He said they told him they was away fishing when she burned. Why should they say that?"

"Search me. How would I know?" snapped Knocker Harris.

"You seen 'em before?"

"No. The bloke what came arrived about nine-ish, like. Said he wanted bait-fish for to-day. I give him a cupper and he give me a quarter-pound plug of chewin' tobacco. They was to call for the bait at eight this mornin'."

"You never seen the fire last night?"

"No. Did you?"

Mr. Luton ignored this question.

"What time did the feller leave your camp?"

"'Bout eleven, I'd say."

"Oh!" snapped Mr. Luton. "Yabberin' with you for two hours while he leaves his cobber in the car on a cold night. Feller in car musta set fire to the car himself to keep warm. What did you talk about?"

"This and that."

"I asked you a question, Knocker!" Mr. Luton roared.

"All right, John. Don't shout at me. What's got inter you? He said he liked this bit of country, and I said it suits me what likes quietness and to be left alone, like."

"What else?"

"Oh, we yarned about old Ben and his weather-predictin', like."

"Tell him what we think about the hoo-jahs?"

"Yair, I did sort of give an idea."

"You would!"

Knocker Harris snuffled, but Mr. Luton probed farther. Asked what else was said about Benjamin Wickham, Knocker admitted he had told the stranger Ben and John had been cobbers for a long time, and that Ben often visited John without looking for a bender. It came out that Marsh had learned nearly all there was to learn. He even asked about Mr. Luton's recent visitor, and was told all about Inspector Bonaparte.

"It seemed all right to," whined Knocker Harris. "Not a local, like, what could get back on something."

Then Mr. Luton asked the question Bony ached to put:

"You tell him all this off your own bat?"

"Don't think I told him anything he didn't ask. He was just sort of interested, like, and wanted somethin' to talk about. Nice bloke, too."

"What else was he interested in?" pressed Mr. Luton. "Who else beside me and Inspector Bonaparte did you talk about?"

"Dr. Linke, the Parsloe woman and the parson. That's all."

"So that's all, is it? What about Dr. Linke?"

"He asked me how long the doctor had been workin' up at Mount Marlo, and if Dr. Linke came here much to yarn with you, like. Hey, when's all this goin' to stop?"

"Why ask me?" snarled the old man, deliberately perverse. "You start something, and then expect me to know when it will end. Leave me and my affairs out of talking to strangers. I don't want them to know how much I got in the bank, or how much I keep under the lino. How d'you know that feller isn't a rob-and-bash man? Could break in here after my dough and murder me for objectin'. Nice sort of friend you are."

"But I didn't mean no 'arm, like, John." The voice was distinctly desperate. "We been good neighbours for a long . . ."

"Well, we won't be if you go gassin' to every nosey tourist what comes along. Now get goin' and don't come back for a week."

"All right, John," agreed the plaintive Knocker. He scraped his feet on the floor and paused just outside the door to add: "If you wants me, like, you know where I hang out. Come Pension Day, you might want somethin' brought out from town."

"That'll be the day," exploded the unrelenting Mr. Luton.

Chapter Twenty-One

THE NIECE FROM MELBOURNE

THE afternoon passed without incident. No voices up top disturbed Bony as he scanned those bulky files resting on the bar counter. The only sounds reaching him were made by Mr. Luton overhead.

The old man had accepted rules against which, under normal circumstances, he would have rebelled. The dogs were not to be chained, night or day. The doors were to be kept locked, and he was to go outside the house only to obtain firewood, feed the hens and visit the meat-safe.

That there would be developments Bony was sure. A pot over a fire of this kind must inevitably come to the boil, and his chief concern was that Mr. Luton should not be scalded. That should have been his main reason for slipping that train. Deep in his heart he knew it wasn't the main reason, but the insatiable lust of the hunter inherited from his mother's people.

He closed the last of the files and returned them to the chest, having gained nothing further from them save clearer pictures of Benjamin Wickham's fight against orthodoxy and for recognition that came too late. The files showed that only in recent months had his completed work on long-range forecasting been rightly evaluated with special implications on international relations.

There were at least two groups most actively interested in locating Wickham's recorded methods. Mr. Luton's knees proved the interest of one of these groups, and it was fairly evident that this was the group that had approached Wickham on July 3, and that, normal negotiations being fruitless, its normal bash-and-torture methods had been adopted.

All this appearing to be gangster warfare conducted on Government level was of itself outside Bony's territory, save where it impinged on his professsional interest in the death of Benjamin Wickham. He had no direct proof that the meteorologist had died of a cause other than that stated on the medical certificate. He would never find direct proof of murder now that the body no longer existed. It was, however, possible to gather sufficient circumstantial evidence to convince any reasonable authority that murder had been done. And while the possibility continued, he would not permit gangsters, foreign or not, to side-track him by pulling strings for his recall.

As he had told Mr. Luton, the opportunity for murdering Ben Wickham was wide open, and the motive for killing could be one of several to activate a number of people.

The night brought no disturbance. Even Knocker Harris did not call, probably continuing to be upset by Mr. Luton's brusque treatment. The evening was spent playing poker, and only once during the night did the roaming dogs give voice to something or other far from the doorsteps.

It was eleven o'clock the next morning when Miss Alice McGorr arrived.

She had been associated with Bony in a case of mass infant abduction, and she hadn't hesitated to act, following the telegraphed request to contact Jessica Lawrence. The car that brought her had stopped at the wicket gate. The driver had carried her heavy suitcase to the veranda, and had waited until the door had opened and Mr. Luton had admitted to his name.

Mr. Luton didn't know what to make of her. There was something the matter with her appearance, but he could not decide what. He liked her brown eyes, and thought it a pity she had a receding chin. He knew at once that set against these negative points was physical and mental capacity beyond that of the average woman.

"You don't know me, Mr. Luton, but I am your niece, Alice McGorr, all the way from Melbourne," she told him, and before he could raise argument he found himself inside the house with her and her suitcase, and the door shut. Subsequently he was to remember the expression of her eyes when she demanded:

"Where is Inspector Bonaparte?"

A sepulchral voice moaned:

"Down among the dead men."

"What is he to you?" asked Mr. Luton, regaining poise.

"Another uncle. Now lead me to him."

Mr. Luton stalked into the sitting-room, Alice McGorr right on his heels. A motion of his hand halted her in the doorway. She watched him gravely move the table aside and, with growing interest, carefully roll the linoleum away from the trap-door. He lifted the trap, held it upright, and Bony emerged to flash a smile of welcome before stepping over the trap.

"Alice!" he said, and Mr. Luton didn't fail to note the gladness. "I didn't expect you, yet."

"It happened that I was home when your friend's telegram arrived," she explained. "Are you all right? You look normal. What's the big idea of being down there?"

"I reside there, Alice. A wonderful place! The finest bar in Australia. Mr. Luton, meet my very dear friend Policewoman Alice McGorr. Alice, I present another very dear friend."

Mr. Luton dropped the trap-door and stepped over the rolled floor covering with hand extended. He was smiling, and again the years vanished from his face.

"Glad to meet you," he said warmly. "Now I'll roll back the lino and we'll celebrate. Just as well I baked them cakes."

"In case a visitor should call, remember that Alice is your niece from Melbourne who intends to stay with you a few days," Bony reminded him. "And if I should disappear, Alice, say nothing and don't worry."

Mr. Luton departed to prepare the party, and Bony asked:

"How did you manage to get away so soon? Superintendent Bolt obviously co-operated."

"Your telegram came just after twelve yesterday, and it took an hour to reach the girl who sent it. The Super was out, and just as well it was my day off duty. He didn't come to his office till six. When I told him I had had word from you, he said: 'Shut that door.' Then he said: 'Now, let's have it.'

"I showed him the telegram and then repeated what the girl had said on the phone. The gist of it was that you were in a spot, and wanted me urgently.

"The Super said: 'In a spot! Well stuck, I'll say. All hell has spewed because he vanished off that train.' He thought a bit, then said: 'Look, Alice, that Bony feller has been prodding a stick into an out-size bull ants' nest. Boase and his Adelaide boys kicked him out of South Aus. and now his Brisbane bosses are kicking a stink 'cos he didn't get as far as Melbourne. So he went to Cowdry, did he? And now he's yelling for help.'

"I said: 'Pop, he's not yelling. He's asking.' Pop said: 'You win, he doesn't yell. Like to go?' When I told him I was going, with or without leave from the Department, he said: 'Go on home, Alice, and pack a bag. I'll work it out.'

"He came to my place about nine last night," Alice McGorr continued. "I could see he was worried, and he said: 'Look, Alice, I don't like the background of this business. I can't nail anything, although I've contacted both Adelaide and Brisbane. Someone's dropped a shutter and no one's game enough to raise it. That means the someone is mighty powerful. Now this is straight. If you barge in, you might lose your job.'

"I said: 'I'd be losing only a bobby-pin, Pop, but you might lose a job worth to you about a hundred diamond watches.' You know how he'd take that, Bony. He said: 'I have a car outside. Old pal of mine driving. He'll get you there sometime to-morrow morning. Take a gun in your kip. And an extra hat-pin. It might be tough. I managed to arrange a week's leave of absence for you. You're running up to Sydney to tend a sick grandmother, see?' And here I am, sir."

Bony nodded, essayed a smile, and left the room to stand facing Mr. Luton's bullock yoke without seeing it. The strength of the Melbourne Superintendent's friendship affected him, for it was no mean thing for a policeman in Bolt's position to put a telescope to a blind eye, such being his faith in another man's integrity. And it was no mean compliment to Bony of the mixed blood.

Great people! Alice McGorr, the daughter of a safe-breaker; the girl of fourteen who cared for her small brothers and a pair of twins when the father was in gaol and the mother dying in hospital. The then Sergeant Bolt had put the father in gaol, and Sergeant Bolt had taken the family under his wing, and given Alice opportunity to educate herself; had got her into the Department, where she became the best policewoman ever. Off duty, it was 'Pop' and 'Alice'. And just 'Bony'.

Someone called from outside the house, and Bony pushed the door to the living-room almost shut. He heard the scrape of a chair and the door being opened to admit Knocker Harris.

"Good day-ee, John! How's things?" came the usual greeting in the nasal whine of the first settlers, handed down to the fourth generation. "Day-ee, Miss!"

"Meet my niece from Melbourne, Miss McGorr," persuaded Mr. Luton. "Alice, this is an old friend who lives up-river a bit. The name's Harris, but we all call him 'Knocker' 'cos he knocks everything down that tries to get up."

The introduction was acknowledged, and Knocker said:

"From Melbun, eh? Long time ago when I was there . . . year that Sister Olive won the Melbun Cup. So you came to visit your uncle, like. Close one, your uncle. Never told me anything about you."

"There's lots I never told you about," countered Mr. Luton, and then raised his voice: "And don't try to make me out a liar."

"I ain't sayin' you're a liar, John."

"Well, don't."

"I'm sure Mr. Harris and I will get along," soothingly interjected Alice. "'You live up the river a little way, Mr. Harris? We'll probably see more of each other."

"Too right," agreed Knocker with no enthusiasm. "Well, John, don't suppose you want me hanging around, like. Pension Day to-morrer, and I thought you might want something."

"You can fetch me a bottle of them kidney pills. I've just about run out of gin. And order me a double issue of bread while you're in there. I'll get the money."

"You stayin' long, Miss?" Harris asked, and Bony detected an underlying note of unease.

"Maybe a week," replied Alice. "Might be a month. See how I like being here, and how uncle behaves himself."

"Why I'm askin' is because there's some funny goings-on around here, like," explained Knocker. "What with a bloke arrangin' to come back for bait, and his car being burned up. And me dog sort of runnin' about sniffin' all the time, like he got a burr up his nose. And three men pretendin' they're fishin' with their boat anchored on a sand-drift only a foot under surface. And there's John here keeping his kitchen door locked of a morning, like."

"Don't be a crying fool, Knocker," shouted Mr. Luton. "I'd

just got back from a walk to look-see that burned car when my niece arrived and we come in the front door. I don't rush about throwing open the doors and flingin' up the winders soon's I get home again. And what's wrong with them three men fishing off a boat? What sort of boat?"

"Open deck motor-boat, like. You can't tell me they'd catch a fish in a foot of water over a sand-drift. Anyhow, I watched 'em going up-river, and they hardly know how to steer the boat. They wasn't fishin', like. They was keeping an eye on this house. Seems like there's no end to this espinage. You had word from the Inspector since he went away?"

"Not yet. But he'll write sometime if he don't come back for more fishing.

"Well, I suppose I'd better be shovin' off, like. You look after your uncle, Miss. He wants feedin' up, like, at times when he ain't so well. I done me best."

Bony heard the door closed. Alice said:

"That's my cue to go ahead with the cooking, Uncle. What have you got on hand for lunch?"

Chapter Twenty-Two

ALICE THINKS IT'S FUN

MR. LUTON'S reactions to Alice McGorr ultimately balanced in her favour. He disapproved of her smoking. He disapproved of her taking complete control of his kitchen-living-room. He wasn't quite in favour of being called 'uncle'. Oppositely, he did like her direct approach in conversation. He did like the way she dressed her blonde hair in a tight bun at the nape of her neck, because he was reminded of the days when he was young, and he did like her brown eyes, which could be so expressive of warmth and intelligence. It was a great pity that her chin was negligible. And as he listened with her to Bony's outline of past events in and about his cottage, he came to admire the manner in which she received the story.

"I am sure, Mr. Luton," Bony continued smoothly, "you are in agreement that the position as it has developed is, shall we say, delicate. We are living in darkness, and all we have seen are shadowy figures best described perhaps as 'sinister'. I am confident you won't take umbrage at what I am going to say—that Alice will be completely able to meet all contingencies.

"When I returned from Adelaide, I considered it necessary to lie low, like Brer Rabbit, and just wait on events. Since then, however, I have found that I must have greater freedom and at the same time be assured of your personal safety."

"I can well look after myself," Mr. Luton protested.

"Of course, Mr. Luton. By the way, is that embrocation doing any good to your knees?"

"It is so. I better get some more from Knocker. Hey!" The old man smiled ruefully. "All right, Inspector. I can't win."

"This house might be attacked front and back at the same time, and the attack might not take the form of gun-play. It might be a matter of being compelled to answer questions, and, because the attackers will be men, let us say, like Boase and Sergeant Maskell, such questions can more quickly be defeated by a woman than by a man. You may find that hard to believe.

"I am asking you to remove from your mind the error that Alice is a weak, defenceless young woman you have to protect. This new niece of yours is tough. I heard it said by an authority that 'when she can't roll 'em, she bumps 'em, and when she can't bump 'em, she tosses 'em, and when she can't toss 'em, she flattens 'em.' All the tricks she learned from the police experts were mere variations of better ones she knew all about before she joined the Police Department.

"I'm telling you this because should anything rough break loose, you must accept orders from her. She represents the Law, whatever that might mean. She is far more responsible for anything ugly that might happen to you than you could be responsible for anything that happened to her.

"So both of you will act normally as uncle and niece. Lock the doors only at dusk. You will do outside chores and Alice will attend to the cooking and the house. Now and then you may stroll about the garden and see to the hens. At night, keep the dogs chained. All clear?"

"Yes."

"A final point. When I decided to lie low on my return from Adelaide, it was less to conceal myself from the police than from those who are interested in Ben Wickham's secrets, and thus encourage them to move. Just now I am reminded of two opposing armies manœuvring for position."

When Dr. Maltby called shortly after three that afternoon, Alice was briefed and ready. She opened the front door in answer to his knock, and his surprise was genuine. Heavy and yet agile, his dark eyes moved swiftly over her, and she said politely:

"Well?"

"Who are you?" he asked, and she could see suspicion in his eyes.

"Who am I!" she repeated. "Who the hell are you is more to the point. What d'you want?"

"I came to see Mr. Luton. Is he in?" countered the slightly nettled Maltby.

"Go down one and come on, mister," snarled Alice. "All I asked you was who you are."

"The name is Maltby . . . Doctor Maltby."

"Oh! I never sent for you. My uncle is all right, so far. What d'you want to see him about?"

Maltby tried to smile. The hard brown eyes and straight brown eyebrows of this person, the small but somehow grim mouth, the direct hostility, were outside his experience as a country doctor.

"I must explain, Miss . . . Miss . . ." Alice declined information. "I live at Mount Marlo, you know, and often I call just to see how your uncle is getting along. He's not as young as he was, and all that. Sometimes . . . er . . . sometimes . . ."

"Sometimes he gets a neck-ache tipping bottles," Alice now assisted. "Still, I'll be knocked flat if you ever reach his age. You needn't worry about uncle, and when he's sick I'll send for you fast enough. He's in bed this afternoon. Got a cold. I sent him there, and there he stays. From what he's been telling me, it's time I turned up. What with people pounding on his door at all hours, and others threatening to put him in an old men's home. Drive anyone screwy. I'd like to hear anyone threaten to put me in an old men's home!" Alice's voice became shrill. "So you live in that great stable of a place on the hill! Well, stay there, and don't come poking your nose into other people's affairs."

"My dear young lady . . ." protested Maltby. But it wasn't any use. She shrilled him to silence, and slammed the door in his face.

Seated at the table with Bony in the living-room, Mr. Luton was startled, until he recalled that Bony had directed Alice to 'receive' Dr. Maltby when he had seen him leave the car. Alice came in from the front room, smiled at Bony's expression of approval, and sat with them. Mr. Luton was asked to step outside to ascertain if the doctor was making for town.

Mr. Luton's hearing wasn't defective. He heard the car crossing the bridge.

"The next caller could be the policeman or the doctor's wife," Bony said, adding gravely: "The latter will extend you, Alice."

"Think so?" she challenged, smiling at him, and making them both oblivous of her chin. "What are they really after?"

"Ben Wickham's will and Ben Wickham's weather secrets. Their immediate interest undoubtedly will be you. I am overwhelmed by the manner in which you repulsed Dr. Maltby."

"Want me to defongerate anyone else?"

"Er . . . yes. And with the hard pedal this time on the rights supposedly remaining to the ordinary citizen from Magna Charta. Should Mrs. Maltby come, you will have to out-talk her, and you could suggest that no one is going to cremate your uncle to get away with any nasty work."

"What if the parson comes?" musingly asked Mr. Luton.

"Alice could deal with the Reverend Weston," replied Bony, "on the lines that she doesn't require any assistance from him in the reclamation of a drunken sot." The light in

Bony's eyes blotted out any intended offence, even had Mr. Luton not understood that these counters were applicable only to each of those persons who had troubled him.

The man who called was neither the parson nor the doctor. Only the dogs gave warning, for he came on foot, and shouted from the outside of the picket fence. From between the hem of the lowered blind and the sill of the window, Bony surveyed him. He had not before seen this character. He was short, and dapper in appearance. He sported a thin dark moustache, and he carried a small suitcase.

Alice went out to the veranda and asked what he wanted, in words meaning the same. The man said he had soaps, lotions, and things for sale. She asked him who he travelled for, and he mentioned a well-known firm. The dogs growled and barked, and Alice raised her voice to a scream, demanding to know where he had come from, how long had he been working for his firm, and so on, until the man was clinging to the fence as though his body was drained of strength. Unable to gain ground, he departed, leaving Bony undecided about him.

The policeman came about four. He had in his car a small terrier that at once infuriated Mr. Luton's dogs. He was, to use a colloquialism, 'right up Alice's alley'. When she opened the door to him, he stepped back at sight of her ruffled hair, the flour on her nose and arms, and the glint in her eyes. As usual he was in civilian clothes. His opening revealed contact with Doctor Maltby.

"Day-ee, Miss. I'm Senior Constable Gibley. Mr. Luton in?"

"Well, he is, and he isn't. What's he done now?" Alice asked, with delightfully assumed concern.

"He hasn't done anything, so far, miss. Who might you be?"

"That's telling. Any reason for knowing?"

"Well, could be. Me and Luton's known each other some time. Him living alone, I call in now and then to see how he's shaping."

"You do, do you!" snapped Alice. "So that's why he's been getting a bad name. The policeman always on his door-step, they say. Questioning him about robberies and hold-ups, and things. Serving summonses on him for alimony and such. Well, I don't like it, Constable."

"So you don't like it! Who are you, if you don't mind me asking, miss?" lunged Gibley with sarcasm.

"I'm his niece, and the name's McGorr. And I'm not telling me age or giving you me fingerprints." Up rose the voice. "And I may as well tell you now as later that I've come to this outlandish place for two things, see? To keep me uncle off the sherry and to keep you from dragging the fambly name in the mud. I know all about you and them who'd send him to a home or something. And if you want to barge in here, show us the search warrant, and if you ain't got a search warrant, get going."

"Now look here, miss . . ." Gibley started.

"I'm not looking nowhere I can't see," she shouted at him. "And I'd like to see you try to drag me to the lock-up. Go on, have a go if you think you can use yourself. No? Right! Then what did you come for?"

Gibley was furious, and somewhat daunted.

"All I come for was to ask after Mr. Luton," he replied with exaggerated courtesy.

"And all I been telling you is that uncle is not stinko, is going to stay that way, and he won't be going to any old men's home. And I'm kept busy feeding him. Anything else you want to know?"

"Yair. I want to see Mr. Luton."

"Not a hope. He's abed with a bit of a cold, and I've hid his clothes."

Senior Constable Gibley shrugged with desperation and strode to the gate. He appeared ringed by dogs, and he drove away with his terrier yapping defiance of the larger dogs, who kept beside the car all the way to the bridge.

And Mr. Luton was roaring with laughter in the room behind Alice, and the smiling Bony standing with him. Abruptly their laughter was stilled. Someone was knocking at the back door.

Bony nodded to Alice. She passed to the living-room, Mr. Luton at her heels and Bony remaining in the sitting-room, behind the fractionally closed door. Mr. Luton crossed to his bedroom, Alice waiting to see him enter it before she opened the kitchen door.

Bony saw her stiffen a moment before she backed rigidly into the room, and then appeared an automatic, followed by the arm of the hand which held it, then the little man with the dark moustache.

The intruder dropped his suitcase to the floor, but not for an instant did his eyes leave Alice, or his automatic waver. At close distance, there was nothing hesitant about him. Reaching behind, he pushed the door shut.

"Move away," he ordered. "Back! Now stop. So! Luton is where?"

"In bed," replied Alice, stiff as a board, but poised on her toes. Mr. Luton made no move, and Bony was thankful that the old man had sense enough to realise that to make a move would certainly discharge the automatic at Alice.

"The policeman coming and going suited me most well," the man said in the precise way which reminded Bony a little of Dr. Linke. "Luton! Come from your room, your hands up."

Bony's case was in Mr. Luton's room. His automatic was in the case, and he didn't blame himself for this situation. Now that Mr. Luton was being cautious, he had no fear for

Alice McGorr. Only a slight unease for the gunman.

Mr. Luton did not appear. Alice began to sway on her toes, her head to jerk. Her knees were giving way, and suddenly she slumped to the floor.

The gunman stared down at her. He commanded her to get up, but Alice was presumably in a dead faint. He again ordered Mr. Luton to come from his room, and although the conversation between Alice and the policeman had told him Mr. Luton was abed with a cold, he did not know which of the rooms off the living-room was Mr. Luton's bedroom.

He could not continue to point his automatic at a woman collapsed in a faint. He could not menace a man who refused to appear. This situation wasn't taken care of when the stick-up rules of procedure were laid down by the gunmen's union.

There was a jug on the wash bench close to the tap, and the gunman was kidded by the old-fashioned theory that to bring a woman from a faint you dashed cold water over her. He moved towards the bench. That was fatal.

It was as though Alice McGorr was shot out of a gun at a fair. She sprang from the floor to the gunman. The gun exploded and arched through the air to land on the floor beside Bony. The gunman rose in the air, too, as far as the ceiling would permit. He was coming down most ungracefully when each ankle was grasped by a hand, and each leg pulled as far apart as a human frame can span. Then he was on his back, and the instep of a shoe was gouging hard into his throat. He began to object, but the split of his legs was widened a fraction beyond possible. He did shout something before realising that surrender was indeed the best policy.

"Bravo, Alice!" Bony cried.

"You wouldn't read about it," chortled Mr. Luton stepping from his room, and Alice said brightly:

"I don't think I'll ever leave the Police Force. It's always such fun."

Chapter Twenty-Three

IN THE FEMININE MANNER

AN interior water-pipe between the living-room window and the wash bench, and Alice's handcuffs, produced no discomfort while the prisoner was seated on the floor.

Small in stature, he wasn't small in courage. For the first half-hour his will-power was strong enough to resist Bony's questioning, supported by Alice. And this brought afternoon tea-time, which, in Australia, is sacred to the god of leisure.

In the Iron Curtain countries they use drugs and implements to make a man talk. In the United States they employ bright light and relays of questioners. In Australia, if a criminal won't talk, they give him afternoon tea; in other words, leisurely soften him with kindness. It is a sad fact that these several methods of extracting information, based no doubt on scientific research and study, were ever man-controlled. Huge steam hammers to crack eggs! But interrogation by women!

Alice addressed the prisoner on the floor:

"I'm giving you a cup of tea and a slab of cake. If you swill tea on the floor, I'll smack your face."

The prisoner, who had shown silent hostility under polite questioning, glared at Alice when she stooped to place the cup and plate on the floor beside him. It is probable that he would have withstood the steam hammers applied with such labour by real he-men with brains. Since he had risen to and descended from the ceiling, he hadn't uttered one word.

At the conclusion of the afternoon tea-break, Alice nodded

to the sitting-room, and Bony and Mr. Luton accepted the hint and withdraw. There Bony again examined the contents of the prisoner's wallet, which told them little more than that the prisoner's name was Tolnic, which could be of Slavonic origin. The suitcase did contain a few packets of soap, boxes of pins and the like.

Into Bony's concentration crept Alice's voice, raised to that shrillness she had used to annihilate the callers. The voice rose to a screaming jumble of abuse, dropped to a nasal whine, and continued. The diatribe was punctuated by the clatter of pots and pans and the banging of what could be a rolling-pin on a pastry board.

Bony watched the clock. When he glanced at Mr. Luton, he saw the old man frowning and wincing.

"Glad I'm not married," avowed Mr. Luton, and Bony smiled thinly.

It wasn't only what Alice was saying to the unfortunate prisoner with such remarkable verbosity; it was the timbre of the voice, which seemed to pierce a man's head like the point of a surgeon's probe. Down through the ages, millions of men have heard this voice, going on and on and on until the mind reels and the stomach suffers as though from the effect of a rough sea.

Mr. Luton rose and closed the door. Bony smiled as he returned to his chair. Mr. Luton closed his eyes and groaned, because the door made no difference. Through it, through a brick wall, through sheet steel that voice would penetrate.

Aware of the purpose of the domestic nagging which, possibly, is the cause of thirty murders in every hundred, Bony became entranced by the raw phrases, the inane questions, the ridiculous charges, the atrocious innuendoes. And, above all, the astounding sincerity of Alice's performance. There wasn't any doubt that a man was being verbally lashed by a furious spouse.

Mr. Luton exploded. "I can't stand it. It's worse than the hoo-jahs. Can I go outside, Inspector? Ought to chop a bit of wood."

"No, Mr. Luton. It's likely there are confederates outside."

"But when's she goin' to stop?"

"When the prisoner breaks. It's her intention to break him."

"But she doesn't know him," argued the old man. "He's not married to her, is he?"

"No, and if he's not married now, he never will be," chuckled Bony.

Still accompanying the terrible voice were crashes and bangs, the clatter of tin-ware, the slam of the oven door. Never ceasing, on and on and on, skewering through your brain, the endless insults, the endless accusations. Rising, falling, swirling, snarling streams of words. Nothing mattered save the shrill voice with the relentless wailing-whine. On and on and on!

Now and then the prisoner shouted. The effect on the voice? Not the slightest. A rhythmic noise, produced by the handcuff on the ankle being pounded against the pipe, was as the feet of King Canute opposed to the waves. Mr. Luton paced the sitting-room, sometimes his hands pressed against his ears, sometimes his teeth biting upward at his moustache. Bony wanted to burrow his head into something, but the linoleum was tacked to the floorboards.

On and on and on! Shrill piercing, hammering at the mind with twenty million blows to the minute. The uselessness of walls and doors to shut it out! The naked defencelessness of the brain!

One hour and six minutes did the trick. The prisoner was screaming "Stop!" Bony opened the door to the living-room, where Alice was still talking and the prisoner watching her with mouth agape and eyes glassy.

"I tell! I speak!" he moaned.

"Of course you'll tell," snarled Alice. "I can go on till to-morrow night without stopping. And I will, too. If you'd lived in our street when I was a kid you'd have talked an hour ago. You tell now, or else!"

"Your name?" asked Bony. "And address?"

"Ivor Tolnic. Two-nine Alford Street, Hindmarsh."

"Why did you come here threatening bodily injury?"

He was an illegal immigrant. When he had jumped his ship at Port Adelaide, he thought he had jumped his country. That was five years back in history. An engineer, he had obtained work as a cleaner in an engineering shop, had joined a union, had married, was buying a home. Then his country had caught up with him.

Tolnic was stopped in the street when going home from work the previous day. The man he did not know. He was told what to do, and what would happen, either way. The man, British, spoke like an Australian. In the car, two men. They were non-British. All three men knew everything about him. No, his name hadn't been Tolnic on the ship, or in his own country, but they knew it.

He had recognised Constable Gibley from the description given by the men, and this was backed by the conversation between the policeman and the young woman which he had overheard from near-by bushes. The presence of the young woman did not affect his determination to stay in Australia. Yes, he would have pulled the trigger if . . .

He ate the meal prepared by Alice when still sitting on the floor. The door was shut and bolted. Without, the world was calm, quiet, and the dogs, unseen, were lazily lying on the outside mat.

This evening the moon was at full. After dinner Bony stood in the dark sitting-room, gazing beyond the window at the trees beyond the wicket fence and the sheen of the river beyond them. The risen moon was tinting the topmost leaves of the trees with silverfrost. In the outer room the clatter of plates and cooking utensils spoke of the washing-up being done by Alice and Mr. Luton.

At this hour Mr. Luton was supposed to be tied up and the doors open.

Into the clearing, to the left, appeared a shape. The shadows prevented Bony from nailing its identity. It came across the clearing towards the cottage and remained mysterious until it reached the car track opposite the gate, where it resolved itself into two men, one following closely the other.

The first man raised the gate-latch. The dogs met them, obviously doubtful. The first man was Knocker Harris. The second man Bony did not know. In the same order they advanced along the cinder path, and Bony slipped to the door and whipped back the bolt.

He could hear the dogs wingeing a welcome. He heard the scrape of boots groping for the veranda steps. He stood braced on his toes, the automatic in his right hand, the door-knob in his left. The two men crossed the veranda. Someone pounded on the door. Then Knocker Harris shouted:

"Don't open the door, John! Keep her locked! Keep her . . ."

Bony snapped the door inward. Knocker Harris was sinking to his knees, writhing in contortion, his mouth wide to scream or shout another warning. He slumped, and as he went down, Bony saw the gleam of steel in the hand of the other man racing for the wicket gate, and slashing at the charging dogs.

He said, in a low whisper:

"Halt! Police here!"

Then fired once.

The second man dived at the gateway and lay still. Bony stooped over Knocker Harris, partly lifted him, dragged him into the house, re-bolted the door and flashed down the blind.

The light went up. Over the prone figure of Knocker Harris, Bony saw the startled Alice McGorr with Mr. Luton behind her.

It was obvious that Mr. Luton's neighbour was *in extremis*. His breathing was difficult. Perspiration soaked his face and hands. The wound was bleeding inwardly from the point of contact above the left kidney.

"What happened?" gently asked Bony.

"Sort of . . . sort of baled up, like. Was comin' along . . . see . . . if John wanted any more from town. Didn't see him. Came behind me . . . prodded with knife . . . told me keep going. Said tell John open up, like. I wouldn't. . . ."

"Well?" softly urged Bony.

"I . . ."

"Please, Knocker."

"I wouldn't say 'Open up'. Told John not . . . not open up."

Harris drifted into unconsciousness, and Bony drew aside to permit Mr. Luton to pour a little more brandy between the partly open lips.

"Did you fire that shot?" Alice asked.

"Yes. Harris was brought to the gate and marched to the door by another man. When Harris's warning was cut off, I opened the door, to see him falling, and the other running to the fence gate. I called out: 'Stop! Police here!' He did not stop, so I fired. Er . . . I hope you heard me order him to stop?"

"Of course, Bony. I hear everything you say. Didn't you know?" A moment later she whispered: "He can't last."

Mr. Luton heard her and looked up. His mouth was slack. His eyes dimmed. He stood helplessly.

"I . . . We must fetch the quack," he said dully.

Bony slowly shook his head.

Knocker Harris attempted to sit up, and Alice held him.

His glazing eyes passed from Mr. Luton, upward to Alice, round to Bony. The voice was almost a gurgle:

"John was me only friend. Got to . . . explain . . . like," he managed. And Bony nodded and knew that Knocker Harris died knowing that no explanation was necessary.

Chapter Twenty-Four

LEAVE IT TO ALICE

THE rising moon was concentrating the shadows. It was touching the points of the picket fence, deepening the shadow beneath as though to delay shedding its light on the form lying in the cindered gateway.

That body was a development threatening to deprive Bony of the initiative. He had planned to go-get a mountain, and the mountain had moved to stand over the gateway. He had sent for Alice McGorr that he might gain greater freedom of action and less responsibility for Mr. Luton, and the little man had come to herald swift enemy counter-action.

From behind the edge of the blind in the sitting-room, Bony watched the front, wondering if the slayer of Knocker Harris was one of those men who had brought Tolnic from Adelaide. The Queensland heeler appeared crossing from the river-bank, and he came on till within a yard of the dead man, where he sat, and lifted his jowl and howled.

"What's going on up your street?" asked Mr. Luton from his guard point at his bedroom window.

"Your heeler has found the dead man at the gate," replied Bony, and then Mr. Luton saw the dog's mate, which, wounded, had run for the kitchen door and died on the way.

"That's what he's crying about," he said, and added: "I feel like crying myself."

"Now you look up cheerful," Alice advised, and the old man's counter didn't register with Bony, because the dog had ceased to cry and was staring along the track to the bridge, stiffly erect, the moonlight gleaming on his fangs.

Bony cautiously opened the front door, no light behind him, the veranda shaded from the moon by its iron roof. Sure that no one stood either side the door, he opened it still wider. Now he could hear the dog's throaty growl, the animal low to ground, legs braced. Some distance away a car engine raced, but this could not be the cause of the dog's attitude.

The picket fence ended at a wire fence keeping the scrub back, and at this point something moved, just beyond the white pickets. It was stalking the dog. Bony heard it say:

"Here, Towse! Lie down, old fellow. Good Towse!"

But Towse wasn't taking it. His spring reminded Bony of Alice going into action off the floor. There was a spurt of dull fire, the metallic crack of a small-bore pistol. Then man and animal appeared for a moment atop the fence, then beyond it on the dusty track.

Unable to leave the door unguarded, Bony called for Alice.

"I'm here," she said within two seconds.

"Wait."

The car he heard had turned off the highway and was coming at speed towards the cottage. The uproar beyond the fence was certainly raised by a man being savaged by a dog, and they seemed like two crocodiles wrestling in a pool of silver. When the headlights of the car found them, Bony pushed back into the cottage and locked the door.

The car was stopped while its headlights still held the combatants. Men erupted from it. They counted seven, and among them were Boase and Sergeant Maskell.

"South Australian police," Bony said sharply to Alice. "Now listen, because this gives you a ticklish job. They'll demand admittance. Remember, you are Mr. Luton's niece come to protect a sick old man from being hounded by violent strangers. Demand the search warrant. They'll have it, more than likely. Rile them for always arriving after a murder, never before. Keep it going. I'll prepare Mr. Luton."

Bony snapped on the bedroom light, saying:

"The police are here. You've got to be ill."

Mr. Luton regarded him with raised white brows and an excited gleam in his eyes. Bony winked. He knelt before Mr. Luton.

"You look quite ill, Mr. Luton," he said, loudly for the benefit of the prisoner. "You must lie down. Take it easy. The excitement is too much for your heart."

Off came the slippers. With Mr. Luton's assistance off came the coat and trousers. Mr. Luton was in his under-vest when there was loud knocking on the front door.

"Hold them, Alice," Bony softly encouraged.

"Get off that veranda," screamed Alice in the best traditions of the inner suburb in which she had been born and had lived for twenty-five years. "I can see you through the winder. If you don't clear out, I'll shoot your whiskers into the river."

"Now, now!" one said, and Bony could recognise Boase. "Police here. Don't be afraid. Let us in."

"Police here!" mocked Alice, scorn enough to wither his soul. "Where's your search warrant? Go and get it. And get yourselves a bitta manners."

The handle of the back door was turned, but even the prisoner wasn't interested. Alice scoffed and abused and threatened. The already splintered door shuddered, and someone said:

"If you don't open up, how can we serve the warrant? Stop your stupid screeching and listen."

"Shove it under the door," yelled Alice, when, attired in pyjamas, Mr. Luton was sliding under the bedclothes. As he was expected to look sick, he suggested the blue-bag in the wash-bench cupboard. A smear of blue on the lips heightened the effect produced by a trembling hand on the coverlet.

Bony returned to the kitchen. The prisoner was terrified. Bony stood before him and said reassuringly:

"The less you say about me, the easier it will be for you."

He went on to the sitting-room door, waited for Alice to pause to tell her to offer no further resistance. He slipped back to Mr. Luton and sat on the chair beside the bed. The front door was giving trouble; he could hear a hinge being torn off. Then light was born in the sitting-room.

"Now where's your warrant?" shrilled Alice. "Police me foot. You're not policemen. Why, you all got hump-backs. Now don't all talk at once. Which one of you knifed poor Mr. Harris? Go on, own up, you murdering lot of scum."

Boase said, with a keen edge:

"Shut up, and look at this."

"Oo-o-o!" gasped Alice. "Superintendent and all." She gave a short pause. "So you are police. And like all your rotten kind you arrive when all the murdering's done. You couldn't have got here before, could you, you great big flat-footed slob."

"Pipe down," snarled Boase. "Dead man outside the gate. Another specimen fighting with an unfortunate dog. Dead man lying right here. What else?"

"What else!" shrilled Alice, thoroughly aroused. "Another gunman anchored to the kitchen bench, and me uncle sick of a heart attack, and him paying taxes and things. Ain't that enough? Wait till I get a reporter. Wait till I tell the papers about all this. Wait . . ."

"If you don't shut up," roared Boase, "I'll have you taken outside and anchored to a tree."

Alice put on a realistic act of hysterics.

In the kitchen a harsh voice commanded the prisoner to get up. The little man moaned, and the harsh voice called Boase to look at the handcuffs.

"Police cuffs, be gob!" exclaimed Boase.

"My equipment," Bony loudly informed him.

Men spun around, then crowded into the bedroom, where there was complete silence seeming to last for a week. Boase stood behind Sergeant Maskell. There were four other men not known to Bony. He said icily:

"You will not make a commotion. The owner of this property, into which you have unlawfully broken and entered, is a sick man, as you must observe. His trouble is of the heart, brought about by the assault on this house by gangsters, and added to by the illegal entry made by yourselves, I presume without a warrant."

"Who are you?" a man asked, and Boase straightened to restrain himself from laughing loudly.

"Him! He's Inspector Napoleon Bonaparte."

The questioner was large and tough and had a face well schooled to evade emotion. He said:

"In that case, Inspector Bonaparte, you're headed for a load of trouble. You better tell us now about these killings."

"You can get out of here," weakly complained Mr. Luton. He endeavoured to rise on an elbow, sank wearily back to the pillow and called Alice. She appeared behind the burly figures masking the door-frame, pushed in between them and stepped hurriedly to the bedside.

"Empty these pests out of my room," commanded the 'ailing' man.

"Yes, Uncle."

Alice straightened, glared at the intruders. She opened her mouth to take in steam, and Boase beat her to it by saying:

"All right! All right! Get out of this, chaps. Anything to stop her starting. Come on, Bony. It's up to you to watch your step." They crowded into the living-room, and Bony freed the prisoner. And then Boase said: "Now, Bony, we'll have it."

Bony leaned against the cupboard beside the stove. His long

brown fingers were suddenly occupied making a cigarette. His eyes were masked, almost sleepy, and a slight smile puckered his lips. He applied a match to the cigarette before saying coldly:

"You will now take it. The man on the bed in there is the owner of this house. I am his guest. We have had trouble from strangers before you came, and when you arrived there was no riotous disturbance in this house. You demanded admittance. When asked for a search warrant, you said you had one. I then asked Mr. Luton's niece to admit you, but you broke down the door before she could do so. Your search warrant—at once."

"Now look here, Bony," began Boase. "It won't work. There's been murder done inside and outside this house. You can't play the fool."

"Waste of time," the pan-faced one cut in. "For your information, Inspector Bonaparte, I have here a warrant for your arrest."

Boase waved him back.

Bony bowed. "I know Sergeant Maskell, Super. Please present your other associates in illegal practices."

"We're Commonwealth Investigation, Bonaparte, and you can chew on that," gave the man with the arrest warrant. "Unless you give tongue, we're taking you in."

Aware of the jealousies between the Commonwealth and the States Police Departments, Bony played it, for the events of the immediate past had befogged issues already involved. Looking to the two South Australian policemen, he said:

"As you know, I am on leave of absence, and the guest of Mr. Luton. On several occasions I met Mr. Luton's nearest neighbour, one known as Knocker Harris. This evening, at about seven-thirty, I was looking out of the front-room window, admiring the moonlit night and considering what bait I would use to-morrow." He then described the actions of the two men who appeared in the clearing, their arrival on the veranda. "I opened the door in time to see Harris collapsing to the veranda floor, and the other man racing to the gate. He still carried the knife and was slashing at the dog. Although on leave from duty in another State, I have duties to observe as a police officer. I called on the man to stop, and when he did not obey my order, I fired to enforce obedience."

"By shooting him dead?" sneered the C.I.S. man.

"In view of what occurred earlier this evening, Superintendent Boase, and in view of the fact that with me in this house is an old man and a young woman, I am prepared at any time and place, either at official enquiry or in the press of Australia, to claim that I did not fail in my duty."

Bony outlined the events of the late afternoon, ending with the entry of the little man armed with an automatic pistol, and his capture and confession—what there was of it. He went on:

"Prior to these events, there have been strange happenings in this part of the State of South Australia; unlawful activities by several persons. One: the office of the late Benjamin Wickham was broken into and ransacked, this crime not being reported, as far as we know. Two: men came here and employed threats and menaces for the purpose of pumping Knocker Harris for information concerning the late Mr. Wickham's work and papers and, three: a Miss Jessica Lawrence was waylaid when she left this house late one night. The car used by these persons was destroyed and reported to the local officer as an accident. Also, a Dr. Carl Linke was removed by persons purporting to be police officers. And I had been enjoying two or three days of peaceful fishing when someone in Cowdry reported to someone to have me recalled to Brisbane, according to what Senior Constable Gibley inferred one pleasant afternoon.

"There, Superintendent Boase, you have sufficient material

on which to base your investigations. The foreign gentleman present will no doubt supply valuable information. The dead man at the gate is obviously his accomplice, and the third man with whom he came from Adelaide is the person attacked by the dog he failed to shoot. There are other matters we can discuss at your leisure."

"Now is the time, Inspector Bonaparte," Superintendent Boase decided, and the left eyelid just barely flickered. "I arrest you on a charge of manslaughter."

"But you can't do that, Super," interjected the C.I.S. man. "I have already a warrant for his arrest, and power to conduct him to any lock-up in the country. You know that."

Boase stretched, yawned, grinned without mirth.

"This is my territory," he said stonily. "Bonaparte is my prisoner."

"But you can't . . ."

"Don't be a blasted fool. Killings are my job."

"Yes, and get to hell out of it!" shrilled Alice, appearing among them. "My uncle wants peace and quiet and something to eat. Now defongerate. This isn't an opium den. Go on! Imshi!"

Chapter Twenty-Five

THE BLACKMAILER

SENIOR CONSTABLE GIBLEY arrived with reinforcements, and thus enabled Sergeant Maskell to relieve Boase of the routine work.

"Bring in that dog-fighting fellow," Bony said curtly, and Boase found himself repeating the order.

The dog-fighter appeared decidedly ill-used. His overcoat and trousers were ripped. He might lose at least one ear, and his hands were lacerated.

"This one of the men you accompanied from Adelaide?" Bony asked Tolnic, and, after hesitation, the little man nodded.

"Very early on Wednesday morning the dog-fighter there was here with another man; not that man found dead in the gateway. They walked into this house, bashed Mr. Luton, lashed him to a chair and kicked his knees. They demanded to know where Wickham kept his papers, and referred to an important notebook. When Mr. Luton declined to say anything, this dog-fighting thug produced a hypodermic and prepared to inject a drug to force the information from Mr. Luton. It was unfortunate for him and his accomplice that I arrived back from Adelaide in time to prevent a most serious crime."

"They came this time for what?" asked the would-be arrester.

"You ask Tolnic. That's your job," Bony replied coldly,

his blue eyes blazing, and reminding Gibley of an uncomfortable moment.

The Commonwealth Investigation man asked. He asked twice, and Tolnic was dumb. From the next room Mr. Luton roared:

"Leave him to Alice. She'll make him talk."

"You be quiet, Uncle," shrilled Alice. To those either side of the dog-fighter she commanded: "Take that stinking thing away." When the command had been obeyed, to Bony's amusement, she turned to the little man. "Now you, Tolnic. Speak up. Remember me? Every time your wife is dissatisfied you will remember me. I'm telling you something. You're in the soup, d'you understand? You'll lose your job and you'll be locked up, but this is a good country, and ordinary people like you and me, and these policemen, don't go in for torture. They won't stand for your wife and kids being badly treated. You just tell the policemen what's what. Inspector Bonaparte's already told them what you told us, but I think there's a bit more. Now, about being stuck up on the street and told to take this job 'or else!' . . . is that true?"

The little man breathed the affirmative answer. Only Tolnic and Boase saw the soft gleam of sympathy in the girl's brown eyes. She nodded encouragingly.

"You tell everything that happened from the time you left Adelaide with these men."

Added to the men's original objective in bringing him, Tolnic's role had been also to ascertain who was in the house with Luton, with emphasis on the man who had frustrated their earlier attempt.

As their car had passed Mount Marlo, they saw a car turn off at the bridge and take the track to Luton's house. They had parked their car deep in the scrub, and they waited there until Dr. Maltby had left.

They had overheard Alice's reception of the doctor, then

Tolnic was instructed to proceed as planned. They had not thought of the dogs now free of the kennels, and the dogs bluffed Tolnic at the gate. From the veranda Alice had further bluffed him, and he had returned to his masters to report.

Then Gibley had called at the cottage. They overheard that Mr. Luton was abed with a cold, that his clothes had been hidden to immobilise him, and when Gibley drove away they were convinced that the only person with Luton was this woman with the devastating tongue.

When the dogs had raced away after Gibley's car, the position was open and shut for Tolnic to offer his wares at the back door. He was to hold up the woman, gag and secure her, then to knock Luton out if he proved difficult. Meanwhile, they would lie in wait for Knocker Harris should he appear, and at dark would take over from Tolnic. Tolnic was to encounter all the risks, and if he was apprehended, and talked, his wife and children were to be bashed. The usual technique!

Alice smiled at him. Then she swung about to face the men.

"Having given you a few lessons on interrogation," she told them, "I am going to make tea and sandwiches. So you all get out of my kitchen, and stay out, see?"

They drifted, and Boase asked with mock humility: "Can't I stay here with Bonaparte?"

"Yes, let's," Bony supported, and they sat at one end of the table and regarded each other like representatives of East and West. After Alice had slammed the door to the sitting-room, there was quiet. Bony said:

"You and I, Boase, have to be good. This affair is big, proved so by the interest of C.I.S., and, I am confident, also by S.S. Politics, Boase. Crime is as a sweet rose nodding in soft sunshine over the black evil of a political cesspool. Admit that the C.I.S. has been putting much over your Department."

"Correct," snapped Boase, taking from a pocket a pipe and pouch. "What annoys me is I don't know how much."

"I could tell you. I know most of it now. They put a lot over me, too. I am not a politician, and no one can be permitted to use me as a scapegoat. To employ an old saying, 'I shall get out from under,' and although in calm moments you won't blame me, you will get hurt in the process. Wait! You and I have always worked amicably. I think we could agree that off duty we have a mutual personal liking. I need your assistance now. You will need mine later."

"What do you want?" asked Boase, eyes small, tapping the stem of his pipe against the stiff hairs of his moustache.

"I must return to Brisbane as fast as I can."

"Oh! Pretty hard—with all this mess. What can you do?"

"The loud pedal will be down hard on the cremation of Wickham's body, in view of the protest made by Luton both to Maltby and Gibley. I must push it down, because, in order to emerge safely from under, I can spare no one. You assist me to get to Brisbane within hours, and I'll present you with a soft pedal that you can push."

"All right, Bony. I'll buy."

"I have proof sufficient to satisfy any reasonable man that Ben Wickham was murdered, how, by whom, and why."

Superintendent Boase actually permitted his chin to drop. It didn't occur to him to doubt, for Bony's reputation was too solidly on the ground of achievement. So he said levelly:

"Blackmail, eh?"

"Blackmail, Super."

"If I don't pay, you let a murderer slip into limbo?"

Bony shrugged, smiled, and Boase burst out with:

"None of your Mona Lisa grin with me, Bony. When do I pay, and when do you?"

"Immediately we reach Brisbane, I shall be on the mat. You will be there; a unique experience for us both. You will hear me contending with stupid officialdom. You will hear me uttering dire threats. And, when you leave Brisbane for your own city, you will acknowledge that I shall ever be the 'Great Australian Blackmailer'. And, Super, you will be rejoicing that the matter of that cremation will never come up to annoy you and reflect on your Department."

"May I confer with my Chief Commish?" Boase said ironically.

"Certainly. We should fly to Brisbane, via Broken Hill. The political police could be a hindrance at Melbourne and Sydney. By the way. Alice, just a moment."

"I'm just serving supper. Sugar, Superintendent Boase?"

Boase looked at her sharply. He had not before heard this voice, this normal voice. And it appeared that not previously had he seen the normal face of this talented young woman. She placed tea-cups and plates before them, added plates of scones and cakes. Then seated herself between the big man and Bony.

"I present, Super, Policewoman Alice McGorr, of Melbourne."

Boase glared at Alice, squinted at the plate of cakes, raised his gaze to meet the laughing eyes of Bony.

"The States, you see, are well represented. Alice—I am sure she will be delighted to be so addressed by you—is on leave, and will be staying here for another week to look after her poor sick uncle."

Bony had purposely raised his voice, and from the bedroom came the lion's roar.

"Poor sick uncle be damned!"

Boase lifted both hands off the table. He said:

"I give up. I give ruddy well up."

And Alice said meekly:

"Now, Super, just drink your tea, and swear after if you want to."

* * * * *

Bony pulled the bell at the front door of Mount Marlo and, while waiting, the moon told him it was about ten o'clock, the moon being less usable than the sun as a clock. To the maid who answered the bell he said:

"I am Inspector Bonaparte. I wish to see Mrs. Parsloe."

He was invited inside and offered a chair in the hall. Two minutes later he was bowing to a white-haired woman, large, austere, and, he was thankful to note, intelligent.

"I have been wondering why you didn't call when you were down last, Inspector," she said. "Please take that chair. It's very easy."

"Unfortunately I cannot stay as long as I would like, madam. I am leaving almost at once for Adelaide. There are several questions I wish to ask, and a service to render which I believe will relieve your mind relative to a certain matter."

Mrs. Parsloe flipped a cigarette from a pop-up box, and Bony was not slow with a match. She looked above the flame and smiled.

"It seems that you are addicted to trading questions, Inspector. We have heard all about you from the Reverend Mr. Weston. I too agree to trade."

"I thank you, madam. Will you begin, or shall I?"

"Perhaps your questions would be more exciting?"

"As you wish. Why did you not report the burglary of the office?"

"I was asked not to report the matter to Gibley, and I would prefer not to mention by whom."

"Was the 'whom' the person you reported Dr. Linke to, the following morning or afternoon?"

"Yes."

"This 'whom' had been in contact with you previously, had he not?"

"Yes."

"You reported Dr. Linke for what reason?"

"My brother's weather calculations and other papers and a book were missing, Inspector. Dr. Linke, a very nice man, is a foreigner. His . . . er . . . work for my brother wasn't quite regular, but, according to my brother, invaluable."

"Have you knowledge or even an idea where he is at the moment?"

"Oh yes. He returned to us this afternoon."

"Ah! I am happy to know that. I must see him, and Miss Lawrence, before I leave." Bony smiled and extracted a sheet of paper from a pocket. "In the course of my . . . er . . . fishing expeditions, I came across your late brother's will. As it was in an unsealed envelope, I took the liberty of reading it. I present you with a rough draft of all the clauses in it."

"You found the will!" exclaimed Mrs. Parsloe, abruptly standing. "And that notebook!"

"Yes, and the notebook. I know that Mr. McGillycuddy was most interested in the notebook, but the will expressly states he is not to have it."

"He wasn't going to get it," Mrs. Parsloe asserted sharply.

"Unless the Commonwealth paid the figure you named to Mr. McGillycuddy?"

"Unless . . . Why, you seem to know everything, Inspector."

"Yes, Mrs. Parsloe, now I know everything. Later, when I have gone, you might ring Mr. McGillycuddy and say I said so. Now, where can I see Dr. Linke and Miss Lawrence?"

Mrs. Parsloe was an angry woman when she left the room. Thirty seconds were given to Bony to admire the pictures, when Linke flung open the door and followed Jessica. She clasped both of Bony's hands, and Linke gripped his arm.

"Bony! Is everything all right?" Jessica asked anxiously.

"Splendid. Mr. Luton is in bed with a slight cold. He is being nursed by the young woman you contacted in Melbourne.

She is very efficient, and will be staying with Mr. Luton for a week at least."

"Yes? Go on. There's more."

"Greedy, are you not? The enemy has been captured, and the police are all over the place mopping up. I am going to Brisbane for a few days, and shall be back for the extension of my leave. Go and see Alice and Mr. Luton to-morrow. You'll like Alice, and she'll like you."

Bony regarded Dr. Linke, smiling and open, and obviously happy.

"I found Ben Wickham's will and the missing green-covered notebook, Doctor."

"Ah! Good! That is very good, Inspectore."

"I had sufficient audacity to read the will. Ben Wickham has treated both of you very handsomely. He thought a great deal of you, and to you, Doctor, he bequeathed that mysterious notebook. Now I must go. Superintendent Boase is waiting for me. Because of the audience down at the cottage, I was not able to say *au revoir* to Mr. Luton. Please give him a message. Tell him I'll be back to stay again soon, and not to disturb the hens until we can rob their nests together."

Chapter Twenty-Six

BLACKMAIL BY INFERENCE

IT was ten o'clock this warm spring day in Brisbane. The staff at Police Headquarters, normally calm and slightly bored, was this morning influenced by an undercurrent of excitement, for the rumour was rife that at long last Inspector Bonaparte was really to be stood on the mat.

The Chief Commissioner was in a wicked mood. He tormented the sheaf of papers on the desk, and now and then would lift himself and the swivel chair and pound it on the floor. His meticulously barbered white hair and the full white military moustache emphasised the dull red of his furious countenance, and his diamond-hard blue eyes bored directly across the desk to the dark, lawyer-type face beyond. His voice, though low, had a penetrating effect.

"I've told you, and I've told others, sir, that Bonaparte isn't a policeman's boot-lace, but he is my ace investigator, and further, and most important, he is a man of honour. If he had been told the true state of affairs down at that damn place called Cowdry, he wouldn't have stirred up this . . . this . . . confounded Commonwealth balderdash and nonsense."

"The fact, Colonel, cannot be evaded that he did not comply with the order to return," calmly argued the Chief Secretary. "Had he obeyed the order, we would not now be embroiled with Commonwealth Instrumentalities. I am afraid that Bonaparte will have to kill the cat."

"Are you hoping he will have to?" demanded Colonel

Spendor, renowned for his loyalty to and protection of his officers.

"Certainly not."

"Then I'll wager you five pounds that Bonaparte doesn't kill the cat."

The legal countenance softened a fraction in what was supposed to be a smile. The Chief Secretary accepted the wager, and rose with the Chief Commissioner.

"Then we'll go along to this Gilbertian court-martial," decided the old cavalry officer. "Lowther! Where the devil are you?"

"Here, sir," replied the gaunt secretary, opening the door for them.

"Bring those damn papers, and for heaven's sake try to appear bright."

Lowther smiled at the ramrod back passing through the doorway, snatched the sheaf of papers from the desk, and followed on. They entered a room much larger than the Commissioner's office, and it was obvious that the space was needed, for, in front of a covered table, sat a row of men who stood until the Chief Commissioner and the Chief Secretary were seated.

To one side of the desk, facing both men and the two Chiefs, sat Bony.

Colonel Spendor bounced his chair, haw-ed, teased the papers Lowther placed before him, glared at everyone including Bony, and opened proceedings.

"Detective-Inspector Napoleon Bonaparte," he said. Bony stood. "You are to understand that this is not a Court of Disciplinary Action, but an Official Enquiry from which recommendation might be made to terminate your appointment. You have been given due notice of this?"

"Yes, sir."

"You may select any officer present to assist you."

"Thank you, sir. Under the circumstances, I will decline assistance. May I ask a question?"

"You may ask questions at any point."

"Then, sir, other than Superintendent Boase and my colleagues, who are present?"

"Representatives of the Chief Secretary's Department, and of the Commonwealth and Queensland Governments."

"Sir," persisted Bony, "in justice to myself, may I be informed whether there are representatives of the Commonwealth Security Service and the Commonwealth Investigation Service?"

"Representatives of those services are also present," replied Colonel Spendor, and hurriedly wrote a note which he passed to the Chief Secretary. Bony sat down. The Chief Secretary read: 'Raise that wager to ten pounds.' Without a muscle moving, the C.S. wrote his acceptance.

"A telegram was sent you at Cowdry, South Australia, to report here without delay," stated the Colonel. "You failed to obey."

"There is no proof, sir, that I received any such telegram."

The Chief Secretary's only reaction was a slight tightening of the mouth. Colonel Spendor haw-ed, bumped his chair, snapped:

"Superintendent Boase. Tell us what action was taken by your Department, in accordance with our request, to notify Bonaparte to report back immediately."

Boase rose to relate that Maskell, at Mount Gambier, had been telephoned to transmit a message to Bonaparte, which had been done per Senior Constable Gibley. When he sat, Bony rose.

"Strange," he said mildly. "I suppose there is proof of this?"

Lowther leaned over the Colonel and assisted him to locate a document. The Colonel cleared his throat.

"This is a sworn affidavit by Senior Constable Gibley that

he, et cetera, et cetera, verbally informed Inspector Bonaparte of the message he was instructed to convey."

Again Lowther leaned forward to assist with a document.

"This," went on the Chief Commissioner, "is a statement made to Sergeant Maskell, of Mount Gambier, signed by a postal messenger at Cowdry. 'On' . . . yum yum yum . . . 'I delivered what I suppose was a telegram inside a buff envelope, to Mr. John Luton, for delivery to Inspector Bonaparte, the inspector being away fishing or something. I did not at any time see the message.' And this," continued the Colonel, "is a statement by John Luton given to Sergeant Maskell. Ah . . . urmph! What the . . . ! This reads: 'I have told Sergeant Maskell, who is a friend of mine, that I'm not a bloody letter-box, yours faithfully, J. Luton.' "

Dead silence. Bony rose to his feet.

"Again I ask for documentary proof that I received a telegram ordering me to report to my headquarters. Gibley's affidavit is unsupported. I don't know Constable Gibley very well. I will not say he is untruthful. I do say that my long study of abnormal psychology has convinced me that the human mind is unreliable. A fantastic thought of to-day can become a strong belief to-morrow."

The Colonel tormented his papers. The C.S. wrote a note to him saying: "One to you, Colonel." Colonel Spendor nodded agreement, his face expressionless. He glared at Bony. He glared at those officials he resented being on his premises, poking their noses into the affairs of his Department. He haw-ed, and loudly bumped his chair on the floor.

"Inspector Bonaparte, I suggest that you address us on your activities of a police nature whilst on leave of absence."

"I thank you, sir, and accept your suggestion," Bony said slowly, and produced a sheaf of notes. He looked intently at the officials before bringing his gaze back to the Chief Commissioner. "I was in Adelaide when granted leave of absence, and decided to spend my leave with Mr. John Luton, who resides near Cowdry.

"Mr. Luton's nearest neighbour was the late Benjamin Wickham, the meteorologist of world renown. Further, Wickham and Luton had been close friends for many years. Wickham died in Luton's house, and because his doctor believed that Wickham's heart was not strong, he signed the certificate that Wickham died from heart disease accelerated by alcohol.

"Luton protested that his friend had never complained of his heart, that both of them were recovering from a drinking bout, and that Wickham died of something not alcoholic. The protest was made both to the doctor and to the local policeman. Both of them told Luton he should be sent to a home in Adelaide, on the grounds that he was of advanced age, that he was living alone, and therefore was a liability. Although a witness to this episode is dead, Luton's suspicions of foul play are general knowledge in the locality.

"This would give you, sir, the distinct impression that Luton was revealing signs of senility, that he was living in squalor, and that he was a liability to both his neighbours and the authorities. The opposite is the truth. Luton is remarkably virile in body and mind; he lives in a well-kept cottage surrounded by a garden he cultivates, and he is in possession of considerable means.

"The fact that he has considerable means was not known either to the doctor or the policeman, who probably thought he had been entirely maintained by the late Benjamin Wickham, and therefore was minus social status, and without influence. I intend to put forward a different interpretation of this attitude towards Luton when he expressed grave doubt that Wickham had died of the effects of alcoholic poisoning. I am convinced, sir, that had Luton been known to be a man of substance his doubt would have been forwarded to Police Headquarters, and that cremation would not have been permitted until after a post-mortem.

"I will conclude this section of my reply by stating that the doctor who signed the certificate was a relative of deceased, that he was short of money, and that he knew he was an important beneficiary mentioned in the will. And that the local policeman was being unduly influenced by an agent of Security Service resident in Cowdry and, as a bank manager, a person of local power.

"It was that reaction to Luton's suspicions, rather than Luton's grounds for suspicion, which decided me to probe a little before deciding to investigate, and I hadn't probed very deeply when I did decide to investigate.

"It may be redundant to point out, sir, that I am a police officer sworn to uphold the law, to prevent a crime whenever possible, wherever possible. That I was not in my own State did not absolve me from my sworn duty. I point out, too, that I was at the time on leave of absence, and that I was breaking no regulation governing my employment."

Bony looked intently into the eyes of every man seated in the row, trying to determine the interest each individual had in these proceedings. Speaking clearly, deliberately, he continued:

"I enjoy an earned reputation for not relinquishing an investigation once begun, until convinced whether or not a crime has been committed. Thus, despite hindrance, I reached the murderer of Benjamin Wickham.

"I will now present in detail the forces which attempted to hinder me, and which, if triumphant, would have blindfolded Justice and must have permitted a murderer to evade the consequences of his crime.

"What are these forces? One is the Security Service; its agents in every town, in trades unions and commercial offices. We know that Security Service has no police powers, and that its function is to report only to the Prime Minister of the day. Outside, no one knows its members and agents. Another force is the Commonwealth Investigation Service, which has power to arrest and arraign for trial. Information from the first supplied to the Prime Minister is passed to the second for action when considered necessary. This we all know.

"In theory, sir, an excellent brake on subversive activities. In practice, a waste of public money, because there are no legal bars to subversive activities unless the country is at war. And the main result of the activities of these services is that, while unable to control subversion for which they were established, they have proved, in this partciular case, a hindrance to the elucidation of crime, prosecuted by an officer of a law enforcement organisation.

"As I shall show. The world knows how Wickham fought for recognition, how he was constantly rebuffed. What is not yet known is that the Commonwealth Government ultimately realised the value of Wickham's meteorological knowledge to the entire world, and particularly to any one country ambitious for world conquest. The Government approached Wickham only after it had learned that several other countries had been and were in contact with him. The disillusioned Wickham wouldn't again treat with his own Government, who then became panicky and set their forces to work to induce him to negotiate, and, failing this, to prevent his recorded knowledge being passed to a foreign country.

"The preliminary contact with Wickham was made through the local Security agent in Cowdry, the manager of the Commonwealth Bank. When I tested him, he fell into my trap and communicated with his superiors, who actually had the temerity to attempt to have me withdrawn from the area by cajoling you, sir, to order me to report . . ."

"I don't think, Inspector Bonaparte, I like that verb 'to cajole'," interrupted Colonel Spendor.

"Pardon, sir. The verb is 'to request'—by requesting you, sir, to order me to report without delay. Had they contacted me and, with reasonable courtesy, explained that they were trying to prevent a foreign power from obtaining knowledge of priceless value to Australia, and that I happened to be stamping on their feet, I would have withdrawn at once, with the intention, of course, of returning and continuing my investigation after they had achieved their objective."

Bony related in sequence the events which led finally to the arrival of Superintendent Boase and the C.I.S. at Mr. Luton's cottage. He told of the attack on Mr. Luton, the threatened waylaying of Wickham's secretary, why he had burned the car, and how later he had learned that one of these men, named Marsh, was a member of S.S. from Melbourne. He told of the 'hawker' sent to spy out the land before another assault on the cottage was made by the foreign agents, his capture, and the ultimate use of Knocker Harris as a Trojan horse.

"These events have additional significance," he went on. "All occurred after I had gone to Adelaide to test a rumour that I had been ordered to report back to my headquarters. Security did not know I was under cover when these events occurred, and yet no effort was made while they were keeping Mr. Luton's cottage, as well as Mount Marlo, under observation, to protect an old man living alone, an old man certain to become the centre of a foreign interest who reasoned as they themselves did.

"What is clear, sir, is that the foreign agents were always ten jumps ahead of the Commonwealth Services, and that I was five jumps ahead of the foreign agents.

"I have placed in safety the will of the late Benjamin Wickham and the book in which he recorded his ultimate calculations. Under the terms of the will, the weather calculations are bequeathed to Dr. Carl Linke, the late Mr. Wickham's assistant. Like many brilliant scientists who have come to this country as displaced persons, Linke has been treated by the authorities in a manner which, in a future age, will cause guffaws of laughter. I intend to see that Dr. Linke receives his inheritance from his friend and co-worker in the field of meteorology, and, if the Commonwealth Government is still interested, I might suggest that Dr. Linke be approached with some degree of deference.

"And, finally, sir, there are two matters of a more personal nature. I have prepared a full report of this investigation to submit to a national journal for publication. I now hand to you my resignation that, following its acceptance, I can release my report to the press."

Bony sat down and crossed his knees, careful not to spoil the immaculate creases. In the room there was not a sound until a chair scraped the floor and a man stood to ask:

"May I speak, sir?"

"Well, what is it?" growled the Chief Commissioner, and from the tone Bony was sure the questioner must be a Security man.

"I would suggest, sir, that Inspector Bonaparte's resignation be not immediately accepted."

The Chief Secretary pencilled a hurried note to the C.C., who, turning disdainfully from the person standing, read:

"I'll pay."

Chapter Twenty-Seven

ALWAYS A TRUMP CARD

IN his own office, Colonel Spendor raised himself and the chair and crashed it enthusiastically, for he was delighted by the trend of the enquiry, which would undoubtedly reach far beyond his Police Department.

The Chief Secretary had departed to confer with the Premier, and Lowther was dictating his notes to a typist. With the Chief Commissioner were Superintendent Linton, Bonaparte's superior, and Superintendent Boase.

"It would seem, sir," said Linton, heavy and red, "that Bonaparte has the game sewn up. The point about lack of proof that he received the telegram could be made the subject of an amendment to the Regulations, don't you think?"

"I'll store that for further consideration, Linton," the Colonel evaded. "First things first. The Chief Secretary will present to the Premier an undeniable handle to turn in the innards of more than one Commonwealth Cabinet Minister. For, mark you, the Commonwealth Government won't face Bonaparte's threat of publicity. The S.S. and the C.I.S. will be so shaken up that they won't recognise each other next week. They've had it coming to them, and by gad! it'll take 'em now by the throat."

"You approve of Bonaparte's tactics, sir?" pressed Linton.

"I do not," retorted Colonel Spendor. "But, Linton, I have to admit to private feeling in this matter, and the result has pleased me greatly. Others in this State will rejoice also. And when you dissect what Bonaparte said this morning, you will agree that he employed diplomatic blackmail like a Canberra veteran.

"I'm sure, Boase, that your own C.C. will concur that the Commonwealth has steadily been edging into our State spheres of police activity. How the Commonwealth deals with subversive activities is of little concern to us at this moment, but when Commonwealth organisations act like a lot of damn school-children playing cops and robbers, resulting in citizens being in physical danger, we are entitled to protest. And now this Bonaparte and his Cowdry affair will arm the resistance movement, as it were. Bony knew this, and he played every trump in the pack. Well, we'll have him in. Lowther! Where the devil are you, Lowther?"

Bony was invited to be seated between the two superintendents. Smartly dressed in a grey pin-striped suit, the tie just one shade too bright and the breast handkerchief a fraction too ironed, he regarded the white head of his Chief Commissioner, and then glanced at the man either side of him. The face was calm, the eyes were masked, the mobile lips were still and gave nothing away.

"Inspector Bonaparte," Colonel Spendor said, a glare in his eyes, "I suggest that you cease believing you are extremely clever, so that you need not be shocked when proved to be otherwise. The verbatim report of the Enquiry into your extraordinary conduct at Cowdry will go to the highest quarters, and the powers may decide that your particular appointment is no longer of use to the State. Meanwhile, I do not accept your resignation."

Colonel Spendor ripped and tore the resignation to tiny pieces and hurled them into the w.p.b.

"I admit, sir, that the act of producing my resignation at the Enquiry was theatrical, and was intended to impress those persons present not of our Department," Bony said. "At the Enquiry I stated bald facts, but clothed them with loquacity that certain imputations should be strengthened, one of them being that outsiders cannot with impunity tread on our toes."

"On our toes!" snorted the Colonel. "On your toes, you mean."

"You pink me, sir. My toes."

"Damn it, Bonaparte!" roared Colonel Spendor. "Is that all you set out to achieve?"

"That is all—at the Enquiry. On all other matters, sir, such as the murder of Benjamin Wickham, the wishes of Benjamin Wickham, and certain property belonging to his estate, as well as the justification for my own conduct of the investigation, I am anxious to be guided by you."

The Chief Commissioner was visibly rocked. He snorted. He haw-ed. There was a note of desperation when he said:

"Then I wish you would be guided by me when I have you ordered to report to Department Headquarters."

"I felt that the order was not in the interests of this Department. Nor of justice."

"Is that so! The message was plain enough. Linton and I agreed it should contain a personal note from him so that you would realise the seriousness of it. You answer me that."

"My wife would call it intuition, sir."

"Eh? Damn and blast your eyes, Bonaparte! So would mine. Now for this murder you say you uncovered."

Bony prefaced his report with Mr. Luton's thesis on delirium tremens, and interpreted Luton's character as the product of that early background of an era so vastly different from the present. He then sketched the people in contact with Luton, and the relationship of Luton with Ben Wickham.

"I tested Luton's suspicion," he went on, "by asking Knocker Harris to put it around in the local township that a police inspector was staying with Luton and seemed interested in the death of the famous meteorologist. The early results were promising. I was questioned by Gibley the local constable, by the doctor, and by the Reverend Weston. And then we had a visit from Wickham's chief assistant, Dr. Linke, accompanied by Wickham's secretary.

"Linke informed me that Wickham had been visited by a foreigner who came from Adelaide in a car registered in the name of a staff member of the Hungarian Consulate. This was followed ten days' later by a telephone call from a person who wouldn't give his name, and whose voice Linke recognised as that of the manager of the Commonwealth Bank. Wickham was absent, so the man called the house when the people were at dinner. That night, at ten, Wickham went to the manager's rooms, remained for some time, and left with two men. I then decided to interview the bank manager, and you know what emerged from that interview in addition to the flat denial that Wickham had ever gone there.

"Linke further informed me that Wickham's office had been broken into after his death and ransacked, and that Mrs. Parsloe had not reported the matter to the local police. An important green-covered notebook was missing when Mrs. Parsloe opened the safe before the burglary. Eventually, Linke was questioned by a C.I.S. man accompanied by Sergeant Maskell.

"All these events occurred before I received the recall message, and I claim that in total they provided grave doubt that Luton was in error about his hoo-jahs. And the prodding of intuition told me that the recall move had originated from persons not of this Department.

"The discovery of the will and that notebook completed the list of those who could have had motive for murdering Wickham. Dr. Maltby was short of money. He knew he was to inherit a large sum, and that his wife also shared in the estate. Luton was to benefit to the tune of £20,000. He had access to the will. The lady secretary also knew she would benefit, and it seemed that Linke knew this, and intended to marry her. In fairness to Linke, I doubted that he knew he was to receive the vital notebook.

"Knocker Harris was a beneficiary, but I could not suspect him seriously, because it was he who persuaded Luton to invite me for the fishing, to hear Luton's thesis. Then there were the two thugs who burgled the office, who attacked Luton—agents of the foreign country who had treated with Wickham. Also there was Gibley. Unlikely, but a possible. Gibley was working in with the bank manager. He could have been in league with Maltby, both he and the doctor threatening Luton with removal to Adelaide if he didn't stop yelling about the hoo-jahs.

"The opportunity to murder Wickham was between four in the morning, and 6.25 a.m. He occupied the front room and, despite the season, insisted on the window being wide open." Bony outlined the process of 'the cure' and went on to tell of entry by one known to Wickham, who brought poison in a glass of gin, tempting Wickham to drink between drinks. During that period the dogs were still chained to their kennels placed two hundred and five paces from the kitchen door. Luton stated that had the dogs barked he would have heard them.

"Motive. Opportunity. Means. The three cardinal points. Motive, yes. Opportunity, yes. Means, no, for the body had been cremated and the ashes scattered. An autopsy would swiftly have clarified the means, when I would have reported the facts to Superintendent Boase, and carried on with my fishing."

"Before you uncovered the person who used the means?" Linton interjected.

"Of course not, Linton," snapped the Colonel. "You know damn well that Bonaparte's just blinding us with science. Go on."

"I have to admit, with a feeling of chagrin, that the extraneous cavortings of these cloak-and-dagger gentry obtruded and so obscured what otherwise would have been a comparatively simple case.

"Belladonna proved to be the means. I recalled seeing in

the garden cultivated by Knocker Harris several kinds of herbs, and when Luton told me that an embrocation he was using had been supplied by Harris, I remembered seeing several plants which could be belladonna. I recalled that the symptoms of belladonna poisoning are similar to those of delirium tremens, with the difference that the victim of belladonna dies in a coma, and he of delirium tremens dies with his eyes wide open. When Luton went to Wickham, the latter was laughing at things on his legs, as I have explained. That aroused Luton's suspicions. When the doctor examined the body and questioned Luton, the eyes were closed and that probably excuses the doctor for thinking that Wickham had died of alcoholic effects on a weak heart.

"That Harris was familiar with herbs, both edible and medicinal, is supported by his origin on isolated farms where people in those days had to have a smattering of medical knowledge. For him the opportunity was wide open. The dogs knew him; even if they heard him about they would not have given an alarm. Luton would not suspect him. He knew the interior plan of Luton's house, precisely where Wickham was sleeping. The means I have outlined. The motive was baffling, at first.

"Here was a man described by the phrase 'a simple soul'. He lived comfortably enough on his pension and his barter trade with fishermen. He had supported Luton's booze thesis. He had urged Luton to send for me when they read in the press that I was in Adelaide. He nursed the 'bender-ees', he tried to reform Luton, but Wickham defeated his efforts.

"He had become attached to Luton, a man miles above him in intelligence and experience, and, like so many women, and men too, the attachment was particularly strong when the object of it was sick. He was jealous of Wickham. Wickham was Luton's friend long before he, Harris, ever met him. Wickham and Luton shared so much from which he was barred. Much younger than Luton, he could see that Luton was growing older and he wanted to live with Luton, to care for him.

"Wickham having been removed, Luton fretted and clung to his suspicions. It was the only subject spoken of when Harris went to the cottage. The doctor shunted the idea of murder. The policeman sneered at it. Then they came on my name, which Harris remembered in connection with a relative I had caused to be put away for life. Safe to send for me. The body was destroyed, belladonna and everything. Let the great Bonaparte meet the impossibility of proving murder, and Luton would surrender his phobia and settle down to a quiet and bucolic existence, when Harris could safeguard him, have Luton all to himself.

"A misplaced, possessive, introverted passion to serve. The night he died, he had wanted to ask if Luton needed anything further brought back from town. With a knife pricking his back, he chose to warn us, not to betray us. Had he been brought to trial, I would have exerted myself on his behalf. When he lay dying, he looked first at Luton, then at me. As his life was fading he tried to tell me he had murdered Wickham and why, and he saw in my eyes that I already knew."

There was silence for perhaps five seconds. Linton broke it:

"So you do admit that you received the recall telegram?"

"There is no proof that I did," Bony countered. "Had I obeyed that recall, I would hate myself now."

Colonel Spendor rose, and they stood before him. The eyes of this beloved martinet softened when they rested on the colourful tie worn by the man who knew himself. He said gently:

"Had you obeyed that order, Bony, I would have been damned disappointed."